## PRAISE FOR THE MADISON NIGHT MYSTERY SERIES

"A terrific mystery is always in fashion—and this one is sleek, chic and constantly surprising. Vallere's smart styling and wry humor combine for a fresh and original page-turner—it'll have you eagerly awaiting her next appealing adventure. I'm a fan!"

— Hank Phillippi Ryan,
Agatha, Anthony, Macavity and Mary Higgins Clark Award-Winning Author of *The Other Woman*

"All of us who fell in love with Madison Night in *Pillow Stalk* will be rooting for her when the past comes back to haunt her in *That Touch of Ink*. The suspense is intense, the plot is hot and the style is to die for. A thoroughly entertaining entry in this enjoyable series."

— Catriona McPherson,
Agatha Award-Winning Author of the Dandy Gilver Mystery Series

"A fast-paced mystery with fab fashions, an appealing heroine, and a clever twist, *That Touch of Ink* is especially for fans of all things mid-century modern."

— ReadertoReader.com

"Vallere has crafted an extremely unique mystery series with an intelligent heroine whose appeal will never go out of style."

– Kings River Life Magazine

"Diane Vallere…has a wonderful touch, bringing in the design elements and influences of the '50s and '60s era many of us hold dear while keeping a strong focus on what it means in modern times to be a woman in business for herself, starting over."

— Fresh Fiction

"A humorous yet adventurous read of mystery, very much worth considering."

— Paul Vogel,<br>Midwest Book Review

"Make room for Vallere's tremendously fun homage. Imbuing her story with plenty of mid-century modern decorating and fashion tips…Her disarmingly honest lead and two hunky sidekicks will appeal to all fashionistas and antiques types and have romance crossover appeal."

— Library Journal

"A multifaceted story...plenty of surprises...And what an ending!"

— Mary Marks,
*New York Journal of Books*

"If you are looking for an unconventional mystery with a snarky, no-nonsense main character, this is it...Instead of clashing, humor and danger meld perfectly, and there's a cliffhanger that will make your jaw drop."

— Abigail Ortlieb,
*RT Book Reviews*

"A charming modern tribute to Doris Day movies and the retro era of the '50s, including murders, escalating danger, romance...and a puppy!"

— Linda O. Johnston,
Author of the Pet Rescue Mysteries

"I love mysteries where I can't figure out who the real killer is until the end, and this was one of those. The novel was well written, moved at a smooth pace, and Madison's character was a riot."

— *ChickLit Plus*

"Strong mysteries, an excellent cast, chills, thrills and laughter, and an adorable dog... if you haven't read a Madison Night mystery, what are you waiting for?" — *Kittling Books*

"The writing was crisp with a solid plot that kept me engaged with Madison, Tex and the other supporting cast." — *Dru's Book Musing*

"The strength of this series that Madison has changed, adapted, and grown over the course of the six books." — *3 no 7 Looks at Books*

"…a well plotted mystery filled with great characters that will keep you hooked until you get to the final page." — *Carstairs Considers*

# LOVE ME

# OR

# GRIEVE ME

A Madison Night Mystery

# Diane Vallere

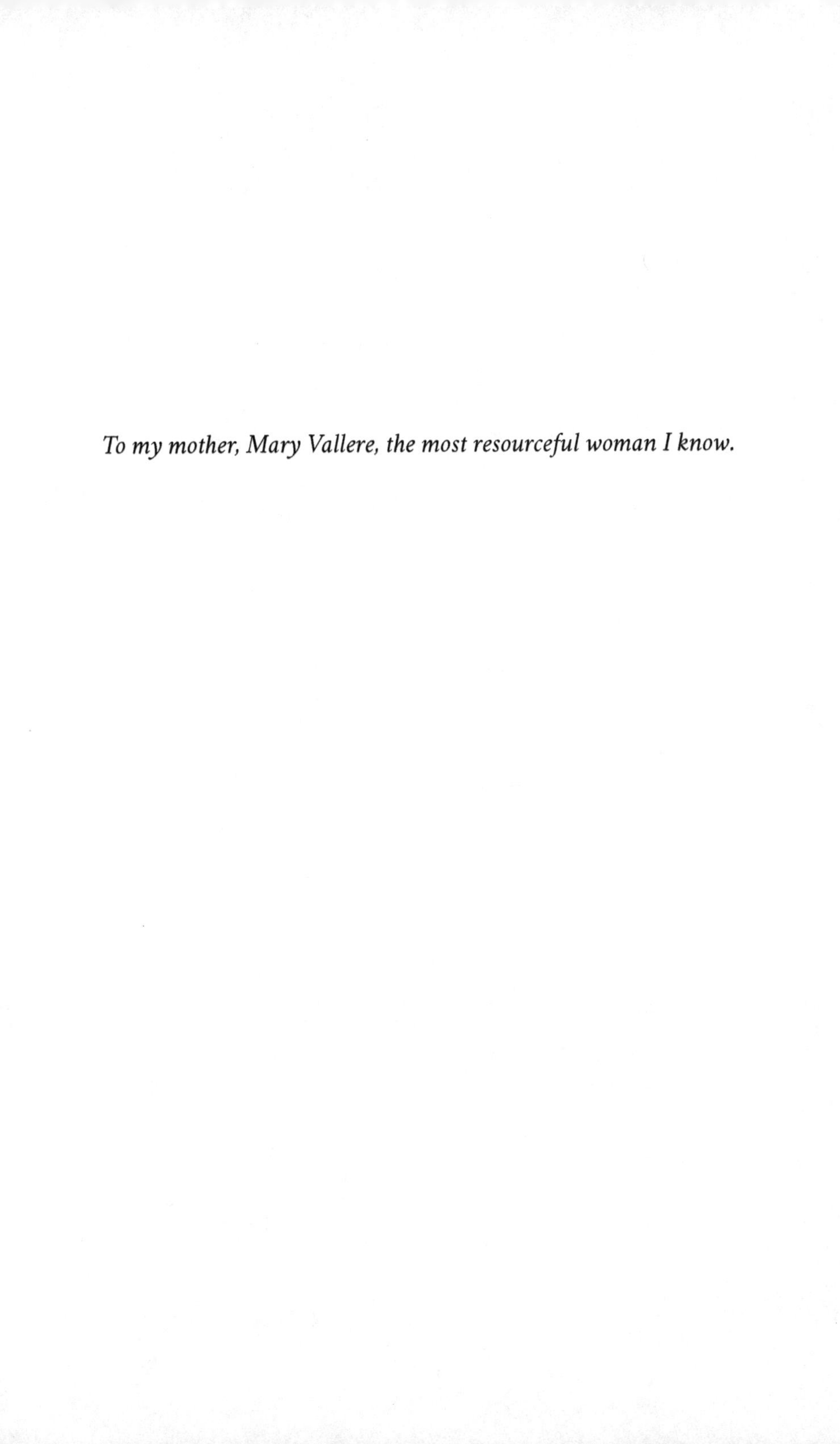

*To my mother, Mary Vallere, the most resourceful woman I know.*

# ONE

There were forty-seven people at my funeral. Forty-seven people who arrived at the Catholic Church of St. Monica on Midway Road dressed as one might have dressed for a funeral decades ago: suits and ties on the men and dresses and hats with netting on the women. Between the sixties architecture of the church and the attire of the attendees, most people would think they'd stumbled onto a film set. Me? I was right at home despite not knowing a single person there.

I learned of my untimely death from an overzealous local newscaster who learned of it from a junior editor at the newspaper (read: intern), who learned of it from a Post-it left on his monitor by a more seasoned reporter who delegated things like death notices of once-famous celebrities—and no, that's not me. I'm an interior decorator who specializes in mid-century design. The celebrity in question was a ninety-five-year-old jazz singer who embarked on a solo career in the mid-fifties and made a name for herself after marrying her power-hungry manager.

We had one thing in common: our name, or most of it, at least.

Addison Nigh, deceased.

Madison Night, very much alive.

I hadn't planned to attend the viewing of the jazz singer who almost shared my name, but my afternoon appointment was a no-show, and I found myself in the area—not exactly a coincidence considering the design district where I spent my morning was eight miles south. Still, it's not every day you get to attend your funeral and live to talk about it, so here I was, morbid curiosity and all.

I sat in the church parking lot in my powder blue Alfa Romeo and watched as the small crowd migrated inside. To me, the church was a marvel of architecture: a cylindrical building of stained glass framed out with a square of concrete. It was as if someone wanted to protect the church within the concrete, as if only those who entered could see the beauty inside. The white structure was defined by a horizontal roof line, fluid, concave waves across the façade, explosive cobalt blue stained-glass windows, and a modern, freestanding white sculpture that contained bells and was topped with a simple minimalist cross. I could spend days wandering the property examining the design details. I'd driven past the church before and had always wondered about the architect. I'd never before had so convenient an excuse to idle here.

I picked up the newspaper that sat on my passenger seat. It was open to the obituary page. And there was my life story. *Madison Night, decorator and amateur sleuth, dies at age fifty-one.* My life, summarized in one snazzy headline. And then there was the article.

*Madison Night, one of Dallas's up-and-coming interior decorators, died on September twenty-fourth. She was fifty-one.*

*Madison grew up in a suburb of Pennsylvania and made Dallas her home in her forties. Her design firm, Mad for Mod, specialized in mid-century modern architecture, a niche market to which she remained dedicated. When she inherited Sweet Dreams pajama factory, she applied for a historical designation and protected the sewing stations by converting the interior into a shared workspace. It is among the more unique properties in downtown Dallas.*

*Gerry Rose, founder of the Design in Dallas Initiative (DIDI), said of Night, "She had a unique point of view. She could have easily had a successful career working for a more established firm, but she was committed to her aesthetic. There's a narrow but loyal market for mid-century design in Dallas, and Night owned that market."* I scanned the rest of the obituary until I got to the last line.

*Ms. Night leaves behind no surviving family.*

I set the newspaper down.

The junior editor at the paper had been tasked with the job of writing an obituary for a local celebrity, but that local celebrity wasn't me.

Once upon a time, Addison Nigh was an in-demand jazz singer, famous for her sultry song styling. She drew dinnertime crowds to hot spots that no longer existed and married her manager, Martin Snyder, eventually falling into obscurity when her looks started to fade. A more seasoned reporter might have recognized her name, but Jimmy Nussbaum, the junior editor on loan from the local high school, did not.

It didn't help that her name had been preceded by an "M" on the Post-it: "M Addison Nigh?" which was intended to indicate Ms. or Mrs. but only confused the search engine Jimmy used to find Addison's life story. He found mine instead, an article about a design competition I'd won two years ago, and called the head of the judging committee for a quote that he inserted into the summary of my life he'd crafted. He submitted the story in time to get back to high school for eighth-period French.

The obituary made the morning edition. The *Dallas Morning News* picked up the obit and reprinted it, as did the *Dallas Observer*, the *Fort Worth Star Telegram*, the *Houston Chronicle*, and the *Austin American Statesman*. By the time the error was caught, the flowers had already started arriving. It was a shame. I would have preferred donations be made in my name to Doris Day's Animal Foundation.

I didn't bother reading the rest of the obituary. I'd had the newspaper in my possession for three days now and I never made it past Gerry Rose's quote. The title indicated young Jimmy had also found out about the various murder cases I'd helped solve, and having lived through them, I didn't need to read the CliffsNotes version. But I couldn't help but wonder what might have happened if he'd called the police captain instead of the head of the DIDI. I'd been dating Captain Tex Allen for over a year, and while his intel would have been more accurate, his quote probably wouldn't have been fit to print.

The sun filtered through the leaves of the trees surrounding the Catholic church, and the interior of my car grew warm. I watched an older man with a cane slowly make his way toward the church entrance. He was head and shoulders shorter than the people who trailed behind him, but something about his presence suggested importance. He wore a black suit with a white carnation on the lapel. A black fedora rested on his head. He favored his left leg as he walked, though his posture was otherwise erect. When he reached the doors to the church, he waited for one of the men behind him to open the door and make way for his entrance.

Proving my stop-off at the Church of St. Monica's on the day of Addison's viewing wasn't a spontaneous thing, I'd dressed in a black vintage dress from the estate of Louise Pledge. She was the organ player for her church for thirty-seven years, and her wardrobe reflected her religious dedication. Today's dress was simple and elegant with a scooped neckline, capped sleeves, and a nipped-in waist above full folds of black fabric. Tiny moth holes had been present on the left side of the skirt, but a talented reweaver had been able to repair the damage. My premeditation didn't stop there. I changed out of my regular choice of Keds into a pair of low-heeled black pumps that I'd tucked behind my seat when I got into the car this morning. It was rare that I spent more than an hour or two in real shoes thanks to a torn ACL and chronic swelling and pain in my knee, but today, the sacrifice seemed worth it. I'd even left my dog, Rocky, a peppy Shih Tzu who never met a pair of ankles he didn't want to sniff, at home for the day.

I slipped on a pair of white cotton gloves in the car and grabbed my clutch handbag. My hands were still recovering from using chemicals to strip the paint off an original maple Broyhill Brasilia bedroom set that an ill-advised previous owner had painted blue. The gloves may attract attention, but they were nothing compared to what people might think if they saw my torn-up skin.

I followed the man to the entrance and slipped inside the church. I felt like Tom Sawyer, sneaking into my own funeral, although the attendees were all strangers. This wasn't about me and I knew it, but I couldn't shake the sense that in some way, it was.

The church was as beautiful on the inside as the out and I sat in a pew toward the back and admired the wooden canework by the altar for a moment, then turned my attention to the event at hand.

A mahogany casket lined in teal velvet sat at the front of the church next to a wreath of blood-red roses. A simple black ribbon decorated the wreath. One by one, people approached the open casket and paid their respects while a small grouping of men stood to the left of the altar talking in hushed tones. Of the forty-seven people, there appeared to be an equal divide between men and women. They remained separate as if this were a Sadie Hawkins dance of the macabre.

A hand touched my shoulder from behind, and I flinched. I looked up and saw a man in a dove gray suit and a nondescript tie. "I didn't mean to startle you," he said. "I'm the funeral director. The family thanks you for coming. There's no service with the viewing, so feel free to pay your respects at any time. The church has suspended services for the rest of the day."

"I didn't know her," I said, but then realized any attempt to explain why I was here would sound thin. "I'm fine back here. I don't want to disrupt the family."

"They'd appreciate knowing a fan came to pay respects," he said. He stepped back and held his arm out, his hand open, gesturing along the red carpet that ran down the center aisle of the church. "There's no rush, but please, don't be shy."

I nodded and then slid out of the pew and made my way toward the casket.

Death didn't make me nervous. Some might say I had a healthier relationship with it than most. But as I advanced toward the casket, I felt conspicuous. I didn't know these people; I didn't know this woman. My business profited from death, from acquiring the estates of people of a certain age and giving their belongings new life through clients who wanted authentic mid-century designs, not reproductions, but my presence today had nothing to do with business. I was here for purely selfish reasons, and they began and ended with the fact that for the briefest moment, I'd taken this woman's place in the obituaries. It would have been silly if the event weren't shrouded in sadness.

Walking past pews of nattily dressed men and women, I stopped by the casket and peered inside. Addison was dressed in red, her signature color, which contrasted starkly with the teal velvet lining of the casket. Her hair was dyed an unnatural honey blond to mimic the shade it had been at the height of her career, and her lipstick matched her crimson dress. Whoever had instructed the mortuary on her appearance had done her a disservice. They'd not acknowledged that she'd aged gracefully but tried instead to cement her in time to a bygone era. Yet despite the makeup, the honey-blond hair, the garish colors of the dress, and the lining of the casket, something about Addison Nigh spoke to me. I didn't know her, didn't know anything about her, but as I stood there, I felt a kinship. I reached out and put my hand on her hand and rested it while an unexpected stream of tears spilled down my cheek.

I swiped at the tears and glanced around. The men who stood to the side of the casket were watching me. My knee throbbed from standing in heels. I smiled and then turned away. I didn't belong here. I hurried down the bright red carpet, out of the church, into the sunlight. I paused when I was outside to catch the breath I didn't know I needed. The doors to the church opened, and the short man with the carnation in his lapel hobbled toward me.

"Excuse me," he said. "I couldn't help but notice how you responded to the sight of Sunny."

"Sunny?" I asked.

"That's the name she went by. Addison was a stage name assigned by her manager. I'm surprised you didn't know that." He rested his weight on his cane and studied me for a long, awkward moment. "May I ask how you knew her?"

"I don't. I didn't."

"You're a fan?"

I shook my head, and then added, "I might be, but I'm not familiar with her music."

"Then why are you here?" he demanded, his voice growing louder. The church doors opened and a younger man and woman, probably closer to my age, exited and came toward us.

"There was a mistake," I said to the older gentleman. "I'm— she's—I should go." I turned to leave, but the man put his cane out to block my way.

"Who are you?"

"I'm nobody."

"Your name, ma'am?"

"Madison," I said. "I'm Madison Night."

And while my name should have served as an introduction, in this case, it did something worse. Upon hearing it, the man clutched at his chest and stumbled backward. He reached out for something to stabilize him and I stretched my arm out too late. He collapsed on the sidewalk, his cane falling to the ground a few feet away.

# TWO

The younger man pushed me out of the way. "Stay back," he instructed. He pulled a small vial out of his inside suit jacket pocket, shook out a white cube, and inserted it into the man's mouth. The woman straightened the older man's legs and propped them up on her thighs.

"What did you say to him?" the younger man demanded. He shrugged out of his jacket and rolled it into a makeshift pillow that he placed under the older man's head.

"Nothing," I said, looking down at the two of them. "He asked who I was."

The man raised his eyebrows in question. It was the question of the hour, and there was no point evading it. "I'm Madison Night."

"You're the decorator," the woman correctly stated. I nodded. At the man's confusion, she explained. "The obituary mix-up, remember?" She pointed at me. "They printed this woman's life story in the newspaper instead of Mom's."

*Mom's.* Addison Nigh was their mother.

The man looked from her face to mine. "You came to your own funeral?"

It felt strange to stand there, staring down at the three of them in various positions on the sidewalk, but there wasn't much else for me to do. "I'm sorry for coming here today. I shouldn't have. It was curiosity, nothing more. When he asked my name…" I looked at the man. His eyes fluttered open and then closed again. "…when he *heard* my name, he—he looked like he was having a heart attack."

The woman stood. "He suffers from low blood sugar. The heat, and the funeral, and then you—I'm sure it wasn't intentional, but it was too much." She held out her hand. "I'm Renee. This is Punch."

"It's nice to meet you both," I said politely. "I'm sorry for your loss."

I'd been preoccupied with the older man, first through conversation and then through crisis, and hadn't paid much attention to Renee or Punch, but as time seemed to slow down around us, I assessed them. Renee had sleek, smooth brown hair, pulled back in a French twist, dark, arched eyebrows and red lips. A red heart tattoo peeked out from under the short sleeve of her black dress. She had a forties throwback style that could easily fit in at one of the many rockabilly concerts in Deep Ellum.

Punch had straight blond hair, parted on the side and longish in the back. His suit was navy blue, with rounded shoulders and narrow lapels. The three of us probably looked either like we were attending a costume party or had been transported here via time warp. I was often the only person in the group dressed in head-to-toe vintage, but amongst these two, I blended in.

I shook Renee's hand then Punch's, though Punch seemed less enthused by the formal introduction.

At our feet, the older man stirred. He put his hand out as if he needed to feel his surroundings before understanding where he was. Punch reached for the older man's hand. "You're okay. Your blood sugar dropped."

"And you left me on the ground? What is it with you people?" He swatted Punch's hand away. "Get me onto that bench." He rolled onto his side and then pushed himself up to a standing position. I lifted his cane and held it out to him, and he appeared to register that I was somehow responsible for his fall. He took his cane and then pointed the end at me. "You," he said. "Sit with me. You two," he moved his cane and pointed at Renee and Punch, "go back inside."

"But—" Punch protested.

"I'm fine. I can tell you jammed one of those sugar cubes into my mouth. It wouldn't kill you to carry candy bars instead."

I stifled a smile. The man may be in his nineties, but he was no pushover.

Renee guided the older man to the bench while Punch picked his jacket up off the ground and shook it out, radiating annoyance at the situation. Impulsively, I put my hand on his forearm. "I *am* sorry," I said. "For causing the stir. My afternoon is clear, and I'd enjoy the opportunity to talk to him."

"I see right through you," he said, "and it won't work. It doesn't matter how much you paid for your vintage funeral outfit. You're not his type." He turned around and stormed away.

I watched a spot on the back of Punch's jacket until he (and his jacket) disappeared back inside the church. Both Renee and the older man remained outside. Renee stood behind the elderly man. Like me, she stared at the church doors where Punch had entered.

"I'm fine," the man said. "Go back inside with Punch."

"I'll check on you in a few minutes." She glanced at me again and then left.

I lowered myself onto the bench. My bad knee throbbed, and I welcomed the opportunity to sit. The hem of my skirt kicked up and revealed the scar that ran across my kneecap from more than one operation. I smoothed the fabric with my gloved hand and then folded my fingers together in my lap.

"Your kids are protective of you," I said.

"Those two? They're not my kids. They're Sunny's."

"How were you related to her?"

"I wasn't. We played together back in the day. I came to show my respect."

"I didn't mean to startle you when I told you my name," I said.

He waved my apology off. "Low blood sugar and heat, that's all. I don't even think of her as Addison. She was Sunny to me. She always shined bright, like the sun." He pointed at my knee. "What happened there?"

"Skiing accident. Torn ACL. There've been a couple of reinjuries since then, but that's where it started."

"Sunny had a similar scar," he said. "Car crash. She wanted to be a dancer, but the accident changed the direction of her life."

I pointed to his cane. "What about you?"

"Shot at a jazz club back in fifty-five," he said. "Jazz isn't for sissies."

Despite the awkward circumstances that led to my presence at the memorial, talking to this man put me at ease. "I never caught your name," I said.

"Jack Folly."

"You played with Addison—I mean, Sunny?"

"I usually played piano, but I could do whatever we needed. Sometimes it was upright bass. Sometimes it was the saxophone. One time on drums."

"That's unusual, isn't it? I thought most musicians play one instrument."

Jack shook his head. Our conversation had turned from Addison's death to Jack's life, and the shift appeared to have brought him some relief from the somber atmosphere.

"I was classically trained. My parents saw something in me and wanted to make sure I had every opportunity, so they sent me to instructors to teach me the fundamentals of any instrument I could get my hands on. Made me more valuable for my range than for my expertise on any one of them." He turned his head toward the church and jutted his chin at the doors. "I met Sunny when her manager brought me in to give her music lessons. She had natural talent but nerves kept her from embracing her abilities. We worked together so much at the start of her career that the only way she would take the stage was if I were up there with her, so I became an honorary member of the backup band."

"You must have been friends in addition to colleagues."

"Used to be. She was a heck of a broad."

"And her kids? You seem to have a relationship with them."

"To those kids, I'm a commodity. The last living link to their mother's life in jazz."

"But the way they looked out for you, it seemed protective. Punch carried those sugar cubes, and Renee said she'd come back to check on you."

"You ask a lot of questions, you know that?" Jack was silent for a moment, and we sat side by side, with the breeze sending a diverting temperature drop our way. "Sunny's son thinks you're a gold digger." Jack's eyes sparkled at the thought, and a hint of the charming man he must have been in his prime was apparent. "Are you?"

It wasn't lost on me that Jack had changed the subject. "I'm a decorator," I offered, "but that's not why I'm here."

"Why *are* you here? I don't believe you ever answered that question."

I shrugged. "Curiosity, I suppose. The newspapers told the city of Dallas that my services were being held at the Church of St. Monica. I didn't plan to show up. My afternoon appointment canceled on me and I found myself in the area with a block of free time."

"You don't find that suspicious?"

"I don't follow."

"Your client canceled because she thought you were dead."

"No," I said, and then cocked my head to the side. That wasn't possible, was it? "No," I said again. "The paper printed a correction the next day."

"Sunny's kids called seven different papers to get the error corrected and the result was them running Sunny's obituary two days later than expected." He gestured toward the church. "They pushed her public memorial to next week because of the mix-up. Today's viewing is for family."

"After the mix-up with the obituaries, I read a little bit about Sunny. About her life."

He looked bemused. "You want to know about Sunny? You won't find anything real in those articles. She was a private person who was forced to live a portion of her life in public. It almost killed her back then. It's why she quit the business."

"And you? When did you retire?"

Jack eyed me sideways. "There's plenty of work out there for a guy like me, and I worked until my seventies."

I could have sat on that bench outside the church talking to Jack for hours, but the doors of the church opened, and a throng of people spilled out. Both Punch and Renee were among them, along with younger children and older couples. A man in a charcoal gray suit slid a door stopper under the heavy church doors to keep them open, and a priest in black robes followed the crowd and mingled with them by the striking stained glass windows.

It was a nice day to sit outside on a park bench: a slight breeze tossed the remaining leaves on the branches overhead and the humidity was at a minimum. October in Dallas was one of my favorite months. The average temperatures hung in the seventies, warm enough to feel comfortable and cool enough to signal change was in the air. Most people loved spring for the newness, but to me, autumn was the season that brought about movement. Falling leaves, crisper temperatures, and the scent of the air shifting from backyard barbecue to homemade pie. This was Dallas, though, so both the barbecue and the pie were from caterers who specialized in bringing the taste of homemade to residents' homes for a nominal fee.

Punch pulled away from the crowd and approached us. "Jack, we need you with us." He looked back and forth between our faces as if he still didn't trust my intentions.

Jack planted his cane on the sidewalk and leveraged his weight against it. He stood slowly. Punch put his hand under Jack's arm and Jack shook him off. "Give a man his dignity in front of a lady," he said. Punch stepped back, and his face colored.

Jack turned to me and held out his free hand. I didn't need the assistance, but I slipped my gloved hand in his all the same. After I stood, I converted our grip to a handshake.

"Mr. Folly, it was a pleasure talking to you about Ms. Nigh. Thank you for sitting with me while I rested my knee."

"The pleasure was all mine," he said. He kept ahold of my hand and leaned in closer. I bent down and turned my head so he could talk directly into my ear. "You sure you're not a gold digger?"

I smiled. "If I were, you'd be the first person I'd tell."

Jack reached into his pocket and pulled out a small ivory card. "If you change your mind, give me a call." He squeezed my hand and then let go.

THREE

The next day, I woke at five thirty and went to the Gaston Swim Club to get in a morning workout. It was the closest thing I had to a routine. I swam for an hour and then showered and dressed in an ivory cotton day dress printed with red and blue dachshunds, blew my ashy blond hair dry and secured it in a low ponytail, tied on red Keds, and collected Rocky from the doggie room where he'd gotten his hour of exercise amongst other frolicking canines. After a little fuss over having to bid goodbye to his new friends, I drove us directly to my studio on Greenville Avenue.

Mad for Mod, my mid-century modern-focused interior design firm, had expanded into a second location that was conveniently located next to the house where I lived, but since I couldn't be in two places at once, I still met clients at the main storefront. My business had been hurt by a legal battle, closing temporarily. After reopening, my client roster had blossomed, but ever since the accidental obituary ran in the paper, things were wonky.

Like the path from the front doors to my office that was

lined with flower arrangements tagged with condolence cards. You would think people sending flowers at the notice of my death would send them somewhere other than my place of work!

I picked up a fully grown and groomed olive topiary. The card read, "Deepest Sympathies. Sincerely, Mrs. Bonneville." Mrs. Bonneville was a long-time tenant at the Turtle Creek Luxury Apartments in Highland Park. I'd first met her while exposing a counterfeiting scheme that involved an ex-boyfriend. I had no reason to keep in touch with Mrs. Bonneville after the case was solved, though truth be told, I had every reason to move on and try to forget what had happened. She must have read the paper and recognized my name.

I tossed the card onto my desk and moved her olive tree to the floor. Another smaller arrangement of bouncing red and white carnations was by my feet. I checked the card. This one was from an FBI agent.

I *had* lived a colorful life.

I moved the flowers to the side to leave a path from the front door to the back and went out the rear exit. My one employee, Effie Jones, should have been around somewhere. I found her behind the building watering a row of potted ferns.

"Hey, Boss," she said. "They keep on coming."

"These were delivered today?"

"Some today, some yesterday. Did you see the lemon tree from Connie's nursery?"

I turned around and glanced inside. "Connie knows I'm not dead. She sent a lemon tree?"

"Her ex-husband did. Talk about out of the loop."

Connie and Ned Duncan were clients who once hired me to design them an atomic kitchen. A few years later, Connie learned that Ned, a band promoter, had been having an affair with his secretary, and she divorced him. She'd since bought a nursery, and I wondered if the tree her ex sent had been an excuse to interact with her via her business. I couldn't fault her for taking his money, though she'd get some ribbing for profiting from my untimely death.

"How did things go with the Ledbetters?" Effie asked. "Did we get the job?"

"They were a no-show."

Effie's brows drew together. "That's funny. Linda called to confirm the appointment twice last week."

I remembered what Jack had said about why my clients had canceled. "Did you happen to follow up with her today?"

"No. Should I have?"

"Come with me." I went back to my desk and found Linda Ledbetter's number inside her client file. I made the call from my yellow donut phone, not the most practical of business tools, but it was functional, and every time I used it, I smiled. When the phone was answered by a familiar female voice, I greeted her. "Linda? This is Madison Night." The other end of the call was silent. "Linda? Are you there?"

"Who is this?" she asked in a shaky voice.

"Linda, it's Madison, your decorator."

"But you're—"

"I assure you, I'm not dead. The newspaper mixed up facts on another person's obituary. Do you have today's morning edition?"

"It's in the recycling."

"I'll wait here while you go check it."

I smiled at Effie, who leaned against the wall in the hallway. Effie was a millennial with a business degree, which put her in the top one percent of people her age. She was hard-working and had shown a desire to organize my business practices and learn about the furniture and design elements I used when doing a job. I'd once thought Mad for Mod would always be a one-woman operation, but I couldn't deny that Effie brought something fresh to the table.

On the other end of the phone, I heard rustling, and then a gasp. And then Linda picked up the phone. "Madison. I'm so sorry. I thought—we thought—you were dead. I can't believe they did that to you."

"It was a simple mistake," I said. "It's been corrected."

"I can't begin to imagine what you're going through."

I chuckled. "Linda, I'm fine. It's a blip of inconvenience."

"Did you contact the credit bureau?"

"Why would I do that?"

"Identity theft. Scammers read the obituaries and then try to establish credit in the names of the deceased. If someone thinks you're dead, they might try to use your name to open an account."

"That never occurred to me."

"Do it sooner rather than later to be on the safe side." She sighed. "I guess this puts us behind schedule."

"I'll keep us on track. Let me get Effie to schedule a new meeting."

I covered the receiver and told Effie what had happened. "The Ledbetter job is a big one. Move other appointments if you need to but get her rescheduled." I handed over the phone.

Linda and Larry Ledbetter were forty-three-year-old hotel owners who planned to renew their vows and wanted me to coordinate the event. It wouldn't be a simple backyard ceremony, either. They were self-made billionaires who'd eloped back when they were in their teens and lived week to week on the money pooled through hostess and valet work at a local hotel. They pinched their pennies and accumulated enough money to invest in a rental property, which paid off within the year. The Ledbetters agreed that if they'd lived this long on two meager salaries, they were willing to do it again, and they did, and after buying into several investments, they ventured out on their own. The Ledbetter Hotel fortune was as much due to savvy investing as it was to Hamburger Helper, their go-to meal in their frugal days.

As they approached their twenty-fifth wedding anniversary, they decided to mark the occasion in style: mid-century style. They purchased a 1955 ranch house and wanted it fully renovated, inside and out, for their vow renewal ceremony. It was a dream job, and it was mine for the taking.

Linda had first learned of me through the man who'd given a quote for my obituary: Gerry Rose. He was a regular at the country club they'd joined and when Linda and Larry mentioned what they had in mind, he was quick to recommend me. I'd introduced him to the mother of his eighteen-month-old son, and either he felt like he owed me something or he believed in my talent as a designer. Considering the woman in question was former police officer-turned-business-owner bombshell Donna Nast, it could have gone either way.

Of course, Nasty, as she'd come to be known, chose to raise the baby on her own and there was a forty-year age difference between them, but nothing in life is easy, right?

While Effie flipped through my calendar and made notations on which appointments to juggle, I grabbed my cell phone and wallet and went to the front of the studio. I dropped into a black leather Forum chair. Designed by Robin Day from S. Hille & Co in 1964, the cushions were mounted to a chrome steel square-section tube and three sides of the chair were framed in rosewood. I'd acquired both the chair and the matching coffee table in landfill-worthy condition at a public auction, eighty dollars for the set. I put five hundred dollars in materials and seventy hours of work into the restoration, but the result was worth it.

I pulled a credit card out of my wallet and called the number on the back. After clicking through several automated prompts, I eventually reached a person. I confirmed my name and credit card number and then launched into my reason for calling. "This may be a preemptive call. I was recently reported as deceased, but as you can tell, I'm not. I'm calling about my business account, and I want to make sure it isn't affected while I clear up the confusion."

"That's smart. Identity theft has been up this year. The first place thieves look is the obituaries. I'll put an alert on your account and issue you a new card. You should receive it in one business day."

I repeated the process with each of my credit cards. Already, my low-level annoyance was creeping into anxiety. The last thing I needed while staring down a job of the Ledbetter magnitude was credit card fraud. My final call was to the credit bureau. The wait time was over an hour, but instead of hanging up, I inserted my earbuds and set my phone on the Forum chair, then grabbed a clean rag and a bottle of leather conditioner and worked my way through the showroom furniture.

I conditioned all of the furniture and then went out back to look for Effie. I circled the block and found her collecting a fresh delivery of funeral flowers by the entrance. I held the door open for her when a white Nissan Altima careened to a stop out front of Mad for Mod. The driver was Punch Snyder, and he didn't look happy.

He got out of the car and waved a newspaper at me. "Was this your doing?" he asked.

I pulled my earbuds out and disconnected the call. "What?"

"Did you do this?" he asked again. He pushed the *Dallas Tribune* into my chest, and I unfurled it. He'd left it open to the obituary page where a new obituary, double in size to the original about me, filled the page. The headline read: *Madison Night, Jazz Singer, Dies at 95.*

I couldn't believe it. The facts of the obit were correct, but the name and picture were not. My name and a bigger photo than the original accompanied the new notice of the late jazz singer's death.

# FOUR

I bit back my first response: *This isn't possible*, largely because I held the evidence that it was. What bothered me more than anything was how I'd wasted over an hour with a phone call to the bank and credit bureau and I'd have to do it all over again. The contents of the obit might have been updated, but in the words of the headline, I was still dead.

I pressed the newspaper back at Punch. "Wait here." I went back into Mad for Mod, clipped a leash onto Rocky's collar, and grabbed my handbag. Effie stood back and watched. "Can you lock up at the end of the day? I don't know how long I'll be."

"Aye aye, Boss."

I carried Rocky out front and approached Punch's car. "Let's go," I said.

"Where?"

"To the *Dallas Tribune*. I want to settle this once and for all."

Punch opened the driver's side. He pushed the door open toward me and I held Rocky to my chest and sat down.

I wanted to be angry with Punch. His attitude from the

moment I met him had been argumentative, abrasive, and all-around annoying.

"I asked around about you," Punch said. "You take advantage of people. You use the obituaries to identify targets who are likely to have estates from the fifties and sixties. It's morbid. Profiting from someone else's mourning."

"Maybe you find me morbid, but a lot of those people appreciate my offers. Estate houses take a sizeable chunk of the profits when they plan and execute a public auction. I walk through a property and make an offer, and if it's accepted, I write a check and arrange to take possession within twenty-four hours. Death is hardest upon the people who are left to grieve, not on the deceased. I provide a mutually beneficial service. Have you ever thought about that?"

Punch grunted something which could have been either an agreement or a dismissal but was unintelligible either way. It also could have meant he had something stuck in his throat.

It was a half-hour drive mostly down Route 75 to the newspaper offices. Rocky stared out the window. We drove the rest of the way in silence. Twice I'd tried to initiate conversation, and twice Punch shut me down. I'd spent enough of my life on my own to be perfectly fine without conversation.

Dallas was an interesting city in that it was zoned commercially, so restaurants tended to be in the same neighborhood, furniture and decorating businesses were grouped, and newspaper offices too. The *Dallas Tribune*, a smaller newspaper that rarely got mentioned in the same sentence as the other news sources, was in a building less than a block from the Book Depository, famous for the JFK assassination. A steady stream of visitors wandered the area every day, but still, Punch got a parking space out front. I set Rocky on the sidewalk, and we followed Punch to the building entrance and then to the door marked "Tribune." Even though Punch had been one step ahead of me the whole time, I asserted myself first.

"Excuse me," I said to a skinny teen while Rocky stretched his leash to sniff the legs of a nearby desk. "Where can we find Jimmy Nussbaum?"

The kid puffed out his chest. "I'm Jimmy. Did I win something?" He looked at our hands. "Where's the big check?"

I snatched the folded newspaper from under Punch's arm and held it out. "Were you responsible for this obituary in today's paper?"

"I fixed that!"

Punch's cell phone rang, and he stepped into the hallway to take the call. I slapped the paper onto Jimmy's desk. "Look at that picture, Jimmy. Look at the picture, and then look at me. What do you notice?"

He did as instructed and then scratched his head. "You look a lot like the woman in the picture."

"I *am* the woman in the picture, and as you can see, I'm not dead." I turned around and glanced at the empty desks. "Is your editor here?"

Jimmy looked scared. "They went out to—to cover a breaking story. They left me in charge."

I lowered myself into a chair. "We'll wait."

Punch came back into the office and tapped me on the shoulder. "Can I talk to you for a moment?" He glanced at Jimmy and then back at me. "Outside?" I stood and followed him to the hallway. "I don't have the time to get this straightened out. The kid knows he made a mistake."

"A *second* mistake."

"Right. He can't do anything about it now. I've got to meet somebody, but I'll pick it up with the paper in the morning."

"I'll handle this." I headed back to the newspaper office and pulled my phone out of my handbag. There was one person to call.

I pressed speed dial, and my call was met with, "Tex Allen."

"Captain Allen, this is Madison Night. I'm a resident in the Lakewood area, and I'd like to report a case of harassment against the *Dallas Tribune*." There wasn't much Tex could do about the error at the newspaper, but Jimmy didn't know that. Jimmy, at the moment, looked pretty scared by what he'd heard.

"Lady, it was a mistake!" the teen said.

"Please hold, Captain." I put my hand loosely over the receiver and addressed Jimmy. "Mr. Nussbaum, did you not report me as deceased in your newspaper? And after the error was brought to your attention and your editor promised a retraction would be printed, did you not make a similar error?"

"I'm an intern on a work-study pass from Dallas High School. I don't even want to be a reporter. It wasn't on purpose —I swear."

I held up my finger in a just-a-moment gesture and returned to the call. "Captain Allen, I really would like you to pay this young man a visit and explain to him his rights."

Tex chuckled. "When I agreed to take a vacation, I thought it would be relaxing. Sit by the pool and work on my tan. Two days in, and I'm ready for action. Thanks for rounding up a bad guy for me, Night."

I stifled a smile. "Shall I wait here?"

"You need a ride home?"

"Yes."

"Give me half an hour. I'm all slicked up with sunscreen."

"I'll be waiting." I hung up and turned to Jimmy. "Perhaps we can go over the retraction you plan to print *this* time."

It seemed an innocuous way to spend a portion of my time:

sitting with an unpaid junior editor while he corrected Sunny Nigh's obituary with her picture and name, but after two strikes, I wasn't risking a third. The phones rang a few times, and Jimmy dutifully answered them, leaving me alone at his desk. When he wasn't looking, I opened the folder marked with the original Post-it: "M. Addison Nigh?" and I flipped through it.

Inside was a black and white photo from the newspaper archives of Sunny Nigh posing with two cigarette girls in short costumes and fishnet stockings. Sunny wore a pale silk gown and had a flower pinned onto the side of her hair. Her life as a chanteuse seemed charmed, and it was a shame by the time the erroneous information was corrected, most people would have forgotten about her again.

"You aren't supposed to look at that," Jimmy said.

"Maybe if you'd looked at it, you might have written the correct obituary." I closed the folder and set it approximately where I'd found it.

"I should have signed up for an extra shop class," he grumbled.

Tex arrived sooner than I expected. He wore a dark gray sweatshirt over a white T-shirt and jeans. He smelled faintly of coconut. Rocky immediately recognized him and yipped twice. "Are you Jimmy Nussbaum?" Tex asked.

"Are you really a cop?" Jimmy asked doubtfully.

Tex raised his sweatshirt enough to display the badge hooked onto the waistband of his jeans. "I'm undercover," he said.

"Like I told her, it was an accident. I'm not harassing her."

Tex looked at me. "Reporting that a living person is dead can have a negative impact on her mindset." He glanced around the empty newspaper office. "Where is your editor?"

"He and the other reporters left to cover a breaking story," I supplied. I turned back to Jimmy. "That is what you told me, correct?"

Jimmy collapsed into his chair. "They left early. There's only five of us anyway, and they don't have to pay me to stay." He looked at Tex. "You're not going to arrest me, are you? My mom will kill me."

"I'll let you off with a warning, but don't let it happen again."

Jimmy looked suitably repentant. "Yes, sir."

"Are you okay with that?" Tex asked me.

"I suppose."

Tex held his hand out and shook Jimmy's. "I'll be keeping an eye on you," he said.

If Jimmy had something he wanted to say, it was quashed by the ringing phone. He answered and scribbled something on the outside of Sunny's file folder. He glanced up at one point, nervously, and then continued to take notes. There was no other reason for us to be there, so we left. A few seconds later, Jimmy caught up to us in the hallway.

"Captain Allen, you need to arrest this woman."

Tex looked bemused. "This woman? The one who brought me here to investigate charges of harassment against this newspaper?"

"That phone call came from the real Madison Night. She said after the first obituary, the banks shut down her lines of credit, and then someone started impersonating her. This woman is a fraud."

# FIVE

Tex learned of my untimely death while working at the police station. A former officer who once went undercover as a tenant in an apartment building I lived in at the time heard the news and sent him a modest plant with a condolence card. He said he dismissed the news instantly, but there'd been something new in the way he held me when I saw him later that night that made me suspect he was lying. I tried to get the scoop from Imogene, the volunteer who handled incoming calls and paperwork filing for the Lakewood PD, but she claimed they'd all been sworn to secrecy. More likely, they'd been threatened with the loss of their jobs. Not enforceable, of course, but it fit Tex's commanding style.

The thing was, Tex knew about the obituary mistake. He knew I was here to straighten things out. And he knew *me.* He knew if anybody was claiming to be Madison Night, it was the woman in front of him. Any other companion, including Punch Snyder, would have considered the accusation—maybe even demanded to see ID—before outright dismissing it.

"A fraud, you say?" Tex asked.

At this point, Jimmy was shaking. "I don't know who she is, but she was going through my desk before you got here," he said. A lightbulb seemed to go off on top of his head and he grabbed a lined yellow tablet and a pen. "Wait! There might be a story here. Can you cuff her and keep her here while I ask her some questions?"

Tex reached around the back of his jeans and pulled a set of handcuffs off his belt loop. He snapped one on me and winked when Jimmy wasn't looking.

"I'm not saying anything until I talk to my lawyer," I said.

Tex turned to Jimmy. "They all get like this. Let me take her downtown for questioning. We'll keep you in the loop if anything comes up."

Jimmy nodded and set the notepad and pen on his desk.

Tex took Rocky's leash in one hand and kept his other on the cuffs behind my back. He steered me out of the building, and I played along until we hit the sidewalk, then turned my back to him. "Undo these handcuffs before you get any ideas."

He looped the end of Rocky's leash around his wrist and whispered in my ear from behind. "You should be so lucky."

"I have been so lucky, remember? I was once arrested for the murder of my best friend."

"That's right," he said. He slipped the key into the handcuffs and unlocked them. I massaged my wrists while he tucked the cuffs back into his waistband. "If I recall correctly, you weren't talking to me at the time. There's a lesson in there. Let's see if I can figure out what it is."

I swatted his arm. Rocky peed on a telephone pole, and then we walked side by side to Tex's Jeep. I scooped up the fabric of my dachshund dress and held it in my left arm while I pulled myself into the seat with my right. Riding around in a Jeep had proven to be one of the more inconvenient things I had to do while wearing vintage apparel, but Tex and I were alike enough to respect our mutual differences.

It was quarter to six. Traffic on the downtown streets was heavy with the influx of drivers getting off work. "Have you eaten today?" Tex asked.

"Not much."

"Are you up for barbecue?"

I glanced down at my dress. Texas barbecue was in a class of its own, and Tex was currently having a love affair with Terry Black's on Main Street. I wouldn't turn down the opportunity to eat there, but my dress would suffer. The meat smokers made it so any fabric in a one-block radius picked up the scent.

"I suppose."

"I brought you a sweatshirt." He bent down to the floor and picked up a gray Lakewood PD pullover which he then sat on my lap. The collar and cuffs were threadbare from several cycles through the wash machine over several years.

"How considerate," I said wryly. I turned the sweatshirt inside out and pulled it on over my dress.

Terry Black's BBQ was about two miles from the *Dallas Tribune*, and we arrived quickly. Already the smoky scent of black pepper and wood coated the air. We parked in their lot, and I picked out a table with Rocky while Tex went through the ordering line, rejoining us shortly thereafter with two trays, a bottle of water for me, and a Lone Star Beer for him. Rocky settled himself under the table and waited patiently for me to feed him something from my tray.

"Do you want to tell me what that was all about back at the paper?" Tex asked.

"Sure." I bit into a burnt brisket end and let it melt in my mouth. I pinched off a minuscule piece and held it under the table. Within moments I felt Rocky's rough tongue on my fingers. "You know about the obituary, right?"

A cloud passed over Tex's face. "Yes."

I wiped off my hands. "Once the newspaper was informed of their error, they promised to run a retraction. I trusted that they would do what they said. I was at my studio when Punch Snyder, the man who took me to the newspaper offices, arrived with today's edition of the *Tribune*."

"Lots of questions here. First: what did the paper say?"

"You didn't see?"

"Been buried in requests for overtime."

I nodded. "They printed the correct obituary, but they used my name and photo. So instead of me being a deceased mid-century modern interior decorator who modeled her life after Doris Day, I'm a deceased little-remembered jazz singer who headlined a local club in the sixties."

"Your name," he said. I nodded. "Your picture." I nodded. "You look pretty good for a ninety-five-year-old woman."

"The photo they used was the same one I used when I renewed my decorator's license. I wore a vintage dress that belonged to—"

"I don't need to hear another obituary."

"—fair enough. Let's just say I dressed to fit the image of the mid-century, so the image that ran in the paper looks like it might have been from that era."

"Have you ever considered rethinking your image?"

I raised one hand and ticked items off on my fingers. "Have you ever rethought your Jeep, your bachelor pad, your reputation as a womanizer?"

"I'm teasing you, Night. You know I love you the way you are."

"And I, you. Now, can we eat?"

Sounds of trays and used flatware clanking into bins, butcher paper being crumbled into balls, and the general tangle of too many conversations filled the background while we devoured our food. Strains of Western swing were barely audible over the din but complemented the general ruckus nicely. From a design concept standpoint, I had to give them credit.

Tex finished his meal first but not by much. He leaned back in his chair and studied me. "You know I didn't mean that, right?"

"The part where you wonder if I'd ever reconsider how I dress or the part where you love me as I am?" I speared my final piece of brisket and popped it into my mouth. I savored the smoky flavors and then swallowed and finished with a sip of water while waiting for his response.

His eyes twinkled, and I knew he knew I was poking at him. "I know you're committed to the Doris Day thing, but if you ever wanted to go Goldie Hawn in the *Laugh-In* years, I'd be okay with that too."

I balled up my napkin and lobbed it at him. Men!

Despite the sweatshirt that Tex had considerately provided, the scent of barbecue penetrated the fibers of my clothes, my hair, and my skin. I headed to the Jeep with Rocky while Tex bussed our table. My phone, which I'd left in the car, showed a voicemail notification from Punch.

What could I have possibly done now?

I called him back and identified myself.

He paused for a brief moment. "Listen, I need to apologize. I went after you hard in the car, but from what people say, you're on the level." Another pause. "And after today at the newspaper office, I get that you weren't trying to make a play for Jack."

"Does Jack know you've appointed yourself the gold digger police?"

"It's not like that. Jack and my mom—a lot of old jazz players —were famous once, but these days, most people see them as old, if they see them at all. You took an interest in him, and that seemed suspicious."

I turned around and scanned the restaurant for Tex. He was standing off to the side of the smokers talking with one of the pitmasters. I feared what ideas he was getting, but he had a rooftop deck at his place and if he wanted, he could smoke barbecued meats to his heart's content.

"That's unfortunate," I said absentmindedly. "Jack seems like a nice man, and I like talking to people who have stories about my favorite era."

"That's why I called. I own a jazz club in Lower Greenville. When I checked up on you, I found out you're a—successful decorator. I'm considering—a renovation. Do you think—" Every sentence Punch spoke had an awkward pause, as if there were a double meaning and he was hinting at which parts were spoken in code. "—you could come by?"

My curiosity was piqued. "Sure," I said. "What's it called?"

"Eight to the Bar."

"When's a good time for me to come?"

"Now would be great. We're closed to the public for a few days, but I'll be here until well past midnight."

I said I'd try to make it, and I hung up.

I glanced at Tex. He'd finished his conversation with the pitmaster and was on his way to the car. I rolled down the window despite the crispness of the October air, hoping to accelerate the process of airing out my clothes. When Tex got closer, I said, "Have you heard of a club called Eight to the Bar?"

"Jazz, right? Out on Abrams?"

When it came to Dallas, Tex was as reliable as Google Maps. He'd been a cop for over twenty-five years and after an awkward transition into the captain chair, had settled in and showed no signs of retiring. All that knowledge of Dallas's dark corners made him a valuable asset, so the city showed no interest in moving him out either. Tex's whole life was based on symbiosis.

"Any chance you're up for another impromptu trip? The club belongs to Punch Snyder, and he said he's considering a renovation. Could be an interesting job."

"I'm on vacation. What else do I have to do?"

He pulled the Jeep out of the parking lot and took a series of lefts and rights to get us onto the highway. Dallas wasn't the most conveniently laid out city, and what would have been about four miles between point A to point B turned into a half-hour drive. Traffic around the downtown area was congested thanks to rush hour, but eventually, we reached our exit and traveled along an access road until we arrived at Punch's club.

The exterior of Eight to the Bar was covered in a white concrete brise soleil. It was an architectural detail of both design and function that encapsulated a building while providing a cooling barrier to absorb the heat from the hot Dallas sun. Brise soleils had been popular in the sixties. In more recent years, the design aspect had been dropped in place of function, with buildings covered in louvered slats that accomplished the same thing.

There was one car in the lot: a white Nissan Altima. Tex left a space between the Altima and his Jeep and parked. Exterior lights cast a hazy glow over the vacant lot, revealing a freshly paved surface and neatly defined spaces. Jazz was born out of the dirtier corners of life, but Punch seemed to have kept his club clean and welcoming.

Rocky and I climbed out of the Jeep and led Tex to the entrance. A wooden wedge held the door open, and we entered. The interior of the club was dark, lit by lights that flooded out of a room behind the bar. Tables were placed evenly around the floor, red lacquered circles with matching red chairs all aimed toward a stage set up with a piano, a drum set, and four microphone stands. Behind the stage was a thick velvet curtain.

"Punch?" I called out. "It's Madison Night."

At first, the only sound I heard was a low hum of electricity, Tex held his arm out in front of me. We both stood there, silently, listening for something more.

There was no reason to be scared, but something about the eerie stillness, the vacant property, and the dark interior of a club I'd been asked to visit put me on alert. I didn't know if Tex had his gun on him and didn't ask. Tex held his finger up to his lip and crept into the back room. I heard the clunk of a switch, and the interior of the club was suddenly flooded with light. After a moment of blindness, I saw the tables and chairs more clearly.

I also saw the body of Punch Snyder lying on the floor.

<h1 style="text-align:center">SIX</h1>

I pulled Rocky's leash taut and called out for Tex. He came from the back room and followed my finger to Punch's body. A dark stain discolored the carpet under his head. Tex bent down and checked his pulse.

Tex straightened up and shook his head. "He's dead," he said. "Do you know him?"

"Punch Snyder," I said. "He's the one who asked me to come here."

"When?"

"We spoke on the phone while you were talking to the pitmaster at the barbecue place."

"Turn on the voice memo app on your phone."

Tex and I had perfected a sort of shorthand in situations like this. He needed the facts—as many as I could remember—while they were fresh in my mind. The longer we waited to have this conversation, the more likely it was that my mind would fabricate information to fill holes in the narrative. First impressions could make the difference between finding out what happened here and not. Tex would record the conversation too and use it as an official record, but by me recording it on my phone, we'd have access to my initial recollection.

After both of our phones were recording, Tex asked, "How'd he sound when you spoke?"

"He sounded," I shook my head, and then continued, "I didn't know him very well, so I don't have much to compare to, but he apologized for his attitude earlier today. He said he checked up on me. He found out I'm a decorator, and he said he owned this club and was considering a renovation." I glanced around the interior. It could use an update, but it wasn't a disaster. "I noticed something about how he spoke. Every sentence sounded like," I paused and thought about the best way to describe Punch's stilted speech pattern. "Like he stopped midway through each sentence to consider if what he was saying was what he wanted to say."

"Do you think someone was threatening him while you were on the phone?"

I thought about it and shook my head. "It wasn't like that. I felt like he had something he wanted to ask me, but it wasn't about a renovation. Almost like he had a secondary agenda for reaching out to me."

Before Tex could prompt me to continue, a door shut at the back of the building. Tex looked at the door and then at me. He pulled out his gun. That answered that question.

I'd gotten used to seeing Tex with his gun. It went hand in hand with him being a cop. He'd taken me to the shooting range to learn how to defend myself too, so I knew how to handle it if need be. But even with a history of finding bodies, being threatened, and in more than one instance fighting for my life, there was something presumptive about expecting the worst.

"Pick up Rocky and keep your other hand on the back of my

sweatshirt," he said. "If you're holding onto me, you won't accidentally touch anything."

"I can wait here."

"Cops don't leave their partners, and I can't have you accidentally corrupting the crime scene."

Tex turned to the door between the bar and the stage. I hoisted Rocky to my chest and grabbed a fistful of Tex's sweatshirt. We moved in step. We entered a hallway with doors on either side, the left side labeled, "Vocalist," and "Office," the first one on the right labeled "Band." The last door on the right was unmarked. The exit was closed, and there was no sign that the door had recently been used.

I knew I was a hindrance. Tex could clear the place in minutes if he didn't have to worry about me and Rocky, but as long as he was employed by the city, he was held by certain codes of conduct. He couldn't risk a civilian's life in pursuit of clues, and I knew he wouldn't risk mine.

He pulled a pair of thin rubber gloves out of his jeans pocket and slipped them on, then tested the doorknob to the rear entrance. It turned. He opened the door, and we tentatively went outside. The door fell into place behind us, a near-silent click as the latch bolt slipped back into the strike plate. He tried the door from the outside and the knob turned again. It was unlocked.

"Call 911 and report the crime. They'll send some unis."

I was about to make the call when a scream pierced the night. Tex grabbed my hand and pulled me as he ran around the side of the building. Rocky jostled against my chest. We returned to the club and found Renee kneeling on the carpet, holding Punch's hand. Her body shook with sobs.

She looked up at us and as recognition hit when she looked at me, her eyes went wide. "You! What did you do to him?" she asked. Her voice had an edge of hysteria to it. I glanced at Tex and then back at Renee.

"You stay with her," Tex said, amending his instructions on the fly. "I'll call it in."

I handed Renee a wad of cocktail napkins from the bar and pulled a chair next to her while Tex stepped a few feet away. "Punch asked me to meet him," I told her. "We found him like this."

"No," she said. For the briefest moment, I feared she didn't believe me. Then she said, "He can't be dead. He can't be." She pressed the napkins to her face and cried harder while she rocked back and forth. There was nothing I could do but sit silently by.

One by one, familiar faces joined us at the jazz club. First, there were the unis—uniformed officers: a five-foot-tall Mexican woman with long hair secured in a tight bun, and a six-foot-five bald Black man, who checked behind each of the closed doors and secured the exits.

Next came the homicide detectives, the two Sues: Ling Tsu and Sue Niedermeier. Ling was athletically built, in her thirties, and Chinese. Sue was a white woman in her late forties. She was solidly built with a layer of pudginess that comes with a taste for baked goods and beer. Tex had them hired during a push to expand the Lakewood PD into something more reflective of the community.

The Sues conferred with Tex then acknowledged my and Renee's presence and walked the building with the unis to get a feel for the crime scene.

The last to arrive was Lloyd, the medical examiner. Lloyd was a hipster. He was thin, white, and bald by choice, with the sort of neatly trimmed facial hair you see on covers of romance novels about park rangers. Lloyd's job was to inspect the body and determine what he could about the time and cause of death. He bent over Punch and did a visual inspection, and then looked up and said something to Ling. She nodded and then waved a pair of EMTs over and instructed them on the movement of the body.

It was unusual for a family member to be at the scene of a homicide, and I wondered about that too, about why Renee was here. I wanted to ask, but between her obvious distress and the officers who would ask her the same thing, the question seemed in poor taste.

Ling and Sue joined us. Ling said, "Hi, Madison." She nodded at Renee and mouthed, *who's that?*

"Detective, this is Renee Snyder. She's the victim's sister."

Ling nodded. She and Sue exchanged glances. Ling said to me, "Can you come with me? I'd like to ask you a few questions."

"Sure." I leaned down. "Renee?"

The woman's hands fell away from her face, but she didn't look up. I glanced at the detectives and then leaned closer to Renee. "These are the detectives assigned to Punch's case. They need to talk to us. Can you do that?"

She nodded. I stood first and then held out a hand to help her up. She dropped the crumpled up napkins and took my hand, keeping her head tipped with her hair shielding her face. I bent back down, scooped up the wad of napkins, and set it on the bar. As shocking as the sight of Punch's body had been to me, it had to be more so for her, and not because of their relationship. She was coming off a memorial service for her mother just yesterday. To have her brother die so soon had to leave her more than shocked.

Rocky and I followed Ling to the parking lot. Rocky seemed happy to have the length of his leash restored. He sniffed the concrete blocks that marked off parking spaces while Sue led

Renee to the other side of the building. I understood the need to get her away from the exit; Lloyd would need to take Punch to the morgue to do a final autopsy. The cause of death may have been obvious, but so many other things, like extraneous fibers, hair follicles, or DNA evidence could help fill in details about what had happened here between Punch's phone call to me and my and Tex's arrival.

Ling pulled out her cell phone and turned on the voice memo app. She held the phone between us. "Captain Allen said the victim asked you to meet him here," Ling said. "What can you tell me about him?"

"His name is Punch Snyder. I met him yesterday at a memorial service."

"Was this a work thing for you?"

"No. Do you know about the accidental obituary?"

Ling nodded. "It made for an interesting day at the precinct. Did Captain Allen tell you what he did?"

"No."

"It's not the right night for that story, but I'll tell you later. You mentioned the obit."

"The woman who died was a jazz singer named Addison Nigh. It was her memorial. I was," I paused, searching for a word she might understand, "curious."

"You went to your own memorial."

People were really hung up on that. "Something like that. I ended up talking to an older man about Addison—she went by Sunny, which might be less confusing—" Ling nodded, "and Punch thought I was making a play for him."

"Let's get back to Punch."

I told Ling about Punch's response to me being at the memorial and about how he showed up with an attitude at Mad for Mod earlier today. I gave her details of Punch's and my trip to the *Dallas Tribune* to clear things up, and how he called me hours later and apologized for his behavior.

"He said he owned this club," I said, and waved toward the exterior, "and he was considering a renovation. He asked me if I could come here to meet with him tonight."

"Did that seem odd?"

"Everything about our conversation seemed odd. I got the feeling he wanted to talk to me about something, but it wasn't a renovation. And tonight felt off too. Sunny had just died, so why was he here? Alone? Why wasn't he with his family? Why did he want to talk about business? None of it made sense."

"If you had to hypothesize about the answers to those questions, what would you say?"

I shrugged. "I suppose he may have wanted to be alone. He said the memorial was for family. Maybe he was going to have the public memorial here, and he wanted to get the place ready. Maybe it's the day of the month he inventories the booze so he can place an order with his distributor. Maybe…you know, he did mention that he had to meet someone."

"When?"

"When we were at the newspaper offices. He said he couldn't stick around any longer, and I said I'd handle it. Maybe he walked into a trap."

Ling tapped the screen of her phone and it lit. The voice memo was still recording. She nodded, then asked, "Were there signs anyone else was here?"

"Captain Allen and I went out the back door. We heard a scream. We ran around to the front entrance and found Renee inside with Punch's body. She was kneeling over him, and she was crying."

Ling pointed to the club with the phone. "Like she was when we arrived?"

"Exactly like she was when you arrived. She didn't move until you and Sue asked to question us."

"Is there something about her behavior that strikes you as off? She came to the club and found Punch's body the day after losing their mother. Screaming and kneeling by his body seems in keeping with normal human response."

"You're right. It is." I stared across the parking lot at Renee and Sue. "But there was something off about Renee's behavior."

"What's that?"

"For as hard as she was crying, when she finally looked up, her face was dry."

## SEVEN

Tex left the crime scene in the capable hands of his team and drove to my studio where my car was parked.

"Are you going back to the club?" I asked.

"No. The two Sues have it under control. I'll follow you to Thelma Johnson's house."

A few years ago, I had the opportunity to acquire the property of Thelma Johnson, a seventy-eight-year-old who'd been part of the case where Tex and I met, for the low price of back taxes. It was in a neighborhood referred to as the M streets: McCommas, Morningside, Mercedes, Merrimac, and Monticello. I wrote the check and moved in slowly, at first feeling like a stranger in someone else's residence, but in time, I made the place my own with a bright yellow kitchen renovation and a space-themed den, among other design choices. Still, I continued to call it Thelma Johnson's house, out of respect for the previous owner (and the generosity of her son).

About six months ago, I surprised Tex by secretly having the freestanding garage on the property replaced with an in-ground swimming pool. A series of recruiting trips for the police force kept him on the road enough that I could schedule construction around them, and the job was complete in under a week. The unveiling went better than anticipated, although when Tex attempted to park his car in the garage upon returning home from a trip, his Jeep ended up a little worse for wear.

We made good time. Tex parked behind me. He got out of the Jeep and met me by my side. He looked at me funny for a beat, and then put his arm around me and led me and Rocky to the door. The temperature had dropped further, and even though I was still wearing his inside-out sweatshirt, I welcomed the warmth of his body close by.

Thelma Johnson's house was a simple two-story Craftsman. There were two entrances: one facing the street and one to the side. The street-side one may have been the official front door, but I preferred to enter through the solarium, where I could shed wet jackets and dirty shoes. (The other opened into the room I'd dubbed the "Glenn Den," a sitting area I'd decorated with a nod toward the Mercury mission astronauts. Some might say it was equally whimsical in its way, though astronauts themselves might scoff at the description.)

We went into the solarium. I unclipped Rocky's leash and he ran to his water bowl. As soon as we were out of the expansive outdoors, the scent of barbecue that clung to us became obvious. I closed the blinds, and we stripped down to our underwear, then tossed most of our clothes into the washing machine. I filled a galvanized tub with lukewarm water, added a capful of Woolite, and submerged my dachshund dress, then followed Tex through my kitchen, up the stairs, and to the hall closet, where he pulled out a T-shirt and drawstring PJ bottoms first, and then handed me a pair of pink Chinese silk pajamas.

"Shower?" I asked.

"You go first. I'm going to check in on Ling and Sue."

After a thorough shower that replaced the scent of barbecue with more feminine odors, I slipped on the pajamas, towel dried my hair, and freed up the bathroom for Tex. He was standing by the window in the bedroom.

"It's all yours," I said.

He nodded. "I recorded a statement of what I saw tonight. Listen to it and let me know if it fits your account."

"Can it wait until morning?"

He shook his head. "Sorry, Night. You know how it is."

I took his phone and sat on the bed. Rocky nuzzled my freshly washed ankles. I listened to Tex's statement. It lined up with my own observations. I set his phone on the bed and bent down to ruffle Rocky's fur. He hopped up onto the bed and walked onto my lap, then put his paws on my chest. "Rocky!" I said with a much-needed laugh. He poked his wet black nose into my face and his pink tongue darted out as he kissed my chin. We spent the next few minutes playing tug of war with his plush carrot, a new favorite toy. By the time Tex returned from his shower, one of us was worn out and the other was apologetic.

I let go of the carrot and Rocky chewed on the stems. "I got distracted," I said, "but I listened to your notes and they match what I remember. Do you want me to get my phone so we can compare them?"

He took his phone from my outstretched hand and set it on my dresser. "It can wait until tomorrow." He glanced at the brass starburst clock mounted on the wall. "It's after midnight. You're not planning to swim in the morning, are you?"

"It's a good way to work off any residual stress," I said.

"I've got another suggestion that's equally effective," he said, raising his eyebrows suggestively.

"You're incorrigible, Captain Allen."

"I am what I am."

———

The next morning, I woke alone in bed. Broad beams of sunlight filtered through the daisy-printed curtains and painted the carpet and the bedspread. Rocky was asleep by my feet. The clock indicated it was long past my usual time to wake. The Gaston Swim Club would be filled with water aerobics classes and water polo players, the worst possible time to try to lap swim for relaxation.

I pulled on a faded pink quilted housecoat with a boxy fit and a stand-up collar then left Rocky sleeping on the bed and went in search of Tex. I found him in the kitchen staring out the window. I tiptoed closer, then stopped when I realized he was on the phone.

"That sounds good," he said. "Keep me posted on what you find out. Thanks." He turned around and pulled white earbuds out of his ears, then tossed the pair onto the placemat on the table. "You're up."

"You didn't wake me."

"You looked too peaceful to wake," he said. "Besides, I thought it might be more fun to swim here."

"My pool isn't designed for lap swimming," I said. I poured myself a fresh cup of coffee while Tex watched me.

He took a pull of coffee. "So, what's on the agenda today?"

"I can't speak for those on vacation, but I'm headed into Mad for Mod. The Ledbetters canceled their appointment yesterday, and the more time that passes before I get access to their new ranch house, the tighter my timeframe to convert it to a fifties pad for their vow renewal."

Tex relaxed against the table. "They really bought a house for the sole purposes of throwing a fifties-style wedding vow renewal ceremony?"

"They did, and we won't criticize them for doing so. Once the ceremony is behind them, they plan to rent it out as extended-stay lodging, so my work will be seen by a constant turnover of people, some of whom might even be looking to move to Dallas. Add in the value of their referral to their friends and colleagues, and this could lead to months of new business."

"Why'd they cancel on you? Not second thoughts?"

This part troubled me more than I cared to admit to Tex. I pulled out a dining room chair and sat on the yellow cotton cushion pad. "Linda saw the obituary. She thought I was no longer a viable candidate to do the work she wanted."

"She thought you died."

"Well, yes." I fiddled with the handle on my coffee mug then looked at Tex. "Linda doesn't know me well enough to think that obituary was anything other than real. At least you had the foresight to check if it were true before canceling our dinner plans."

The obituary first appeared in last Thursday's *Dallas Tribune* and was picked up in each of the major papers by Friday. At the time, I'd been on my way to the world's biggest flea market in Canton, and it wasn't until far later that I realized I'd forgotten to pack my phone charger. I certainly didn't need my phone's GPS since I was back and forth to Canton First Monday Trade Days more times than I could count, but my battery was low thanks to a full day of texting photos to Effie to check against our inventory before haggling and calculating the total of the items I purchased.

The hours listed on the First Trade Days website are sun-up to sundown, and on that wet, late September day, sundown closed in around seven-thirty. I made one last lap of the place to procure any end-of-day bargains, (a never used 1950 Hammond Home Party Package that included dance diagrams, illustrations, recipes, songs, and tips for a successful party) then pulled the truck I'd rented for the weekend around to the pick-up area and packed the last of my purchases, a set of tension-rod pole lamps and a box of milky white glass globe lights, into the back. It was then I discovered my cell phone power cord oversight and decided I'd gotten enough bargains to justify heading home instead of staying locally for a second day of thrifting. I tried to call the motel where I often booked a room to cancel my overnight reservation, but reception was poor, so I drove directly there and canceled in person. I was a frequent enough guest that they returned my deposit.

The drive from Canton to Dallas is roughly an hour and a half, two on a busy day, and three when it rains. I was at eight percent battery capacity when I turned the phone off to conserve what was left in case of emergency.

When I got home, I plugged my phone in and then unloaded the contents of the truck into the warehouse/satellite office next to Thelma Johnson's house. It was after midnight, which meant my truck rental had already crossed over into a second day. I left it parked by the curb and went inside, where I showered off the grime I'd picked up, put on fresh pajamas, and promptly fell asleep, never once learning that, to the rest of the world, I was dead.

That didn't happen until the following morning.

There's this thing about being a single, independent woman. You get to the point where you live your life without thinking about checking in with anyone because there isn't anyone with which to check in. You attract like personalities, others who have their own lives, and it seems normal, healthy even, to take off at a moment's notice, to make spontaneous decisions, and to sometimes go to bed without calling your boyfriend to tell him you decided on a change in plans. You might even forget to turn your phone back on when you plug it in, not because you're avoiding anyone or perpetuating the misinformation that you're dead, but because there's a part of you that doesn't want to walk back downstairs on a knee swollen from a full day of flea marketing.

I didn't know the details of how Tex reacted when those flowers arrived at the police precinct. He wouldn't say. I only knew that the following morning, when I returned the truck rental, Frank, the owner of Frank's U-Haul, stared at me as if he'd seen a ghost.

"You're alive," he'd said.

"Yes," I'd replied. "Is that news?"

He handed me a newspaper. It was open to the obits. The headline told me what he hadn't.

It's funny how an innocent mistake can have repercussions; ripples in an otherwise calm day that are farther reaching than one might imagine. As soon as I saw the paper, I called Tex.

"I'm alive," I said before he answered. "Nothing bad happened to me. I'm at the U-Haul in Lower Greenville."

"Stay there. I'm on my way."

Linda Ledbetter was a new client who'd hired me based on a recommendation. I could understand how the newspapers might have informed her decision to cancel her appointment with me; that was a perfectly normal reaction. But Tex and I were something different and from the way he held me after arriving at the U-Haul, to the way he looked at me now, I could tell things had changed. I wished I knew how he responded to the news, but he brushed off my questions every time I asked.

And then I remembered what Ling had said to me last night: *it made for an interesting day at the precinct.*

So there *was* a story. Tex may have decided to entrust the details of the investigation to his team while on vacation, but nothing stopped me from asking a few follow-up questions of my own.

EIGHT

—

I changed into a yellow plaid circle skirt, a white cotton shirt with a rounded collar, and a yellow cardigan, all of which came from the estate of Melissa Kay. She'd been the English teacher for the local public school system, and her estate came with boxes of classic literature. She favored Hemingway to Jane Austen, and under the circle skirts and cardigans, I'd found twelve pairs of well-worn dungarees, indicating she'd had an interest in adventures as well.

I clipped a yellow leash onto Rocky's collar. Tex stuck around until I was ready to leave, but we parted directions at the first stop sign. It was a cloudless day with a blue sky and temperatures in the low seventies. The sun would warm things up considerably by noon, but for now, Rocky and I enjoyed open windows and wind on our faces.

I drove to Mad for Mod. Effie was already at her desk when I arrived. "Hey, Boss," she said. "Are you okay after last night?"

"How could you possibly know about last night's murder already?"

"Murder?" she repeated. Her eyes went wide, and her voice

shook. "Last I saw you; you and that angry man went downtown to talk to the *Dallas Tribune*. Who was murdered?"

"The angry man I left here with yesterday."

I didn't know her eyes could grow any wider, but they did. "Did you—you didn't —did you?"

"Of course not!"

"Did the reporter?"

"No!" At least, I didn't think so. "The police don't know who was responsible for the murder."

I told her about my evening: getting barbecue with Tex and then going to Eight to the Bar to meet with Punch. I told her about arriving at the jazz club, going inside, and finding Punch's body. I told her about Renee showing up shortly after Tex and I did, and the ensuing aftermath replete with uniformed officers, homicide detectives, and the medical examiner. Effie maintained a True Crime curiosity about these sorts of events as long as there were six degrees of separation between her and the bodies.

"They ruled you out as a suspect, right?" she asked.

"Why would I be a suspect? I barely knew the man."

"I've been watching this documentary about a woman serving a life sentence for killing a man she barely knew. It happens. I figure Captain Allen will keep them from railroading you, but he's got numbers to make too. Uh-oh."

Effie had a habit of hypothesizing about Tex moments before he walked through the door. It was as if he were Beetlejuice and she'd conjured him by saying his name three times.

I turned around. Tex was behind me. "Hi," I said.

He looked past me at Effie, with his stern cop expression in place, and then back to me. He pointed to the front of the showroom. "Let's talk."

I followed him down the hallway to the back of my arranged seating clusters. Today, he sat in a black and chrome Wassily chair that I'd found on trash day several months ago. The chrome frame was in near-mint condition, but the leather straps had been chewed through by a pack of wild dingoes (or so it seemed from the sheer quantity of chew marks). Since it was near impossible to replace the straps in a DIY project, I enlisted the help of a local cobbler who worked on the project between sole replacements. I paid him handsomely for a job well done and marked the chair up an extra twenty-five percent so it would remain in my showroom longer than it otherwise might.

I dropped onto the end cushion of a mustard yellow modular sofa that was perpendicular to Tex's black-and-chrome seating choice. I called this arrangement my Mondrian corner. A red square rug sat under the furniture, and an Alexander Calder mobile in primary colors dangled over our heads. "Have they found the killer already?" I asked.

Tex shook his head. "Everything points to Renee. She could have been there when we arrived, left out the back door, and then reentered and screamed to either get our attention or cover up questions about her presence."

"Where is she now?"

"She's at the station. It's Saturday, so we've got until the open of the courts on Monday morning to convince a judge to sign off on an arrest warrant."

"She lost her mother and her brother in the span of a week. There's not a lawyer in Dallas who wouldn't make a case for getting her released."

"Sue ran her name through the system and came up with thirty-eight unpaid parking tickets. It's enough to keep the lawyers at bay."

"Why are you here?"

"This case is moving fast, and I need to know if you saw anything last night, anything you might not have remembered when you gave your statement. I know you're thorough, and I know you're cooperative, but—"

"Renee didn't cry," I said.

"What?"

"I already told Ling. When we waited for the officers to arrive, Renee appeared to be sobbing, but there were no tears."

"How do you know this?"

"I offered her a stack of napkins from the bar. The way she was shaking, I assumed she would appreciate them. But when she stood up and went with Sue, her face was dry. She dropped the napkins and I picked them up and put them on the bar. They were dry too."

"That doesn't fit with how she appeared to respond."

"I know."

Tex leaned back against the black leather. He looked at the display of clocks, and then checked his watch. He pointed at the clocks. "The time's not right."

"Those are seven-day clocks. I wind them on Mondays."

"You have three of those at your house and I've never seen you wind them."

"I took mine to a clock shop and had the timing mechanism replaced with a more twenty-first-century option. I thought clients would appreciate the update, but I'm three for three on rejections."

"What's the reason?"

I already knew this wasn't about my clocks. When Tex discovered details like this, he explored them. Not from a decorating aspect, but to understand the thought process behind the choice. Tex's world revolved around thought processes: motives of suspects to commit crimes, to cover up evidence, and to believe they're too smart to be caught. In understanding the psychology of the criminals in his district, he and his team closed a high percentage of cases.

"A seven-day clock is one week. And back when that was the only kind of clock people had, they relied on it to keep their lives on track. Winding the clock became part of the family ritual as much as tuning in to watch *I Love Lucy*. They were aware of time ticking by in a way we aren't—time is always there, always available, and we don't have to do a thing to maintain it, but back then, time could stop. Imagine what that could do to a household: the father is late for work, the mother doesn't make dinner, the kids miss school. Medications get forgotten, bedtime gets overlooked, payday never arrives."

"Chaos."

"Right."

Tex stared at the clocks on the wall. I sensed they made him think about something that had nothing to do with mid-century design, but I didn't ask. I'd long ago learned that when he was in the throes of a case, he thought about little else.

A few seconds later, he returned to our conversation. "Anything else you remember about last night?"

I studied him closely. "Why didn't you ask me these questions this morning? And why are you asking me and not one of your detectives?"

"I'd like to keep you distanced from this one."

"Why? It's a matter of public record that I was with you. I gave a statement. Five members from your team saw me, as did your main suspect."

"This looks like a straight shot with Renee, but the obituary mucked things up. You're one of the last people to talk to the victim. It would be best if your name stays out of the public part of the investigation. I'll keep it contained from my side." He leaned forward and held his hand out toward my face. His thumb grazed my lower lip. It was an unexpected gesture of intimacy in the middle of my studio in the middle of the day, and it caught me off-guard. Tex seemed to realize it as suddenly as I had, and he pulled his hand away. He stood. He held out his hand and I grabbed it, and he pulled me to my feet.

"I can cancel my fishing trip if you want," he said. "Lloyd and I've taken the boat out almost every weekend since I bought it."

"Go," I said. "You're on vacation. I'll be fine."

"Concentrate on the Ledbetter job, okay? That should be your priority."

"Right."

"Okay. I'm going to violate the terms of my vacation and go to the station before we leave."

"I'm surprised you lasted four whole days."

He grinned and then left.

A few months ago, Tex had scheduled an unusually high number of recruiting trips for the police department. It was then that I had the pool installed. The pool was mainly a set for me to decorate and photograph for client solicitation, but it increased the value of my property and doubled as a surprise for him.

But he'd had a surprise too: those recruiting trips weren't about recruiting at all. He'd been shopping for a fishing boat. And once that boat came into our lives, Tex, his cousin Mickey, and Lloyd, the medical examiner, started a routine of heading out on Saturday mornings and coming home on Saturday nights, usually with dinner. And while my lifestyle appeared to be rooted in the fifties, I refused to take on the task of gutting and cleaning the fish he caught, so Tex tied on a vintage apron and did it himself. (I'd tried to get pictures, but he confiscated my phone.)

After Tex left Mad for Mod, I returned to my office and poured a cup of coffee from the electric coffee pot. Today's copy of the *Tribune* sat on the corner of Effie's desk. I flipped to the obituary section. At the bottom of the page, after all of the listings, was a tiny correction. *This paper incorrectly reported the death of local decorator Madison Night instead of jazz singer Addison Nigh. A full obituary dedicated to Ms. Nigh's life will be printed in Sunday's paper. To the chagrin of this paper, Ms. Night remains very much alive.*

Well, it was something.

"Where are we with the Ledbetters?" I asked Effie.

"Linda rescheduled for today. She wants to meet you at the property at one."

I glanced at the clock, this one plugged into the wall. On any given day, I'd have had a full day by now, but today I felt unproductive and sluggish. It was already eleven thirty.

"That gives me an hour and a half," I said. I picked up my handbag and keys. "I'm going to work from the satellite office until the meeting" I said. "With no distractions, I can get my thoughts onto vision boards and have something to show Linda when we meet. Can you watch Rocky for a few hours?"

"Of course. Come here, Rock. I got you a new vegetable."

She pulled a plush broccoli out of her oversized black leather tote bag and held it toward Rocky's face. He sniffed it a few times and then chomped down on the head and tugged. A few seconds later, when she released it, he took off toward the showroom to have his way with it.

———

I parked alongside the curb in front of my satellite office, which conveniently sat next to Thelma Johnson's house. Last year, the owners of the property decided it wasn't worth the price of upkeep, and they listed it on the market. I was working toward my MBA at the time, and the idea of expansion took root. Mad for Mod had started as a one-woman operation, then expanded with Effie as a volunteer and then a part-time employee. But after my business expanded, successfully, into commercial properties, I lost it all in a legal battle.

The new Mad for Mod was still a product of my passion, but this time around, my inventory acquisition was more strategic. I still bought estates from families I identified in the obituaries—that part of Punch's accusation was true—but I supplemented that with dead stock purchased in bulk from the original companies who produced it, and I spent nights and weekends taking courses on laying tile, refinishing floors, and rewiring fixtures. I used to keep a handyman on speed dial, but I found there was something satisfying in knowing how to complete these tasks myself.

I set my handbag on my desk, a maple dining room table that gave me ample space for swatches, paint chips, and sketches, and then pulled a fresh piece of 16x20 gatorboard out of my stash and set it on a tilted drafting table. Most of the world had moved from cut and paste to digital work, but I enjoyed the tactile aspect of pulling together a mood board. Linda Ledbetter's ranch house had been sold by the owner for the value of the lot. The owner refused to show the house as a condition of the sale, which led to the listing occupying virtual space on various real estate websites for close to three years. Linda and her husband purchased it for the asking price of one million dollars, which meant they would probably never recoup the costs.

Often, it was the challenge of a job that got my creative juices flowing, but in this case, the job was wide open with no boundaries. My sketches and mood boards felt flat. I'd hit upon all of the expected details: Danish Modern furniture, George Nelson bubble lamps, linear sofas and chairs, and authentic knick-knacks, but something was missing. Personality.

Reluctantly, I packed my concept boards and drove to the Ledbetter property. I arrived ten minutes early and parked behind Larry's BMW. A red Lexus was also parked in the driveway, and a woman with long honey blond hair sat in the passenger seat reading a book.

I got out of my car and spotted Linda and Larry holding hands and walking around the perimeter of the property with a stocky man in an athletic-cut suit. I recognized him as Kip Bledsoe, a former football player turned local realtor whose picture now decorated bus terminals around town. Kip had helped me out of a jam once but not without some drama first. Some days, Dallas felt like a small town. Today was one of those days.

I waved. Linda and Larry waved back, and Kip shielded his eyes and then furrowed his brows. He turned to the Ledbetters and said something; Linda shook her head no, then said something that caused Kip to look at me again.

"Hi, Linda, Larry," I said. "Hello, Kip. I didn't expect to see you here. I thought this sale wasn't represented by a real estate agency."

"You two know each other?" Larry asked. After I nodded, he said, "Kip owns—owned—the property. We found out when we arrived to collect the keys."

I nodded. Kip stared at me. I turned away from him to see if Linda and Larry thought his behavior was as odd as I did. Linda said, "He thought you were dead like we did."

"My agency sent flowers to the church," Kip said. He was struggling to justify my presence with the information he'd read in the paper.

"The paper made a mistake," I said. "I suppose congratulations are in order for all of you. A sale and a purchase?"

"You too," Linda said. She held her hand out with a key dangling from her finger. A small bride and groom hung from the keychain. "A key for you. I couldn't resist the keychain."

I smiled at the key fob. I took the keys and dropped them into my handbag. "I brought some concepts, but I'd love a tour of the place first."

Kip seemed to wake from his stupor. He checked his watch and then stepped away from the Ledbetters. "I've got a meeting back at the office. Congratulations to both of you."

"Congratulations to you too," Linda said. She and Larry took turns shaking Kip's hand. He looked at me again, said nothing, and left.

"Well?" Linda said to Larry. "Time to see our wedding present." She slipped the key into the front door lock and after some jiggling, gained access to the lobby—and it suddenly became clear why Kip had sold the house as-is with no interior photos.

The exterior of the property was impressive: new roof, power-washed brick, freshly poured driveway, inground pool, and manicured lawn, but it hid the house's true secret: a tree had fallen through the original roof and remained inside the property, knocking out support beams and room dividers in one fell swoop.

# NINE

Linda may have gasped. It was hard to tell if the sound I heard came from her or the family of squirrels that ran away from the tree when we entered the property. Larry turned around and left. When he returned, his face was red. "Kip Bledsoe took off."

"He should have told us," Linda said.

I assessed the damage from where I stood. The tree, an oak, lay on its side across drywall debris. Underneath were irreparable remains of furniture that looked impossible to remove while the tree was in place. The ceramic floor tiles under the tree were cracked, and dried-out leaves had fallen off, making it appear as if potpourri had been scattered onto the floor. It was a mess, a nightmare, and a pain in my butt, but there's one thing it wasn't: Kip's fault.

"Kip wrote the listing in a way that protected him from disclosing the damage," I told them. "This property has been on the market for three years. He was clear about his terms: the price was set for the value of the lot, and the house would not be shown. Room stats and measurements were given, but even in the listing, he says it is a generously sized lot in a desirable area and would be great for an investor or property developer. He wanted a buyer who would raze the house and start from scratch, and if that were you, this wouldn't be an issue."

"But there's a tree in my living room," Linda said.

"Yes," I said. "Yes, there is."

The benefit to wearing Keds instead of real shoes was that I didn't mind walking through construction sites or, in this case, loose branches. I looked around for a place to set my portfolio and handbag, and eventually bent down and leaned them against one of the walls that had been undamaged by the fallen tree. There was no denying the tree would affect both the concept and the timetable I initially planned.

"We didn't know what we would find inside, but this could be a blessing in disguise," I said.

"How so? We paid a million dollars for a tree."

"You paid a million dollars for a wedding venue," I corrected. "A project house. We knew going in we might have to knock down walls. That part of the job's already been started. The exterior is in great shape." I turned my back to them and scanned the living room, where I'd hoped to set up for the wedding ceremony. Beyond the tree hung floor-to-ceiling curtains. I scooped up the fabric of my dress and stepped over the base of the tree, approached the curtains, and pulled them open. The windows were dirty, but out back was a sizeable patio and a stretch of neatly trimmed lawn. "I say you plan an outdoor ceremony and use the house for gifts and entertaining."

"But there are no walls," Linda stated, as if I'd somehow missed that detail.

"Walls are easy. The local trade school can give work-study credits to students who work on structural damage while I prepare the design concept. This may look like a tragedy, but it's merely an inconvenience."

Larry put his arm around his wife, kissed her forehead, and then looked at me. "We've told everyone to save the first weekend in November. That's a month away. Is that still doable?"

"Let me make some calls. I'll have a better answer tomorrow."

The truth was, I wouldn't know the extent of the problem until I had a chance to go through the house room by room, but I feared if Linda were with me, every corner would bring another concern. The best thing about working with old architecture was that most of it required some TLC, so I was experienced in dealing with unexpected problems. This was the first time I'd ever found a tree inside a house, though, so I didn't want to overpromise on what I could deliver.

I instructed the Ledbetters to contact Effie and schedule a meeting at Mad for Mod and then pretended to study the gardens while they pulled through the *porte cochere* and drove away. I watched their taillights recede down Northwest Highway. That was the downside of their newest purchase: the constant stream of traffic buzzing by.

Once I was certain the new owners weren't going to return, I retrieved a pair of white leather work gloves and disposable plastic glasses from the trunk of my car and carried a pair of vintage Dickie's coveralls with me inside the house. Effie obtained a box of them from the estate of an auto mechanic named Trace Hartman. A series of vinegar and bleach treatments left the garments soft, white, and free from car smells. Effie ordered a stencil from the internet and spray painted my logo onto the back of each pair and then boxed up the set and gifted them to me on my most recent birthday. It was among the better gifts I'd received.

Once inside the house, I stepped out of my skirt and into the coveralls, tucked my phone into a cargo pocket, and then assessed the damage. Now that my hands and limbs were better protected, I grabbed onto the tree and pulled. It shifted about a foot, which was promising. It wouldn't be impossible to move it, but it would be far more efficient with more than one person. That would be task number one.

The tree had fallen onto a dividing wall between the kitchen and living room, which was a load-bearing wall. When the roof was replaced, makeshift support beams had been put into place, leaving behind a skeletal structure that designated where the new wall would go. That would be task number two.

I left the worst of the damage and checked out the three bedrooms and the two baths, taking pictures of everything along the way. The bedrooms were mostly unscathed, dirty, but intact. I'd convert one to a coat check, for people to drop off any personal items they didn't care to carry. I'd convert the other two into changing rooms for the women and the men. That would require shampooing the pink carpet in one and refinishing the hardwood floors in the other, bringing in lounging furniture and a vanity for the ladies, and a braided throw rug and valet for the gents. Task number three needed truck rental and manpower. I liked a challenge, though, so I made a notation to go through rolls of vintage wallpaper to see what might work to dress each of these rooms up a bit more.

The first bathroom was filled with Mamie pink fixtures, which was always a delight. The sink, toilet, and tub all came from the same catalog, and the pink and white tiled floor set them off perfectly. Repair work was needed for a few cracked tiles around the room, but I'd perfected individual tile removal long ago. Once I chiseled out the grout surrounding the tile, I could replace the broken tiles with something more unexpected. Perhaps white with a starburst pattern, or silver glitter to coordinate with the chrome faucets. The toilet appeared to be in working condition, but I'd leave that for a plumber to determine.

The second bathroom was a bit more sophisticated. The walls were black, as were the built-in storage unit and the carpet, but curtain panels on either side of the Cinderella square tub in the corner were petal pink, the same shade I'd hoped to use in the living room. The porcelain fixtures were white, which would have otherwise felt lackluster but in this case set the color palette off perfectly. The black shag carpet needed a thorough shampoo, and bare shelves needed to be stocked with fresh towels, guest soaps, and maybe even some vintage perfume bottles for a note of whimsy. In a house half-filled with a tree, finding two near-perfect bathrooms was a score. Task number four would be easy.

I returned to what had originally been the kitchen and sat on the trunk of the fallen tree while I made notes. I had a month to make this house safe and hospitable for Linda and Larry. Aside from the room concepts and fixture installations, which I could do in my sleep, the tree removal and structural repair were ninety percent of the problem and for that, I needed help. I pulled out my phone and thumbed through my contacts and nearly jumped out of my coveralls when my phone rang.

"This is Madison," I answered.

"Madison, this is Ling. I have a few follow-up questions about your statement from the other night. Is there any chance we can meet up somewhere to review it?"

"Sure," I said. "I'm at a job site now, but I'm mostly finished. Would you like me to come to the station?"

"No," she answered almost too quickly. "That's not necessary. I can come to you."

I glanced around the interior of the house. "I don't think that's a great idea either."

"Can you meet me at Eight to the Bar?"

"You're inviting me back to the scene of a crime?"

"As I said, I have some follow-up questions. It might help jog loose some details if we're there."

"Sure. I can be there by the top of the hour." I finished my notes and left.

Ling was waiting for me when I arrived at Punch Snyder's jazz club. Ling was a Chinese woman with bone-straight black hair that she'd recently cut into a pixie. It was parted on the side and slicked back with something that both held it into place and gave it extreme shine. I had a good relationship with Ling, but we hadn't yet reached the stage of swapping beauty secrets, so I kept my curiosity to myself.

I met her by the front entrance. She was inspecting the door. Instead of saying hello, she pointed her phone at the doorknob. "Does that look right to you?"

"The doorknob?"

"The door. The knob. The lock. All of it." She held out a set of rubber gloves, and I put them on and then looked more closely at the door in question. I was frustrated to discover I needed my reading glasses to see the details clearly, so I slipped them on and glanced at Ling to see if she had a comment. She held up both hands. "I've been wearing contacts since I was thirteen. I'm blind without them. No judgment here."

I wasn't sure what it was she wanted me to see, but nothing about the door seemed off. After careful inspection, I straightened up and said so.

"That's what I thought, too. No signs of forced entry. No signs of stress. No signs of anything."

"Why is that important?"

"It fits with what Renee told us. She said Punch asked her to meet him here. She said he suspected someone was stealing from the club and wanted to go over a few things with her."

"You seem troubled by the fact that her statement checks out."

Ling sighed. "That's the thing. Renee's been completely cooperative. After I talked to her, Sue talked to her. There's nothing about her statement that raises a flag."

I understood why this was a problem. Ling and Sue had the highest confession rate in the state. They had their own meme: YOU'VE BEEN SUED!, and Tex regularly fielded requests from neighboring police stations to have them teach their methods. If Renee were hiding something, chances were one of the two Sues would have found out.

The fact that neither woman's internal lie detector had gone off pointed to something else: Renee wasn't guilty of the crime in question. And if that were the case, they were holding an innocent woman while the trail of the guilty party went cold. That in and of itself wouldn't be too big of a problem to correct, but I sensed there was something else bothering Ling.

"What's the real reason you called me here?"

"We're under pressure to wrap this up quickly," Ling said.

"Why this case more than any other? There's no political aspect to it, and surely after Lloyd comes back with a full report on the cause of death, you'll have more to work with. I don't see the problem."

"Captain Allen. He's the problem."

"Captain Allen is on vacation."

"Right," she said. "But he's riding us to get a confession so we can get a judge to sign off on a warrant for Renee's arrest. He hasn't said why, but I think it's because of you."

"Me?"

"He's been off his game since he first saw your obituary. Now you're connected to this murder. We don't have a motive or a murder weapon yet, but he's got it in his head that we're solving this case to keep you safe."

I shook my head. "I don't believe he would see it that way. He knows the obituary was a mistake made by a junior editor at a tiny newspaper. Most people don't even remember who Sunny Nigh was, and if they did, they thought she died decades ago. How could that have any possible bearing on me? How could her death lead Renee to murder her brother?"

"We don't have a clear motive, but it could be financial. Ms. Nigh's death left behind a vast catalog of music. Decades of recordings. It might not have meant much when Sunny was a forgotten jazz singer, but if there's a scandal involving her obituary that brings her legacy some attention, well, that could be potentially worth millions."

# TEN

It never occurred to me that the erroneous obituary was anything more than the result of an intern's oversight. "Is that Captain Allen's theory?" I asked.

"It's a stretch," Ling said. "But the obituary mix-up raised more publicity about Sunny than it otherwise would have, which will boost the value of her intellectual property."

"But wouldn't the estate get divided between her children?"

"Yes," Ling admitted. "That's part of the problem."

I thought back over the bins of albums I'd accumulated through years of buying out estate sales. Like most of the men's clothes I obtained, I often sold the records in bulk to a third party that specialized in music.

"She didn't write her compositions, did she?" I asked. "It would be unusual if she did."

Ling held up her hands. "I don't know anything about Addison Nigh except for her nickname. She was ninety-five, and as far as I know, there was nothing unusual about her cause of death. Renee refused an autopsy, saying the family has been through enough."

"What do you want me to do?" I asked.

"Get Captain Allen off our backs. Just for a few days. I don't like Renee as the killer, but Sue and I haven't had a chance to hash out any other theories. If we don't have enough evidence for a warrant by the end of the weekend, Renee will go free, and the captain might put his other fist through a wall."

"His *other* fist? What do you mean?"

Ling looked apologetic. "Forget I said that. Just—can you get us some breathing room?"

"On one condition," I said.

"Name it."

"You let me talk to Renee first."

—————

It wasn't common for a civilian to talk to a murder suspect, but when it came to my relationship with the local police department, there were all sorts of shades of gray. I was back in my plaid skirt, my coveralls now balled up in a corner of the Ledbetter's foyer for my return trip. I followed Ling to the station and waited while Sue brought Renee to an open interrogation room. Renee seemed surprised, but not angered, by my presence. Ling left us alone, though I knew she was watching our conversation from the closed-circuit camera mounted in the corner. Sue leaned against the wall and let me take the lead.

"I didn't expect to see you again," Renee said.

"This is unusual, I know. Do you remember me being at Eight to the Bar when you found Punch?"

She nodded. "He told me he was going to call you. After he checked you out, he knew you had nothing to do with the obituary. He felt bad about the way he treated you, and he wanted to gauge your interest in joining him in the lawsuit."

My antennae went up. "Punch didn't say anything about a lawsuit."

"He was going to sue the newspaper," she said. "He said there was a case. I told him to let it go, but he said someone needed to be held accountable."

I felt my body tense. I leaned back and held up both hands. "I've had my share of legal battles recently," I said. "I'm not a litigious person by nature, and I'd rather move forward than dwell on someone else's mistake."

"That's what I thought you'd say, but he wanted to ask you himself."

"Punch asked me to the club, but he said he was planning on renovating. He mentioned my decorating business. To be honest, if he'd mentioned a lawsuit, I'm not sure I would have met with him." I was troubled by this disconnect, which was compounded by something Renee had told Ling. "Did Punch tell you he thought someone was stealing from Eight to the Bar? Is that why you went to the club that night?"

Renee looked directly at me. At the memorial service, her appearance had been retro forties, rockabilly glam. But today, stripped of the artifice, she looked like a middle-aged mom. Her hair had flattened against her head, and her lips were dry, splotchy where she'd bitten at chapped skin. Patches of rosacea were present on her cheeks. Renee took great pains to enhance her features with extreme hair and makeup, and without them, she seemed defenseless.

"Punch didn't tell you about the thefts," she said. Her gaze was steady, and her demeanor confident but not arrogant. "The Asian detective told you that, didn't she?"

I didn't say anything.

"What is this?" Renee looked up at Sue. "Why did your partner tell Madison what I said in confidence? What's going on?"

"Renee, you already know I was at the club the night Punch was killed. I'm helping the police determine what happened. They thought, I thought..." My voice trailed off. I felt the energy in the room shift. Renee had gone from friendly to hostile, and whatever I said next would either bring her back or push her farther away. "...I don't think you did this," I said, "and I'm trying to help find out who did."

"You don't think—you think—they think—" Renee stood suddenly and the metal chair bounced backward and tipped over. "The police think I killed him?"

"Ms. Snyder, please calm down," Sue said.

"I will *not* calm down. Nobody told me I was here as a murder suspect."

"You're not," Sue said. "We asked you here to talk to us so we can get a clearer picture of what happened that night. We've taken statements from Ms. Night here, and our captain was already on the premises when you arrived at the club. This is all routine."

Renee seemed to sense that "routine" could tip in a moment into "Person of interest" or "suspect." "I've cooperated because I want to help you find out who did this to my family," she said. "My father died when I was a kid. I've lost my mother and my brother in the same week. Now I have nobody. Do you believe I would do that to myself?"

Sue remained silent while Renee lashed out. Even though I was in the room, I knew Renee's anger was directed at the police and not at me. She put her hands over her face as she had at Punch's side, and I willed her to cry, to show some sign of remorse for what had happened or what was now happening to her.

I turned away from Renee and looked at Sue. I pointed to her and then to the door. She thought about it for a beat and then nodded and left the two of us alone.

"Renee," I said gently. "I don't believe you did this. I know you don't know me very well, but I want to help. Please. If there's anything you know that can point the police in a different direction, if there's any evidence that indicates who was behind this, tell me and I'll make sure they check it out."

She kept her hands over her face and rocked ever-so-slightly in her chair. It was almost rhythmic the way she moved, a steady beat playing internally to which she kept time. I let my promise hang in the air for upwards of a minute while I waited for a response.

Slowly, she dropped her hands to her lap. She stared at the desk. "Punch and I were working on a retrospective of Jazz memorabilia to showcase our mother's life. The attic is full of her belongings from when she was at the height of her career. Our first press release was sent out last week, and someone killed Punch because of it. Somebody's afraid of something my mother knew, something she kept secret. Something our retrospective will reveal."

"Did you tell this to the police?"

She shook her head. "I've answered their questions, but so far they've only asked about the night my brother died. I want to cooperate, and I've told them everything I remember. If I'm right, then I'm the only one left who has access to the truth. Go to my mother's house. Everything we've collected is in the attic. Please Madison. I don't know who else to ask."

"I'll see what I can do." It was the vaguest of vague promises, and I owed Renee nothing. But my curious side, the part of me that loved going through estates and learning about the person who once owned them, was tingling all over. Surely, this was no different than the hundreds of times in the past that I'd acquired permission to do the same from next of kin?

Any lies I told myself about why I wanted to go through Sunny Nigh's belongings vanished when Renee told me where to find her mother's house.

"She lived in a ranch house on Monticello Avenue," she said, following it up with the house number.

I almost didn't register the details after I heard the street name. Turns out M. Addison Nigh, Sunny to her friends, lived on Monticello Avenue, just like me.

# ELEVEN

I tried my best to hide my response to this information. It was one more piece that confused me with her: two similar names, two knee injuries, and two addresses on the same street. Two lives that were tangled together at every intersection.

I promised Renee I'd look into her mother's archives, and then I left, but not before glancing up at the camera in the corner. Because without spelling it out, I knew that promise had taken me from being a typo in the newspaper to being a part of the case. I wondered how Tex would feel about that.

When I left the interrogation room, Ling was waiting for me in the hallway. "What are you going to tell the captain?" she asked.

"Renee is the heir to a sizeable estate. I'm in the business of acquiring estates. As far as me doing things that are outside of my normal routine, this isn't it."

"He's going to have an opinion about you obtaining this particular estate."

"You asked me to keep him busy, right?" She nodded. "Trust in the process."

I stopped by the front desk to chat with Imogene before I left. Imogene was a wannabe mystery writer who volunteered at the police station to give her experiences to inform her work in progress. She was insatiably curious about police procedure and on slow days could be found rewriting passages from her novel at her desk. She'd brought the precinct's various half-dead plants back to life, which helped counter the dying atmosphere of toxic male with a literal breath of fresh air.

"Hey, Madison," Imogene said. She sat at her desk. The floor behind her was covered with floral arrangements in baskets, vases, and one on a metal stand. "Did you bring a truck?"

Conversations with Imogene, I'd learned, often left me in a state of confusion and this was no different. "I came here to talk to—" behind Imogene, Ling shook her head rapidly. "—get something from Captain Allen's office."

"Sorry, strict orders. Nobody goes in there but me."

Ling, Sue, and I knew the reason I was there, but now, I was curious. "Sure," I said. "I'll tell him you were doing your job."

"He asked you to bring him something. Hold on, let me call him and see if it's okay."

It would not do to have Tex know I was here! "No, that's okay. I'll explain tonight. The man needs to learn how to take a vacation."

"Right," she said. "So, how many do you want to take?"

"How many what?"

Imogene turned around and gestured toward the varying plants and arrangements behind her. "Flowers," she said. "They started showing up after the first obituary ran." She checked her watch. "The afternoon deliveries should come in any moment."

I counted the arrangements. "That's not so bad," I said. "I've got my Alfa Romeo, but I think the smaller ones will fit on the back seat."

"You don't understand," she said. "This is what came in this morning. One of the rookies is allergic, so I've had to move the others out of the way."

"Where did you put them?"

"Captain Allen's office. It's so full it looks like an explosion at a flower show."

I pulled out my phone and called the truck rental agency. "Frank, this is Madison Night. Is there any chance I could get a driver and an empty truck on short notice?" While I was put on hold, I covered my phone and whispered to Imogene, "Give me a moment. I'll have this handled today."

But like every other one of my currently mounting problems, this one didn't have an easy solution. When Frank returned to the phone, it was with unexpected news. "I've got the truck and the driver, but I can't let you have him until you provide an alternate form of payment."

"Use my line of credit," I said. "I'm nowhere near the limit."

"I tried. Twice. Sorry, Madison, your line of credit's been frozen."

"Repeat that," I requested, even though I'd heard him correctly the first time.

"I just got off the phone with the bank," Frank said. "Seemed unusual, what with your recent business expansion and all, but maybe you haven't been keeping up with your loan payments?"

The last thing I needed was a critique of how I ran my business. "I'll call you back," I said and then hung up.

I turned to Imogene. "The flowers are going to stay here a little longer. Can you handle that?"

"As long as Captain Allen doesn't need his office, we're fine. But when the guy comes to fix the wall—" she stopped talking and clamped her hand over her mouth. "Whoops. I'm not supposed to talk about that."

"Imogene, exactly what happened when Captain Allen received news of my death?"

She looked unsure for a moment, and then, as if reaching some inevitable conclusion, shrugged. "You of all people should know. Come with me."

Imogene stood up and pulled a set of keys out of her desk drawer. She led me past the holding cell, currently free of temporary residents while Renee sat in the interrogation room, to Tex's office. Two members from the more recent class of graduates of the police academy passed us in the hallway and then turned around and watched Imogene insert her key into the lock of Tex's office. Before she turned the knob, she turned to them and said, "Don't you have paperwork to file?"

"Don't you have a rejection letter to read?" one of them retorted.

Both questions went unanswered.

Tex's office was filled, and I mean filled, with flowers. His desk, his chair, the floor from the door to the window, and the windowsill. The air had a pleasant, sweet smell that was at odds with the otherwise masculine energy of the building, and while I enjoyed the scent at first, I could already tell extended exposure would bring on a migraine.

"Does he know about this?" I asked.

"He was here when they started to arrive. That's how he found out." She bent down and picked up two potted plants and then shifted some smaller vases with her foot. "When they kept showing up, he pulled off the cards and told the officers to take the plants home. That took care of the first two days."

"And then he started his vacation," I said.

"He has no idea they're still arriving, and short of tossing them into the dumpster out back, I don't know what else to do."

"You said something about the wall."

Imogene turned bashful. "Yeah, that's not supposed to leave the precinct."

"I'm right here. You can tell me without breaking your word."

"It's not so much my word as a fireable offense."

I crossed my arms over my chest. "Which wall, Imogene?"

She pointed to the one behind me. Several ferns, a lemon tree, and a Dracaena had been positioned in front of it. I put my arms between branches and separated them until I saw what they'd all been talking about: a fist-sized hole in the drywall of Tex's office.

"He did that?"

She nodded.

"When he read my obituary?"

She nodded.

"What happened?"

She shrugged. "I brought him the flowers. He read the card and shut the door. I went back to my desk and noticed the light for his direct phone line was lit. And then we all heard this loud boom."

"And?"

"Sue tried to get into his office, but the door was locked. She pounded on the door. Another deliveryman came with flowers and this time I—" she looked over both shoulders, "—I pulled the card and read it. I gave it to Ling, who gave it to Sue."

I thought back to the day the obituary had been printed. Arriving at Frank's U-Haul and having him show me the obituary. Instantly understanding how the news must have reached Tex and calling him. And the silence on the other end of the phone. That silence that told me he'd believed I was dead, and what it took for me to bring him back from that edge and process that it was all a mistake.

I ran my fingers over the rough edge of broken drywall and then added, "I never saw this," I said. "Do you understand?" She nodded. "You didn't tell me anything."

# TWELVE

I left the police station. I wasn't as surprised by the hole in the wall as Imogene might have expected; Ling had already said as much. Tex had a history of bottling up his emotions, his stress, and the pressures of his job, from way before he took the job of captain. I couldn't fault him for it because I did it myself. It kept us compatible, with mutual respect, but it also made it difficult to get close. Like two porcupines mating. We both had sharp edges and battle scars and a lifetime of habits designed to protect us from getting hurt.

Asking Tex to help with my business needs wasn't the worst idea in the world. Tex had free time on his hands, and I had access to an estate that may or may not hold a clue to a murder. But first, I wanted to see it myself.

I drove from the Lakewood Police Department toward Thelma Johnson's house on autopilot. It didn't surprise me that I'd never befriended Sunny or even knew she lived near me. The community was split: residents who'd been there for decades and mostly stuck to themselves, and newer families who moved in based on the affordability of the houses. The houses had driveways that kept the street mostly clear, except for the occasional party, and alleys behind properties kept unsightly trash bins from littering the curbs. Most back yards were contained behind fences, concealing toys and the occasional in-ground pool.

I passed my satellite office and property and continued until I reached Sunny Nigh's address about a mile and a half down the street. It was a charming white ranch with a blue front door and matching shutters. The front garden beds extended a few feet from the exterior of the house and contained colorful blooming flowers. The grass was green. Someone had kept up with the yard work after Sunny died.

I pulled into the driveway and parked. Renee had given me the location of the key, which I found in a fake rock two feet from the door. It never ceased to amaze me how people installed elaborate deadbolts and fancy security systems yet didn't trust themselves to remember their keys when they left.

Properties from the fifties fell into one of two camps: time capsules decorated in the style of the era, usually lovingly maintained by the owners, or bland boxes, stripped of era-specific personality, gutted, and then refinished by people who binged house-flipping shows on the weekend. But whatever I might have expected upon entering Sunny's house, what I saw wasn't it.

Sunny Nigh lived in a house dedicated to music. Curtains made from fabric printed with sheet music hung in the kitchen and dining room. Tea towels hanging from the oven were embroidered with musical notes. Small instrument-shaped ornaments dangled from the curtain rod above the window, catching the sun and reflecting shades of turquoise, red, gold, and silver. A red and white runner illustrated with couples dancing accented the dining room table.

I set the keys on the table and went into the living room. A grand piano took up the majority of the living room. Behind the piano were built-in shelves that held a vast record collection and a stereo system that looked like it could launch missiles into space. A microphone stand was positioned a few feet away from the piano, and chairs were lined up in rows facing the instruments.

A flyer sat on one of the chairs. I picked it up. It was the program for a recital that took place earlier in the month. In small typeface at the bottom of the program, was a line: *The organizers of this recital wish to thank Madame Addison Nigh for her generosity.*

It felt like a grand gesture, a lady of jazz opening her house for a recital of burgeoning jazz singers, and I was warmed by the notion that in her way, she helped cultivate a new generation of vocalists. I opened the program and scanned the names and song selections. The titles were familiar, mostly Cole Porter and Irving Berlin classics, two by Gus Kahn. The closing number, "Fascinating Rhythm," a classic by George and Ira Gershwin, was to be sung by someone named Natasha. She must have been good; it took guts to perform Sunny's signature song in the singer's own house.

One of Sunny's albums sat on a stand displaying a much younger version of the woman I'd seen in the casket at the memorial. It struck me as odd that she displayed her album at a concert featuring other vocalists. Was that a subtle show of power? Was this open invitation to the next generation meant to cultivate or intimidate?

I checked the turntable. The record was still on the platter. I picked up the album jacket and flipped it over. A slip of yellowed newspaper fell out. I bent down and retrieved it and then read the clipping. It was an article dated May 26, 1955, about a missing twenty-one-year-old cigarette girl who worked at a local jazz club. Her name was Julie May. I didn't recognize the name or the venue. I slipped the newspaper clipping back into the album jacket and returned it to the stand.

I went in search of the pull-down stairs to the attic, which I found in the middle of the hallway. The first level of the house was similarly laid out to the one I lived in, though mine had a second floor. I unfolded the stairs and climbed up, careful to keep my arms and legs from coming into contact with splinters from the unfinished wood.

For as empty as the house appeared to be, the attic was the opposite. Brown cardboard banker boxes were stacked along the back wall, five boxes high and three boxes deep. Trunks were lined up along the side, and in the center were two folding chairs. A heater and a fan were both plugged into an extension cord that ran to the wall. Renee said she and Punch were in the process of organizing a retrospective of Sunny's life, but she hadn't mentioned how long they'd been at it. This didn't look like the kind of project you take on for a weekend.

Once I understood Renee and Punch's organizational system, I started digging. The press release that Renee mentioned was in a folder on top of the front row of boxes. The details were concise.

*The estate of Addison Nigh is coordinating a retrospective of her life in jazz. Displays will contain costumes and music memorabilia, along with a timeline built from newspaper clippings that indicate the singer's early years as she developed her voice, her time singing with big band legend Percy Faith, and her solo career as a torch singer. Home movies will be shown in a private theater setting, and an interactive sound booth will allow aspiring vocalists to sing along with her on an unfinished recording.*

Additional details projected a timetable for opening and

gave contact information for inquiries, donations, and gifts. Punch's name and contact information was listed.

It was hard to imagine a press release for a jazz retrospective of a career that hit its peak seventy years ago would be a motive for murder, but Renee had sent me here in search of something that connected back to Punch's death. I owed her nothing, but already I was hooked. Even when a mystery wasn't involved, I loved piecing together details of a stranger's life to understand who they were. It was my way of honoring them and their choices after they were gone.

Once I got into the boxes, it was difficult to stop. I lost track of time, stopping when my need for a bathroom became more pressing than my need to go through one more bin. It wasn't until I went downstairs that I discovered several hours had passed. I used the facilities and then grabbed my handbag from the piano bench where I left it and was about to leave when I noticed something was missing.

The record album that had been sitting on display.

A sudden chill took over my body and my legs wouldn't move. I had set the album cover back on the stand; I was sure of it. I looked at the floor, and then pivoted in a circle and checked the rest of the room. The album wasn't there.

That meant someone had taken it.

That meant someone had been in the house.

While I was in the house.

While I was upstairs in the attic, with the pull-down stairs unfolded, all but leaving a sign that said, "there's a person up here."

One person knew I was at Sunny Nigh's house: Renee, and she was being detained at the local police station.

"Hello?" I called out. The house did not answer.

There was nothing dangerous about entering the property. Logically, I knew that. I'd been asked to enter and directed to the spare key. Plus, this was what I did for a living, and I'd done it hundreds of times. But all of that changed in an instant, and I needed to leave. I pulled my keys out of my handbag and dashed out the back door, pulling it shut behind me. It wasn't until I was inside my car that I remembered the spare key hidden in the rock and how I left it somewhere inside. Without a locksmith, there was no going back.

With my nerves on edge, I drove to Mad for Mod to pick up Rocky. It was after five, and the sky had taken on a dusky color, all of the brilliance dulled with a cast of mauve. I rolled down the windows. The air smelled of mesquite, probably a backyard grill cooking an early dinner. The temperature was a few degrees cooler than it had been earlier and would drop more when the sun fell below the horizon, but not enough to warrant a change of clothes.

When I arrived at my studio, the interior was empty. Effie had left a note taped to my monitor saying she and Rocky were on a walk around the block. I was lucky to have such a dedicated employee who understood the needs of my business occasionally involved the needs of my dog, but my workaholic tendencies were setting a bad example. Despite Effie's protests to the contrary, I didn't expect her to keep the same hours as I did. I happily paid her overtime, but I was probably due to hire another employee. Mad for Mod had been my baby for so long that it was difficult to trust it to a stranger.

The back door opened, and Rocky charged in. He stopped by his water bowl and lapped up several gulps, and then came over to me and pawed at my knee. I greeted him with similar enthusiasm while remaining in my chair.

"Hey, Boss," Effie said, rounding the corner. "We have a problem."

"What's that?"

"Four more cancellations. I did sell a pair of nightstands from the showroom so today wasn't all bad. I put the money into your Venmo so you're liquid until you straighten out the banking error."

Effie was a millennial. Her generation embraced payment apps in a way that seemed foolish, but I couldn't deny that this solved a particularly timely cashflow problem.

"Did the clients say why they canceled?"

She tapped the newspaper. "News travels fast. Condolences started coming in on our social media accounts. I spent the afternoon replying to posters and hiding comments."

"If we'd never opened those social media accounts, we wouldn't have to worry about that."

"If we'd never opened those social media accounts, your business might not be running a two hundred and eighty-three percent profit."

"Point taken." I picked up my desk calendar. The month had been full, but four red Xs now blocked out new business. The sole remaining job was the Ledbetter gig. "Maybe it's a blessing in disguise. Now I'll have more time for the Ledbetters."

"How'd the appointment go?" she asked.

"Not exactly as I'd hoped." I rested against the arm of a tweed chair and told Effie about the fallen tree, then went on to describe Linda's response and the new challenges involved in the job. "I'll have to move the ceremony to the backyard, and I have ideas for most of the indoor space, but I can't do much until that tree is handled."

"I can't believe Kip sold them a house with a tree inside."

"Kip knew what he was doing. The MLS listing clearly states the conditions of the sale, including that he wouldn't show the interior. He even says the ideal buyer will see the value in the lot, not the house."

"Kip's business comes from property flippers. I'm surprised it's taken this long for someone to bite."

"I can't imagine this is a desirable location for a high-ticket property. The lot might be big, but it faces a highway, which means noise and a certain lack of privacy. Kip got lucky on this one. Buyers like the Ledbetters come along once in a lifetime if that."

I wrote out Effie's paycheck while she played with Rocky, then bid her goodnight. I wandered into the showroom. In Rocky's puppy years, he'd been a menace to the floor and table lamps, but as he got older, he liked to hide his plush toys under chairs. I quickly identified the display that Effie had sold by the plush celery and carrot that sat where the nightstands had been. I had a never-ending supply of end tables at my satellite office, and I could bring a pair in the morning. For now, it was time to go home.

# FOURTEEN

The next morning, I woke early, collected Rocky, and went to the pool for my morning swim routine. I was among the first to arrive and had a lane to myself. The water helped me work out the kinks in my muscles, but instead of clearing my mind, it left me anxious about everything on my plate. After an hour, I gave up trying to relax and headed to the locker room.

It wasn't unusual for me to know the women who shared the pool with me. Six o'clock swimmers tended to be upwards of seventy years old, and I was often the lone exception. Today, I was happy to find Clara Bixby, a mid-nineties native Texan who once worked at a pajama factory I'd since inherited.

Clara was an example of elderly chic. She had close-cropped white hair and regularly dressed in colorful boucle skirt suits with patterned silk blouses and low-heeled shoes. She and her sister had done some modeling back in the fifties, and she carried that same glamour with her today.

"I sure am happy to see you," she said. "Those newspapers made a real mess of things, didn't they?"

"You don't know the half of it. The banks put a hold on my

credit and I've lost four clients already this week." I ran a microfiber towel over my ashy blond hair, rendering it nearly dry in one efficient swoop. "How about you?"

"I was friends with Sunny Nigh, so while I was happy to learn that the newspapers made a mistake, the correction wasn't good news."

It made sense that Clara knew Sunny. The two women were of similar ages and backgrounds. "How did you two meet?"

"We attended grade school together," Clara said. "but Sunny dropped out for a chance to audition for a local jazz band. Several of the girls were jealous and quite catty about it if I remember clearly, but Sunny's success shut them up."

I dressed in a red and white plaid shirt and sanforized denim jeans with red topstitching and plaid cuffs and then sat on a long wooden bench along the wall. "I've taken an interest in Sunny since the obituary mix-up. Did you follow her career after she joined the band?"

"Avidly," Clara said. She stared at her reflection in the mirror and applied her signature Revlon Fire and Ice lipstick, then pursed her lips and dabbed at a small amount that bled into the bow of her upper lip. She capped her lipstick and tucked it into her handbag and then turned to me. "I married young. My first husband, Vernon, loved Jazz." I didn't remind Clara that I remembered a thing or two about her first husband from an earlier case and let her continue. "He took me to see her sing. I remember sitting at that small round table inside the jazz club, watching her on the stage backed by that orchestra, and thinking she had it made. She went out on the road and traveled all over Texas while I cooked and cleaned and kept house."

"You've had a very rich life," I said.

"Don't get me wrong. I have. Most of it happened after I divorced my first husband. I got a job as a cigarette girl at that very jazz club. Gimpy's. I knew Sunny up to that point, but that's when we became close."

"If you knew Sunny, then you must have known Jack Folly, too."

"Jack," she said wistfully. "All the girls loved Jack, but Jack only had eyes for Sunny. It's too bad—" Clara stopped suddenly and looked over the top of my head. A pair of women I didn't know entered the locker room. Their arrival broke the spell of Clara's memories, and she raised her hand as if brushing her thoughts away. "It's all in the past now," she said. "What's done is done, and pretty soon, nobody will be around to remember those days." She picked up her tote bag. "Nice seeing you, Madison, today more than usual." She smiled genuinely and then left.

I wasn't completely ready to face my day, but I wanted to keep talking to Clara about her time working at the jazz club. I threw my wet towel, suit, and cap into my bag, collected Rocky from the dog room, and caught up to her in the parking lot.

"Clara," I called. She turned to me and smiled. "Did you know the girl who vanished from the club? She was a cigarette girl, too. Julie May."

"How did you hear about her?"

"I found a newspaper clipping at Sunny's house. It was a brief notice of her disappearance. Were you friends? Did she ever come back?"

Clara was silent for a moment. She had perfectly erect posture but everything about her seemed to slouch a bit, as if an invisible force were weighing upon her. "We were work friends. You know how that goes. When Julie didn't show up for work that night, we were surprised, but nobody knew enough about her private life to know where she might have gone."

It took Clara a moment of thought to return to what she'd

been saying. "It's too bad those days couldn't last forever," she said. Clara had always been a straight shooter to me, but I got the feeling she was holding something back.

"What happened?"

"Sunny, Jack, and I were tight until Sunny's manager sent her on the road and they came back married. Jack was in Europe by then, but everything was different. Even when he came back, you could see it in his eyes any time you mentioned Sunny's name. She broke his heart, but he never stopped loving her."

———

It had been almost a week since I met Jack outside the Church of St. Monica in Dallas. I hadn't taken the time to follow up on his request that we stay connected. I rooted around inside my handbag and pulled out a small ivory calling card with his name and number. I called the phone number on Jack Folly's card.

"Jack Folly here," he said.

"Mr.—Jack, this is Madis—this is the woman you spoke to at Sunny Nigh's funeral."

"Madis? I don't know anybody named Madis." The phone was silent for a moment. "Are you that pretty blond lady who was hitting on me?"

"That's me," I said.

"What can I do you for?"

"I don't mean to be forward, but I wondered if I could pay you a visit?"

"Sure," he said. "I'm not all that thrilled with the biography I started last night. I could use the distraction."

Jack Folly lived a few miles from Mad for Mod, and I found him sitting outside under his pergola when I pulled into his driveway. He looked the picture of effortless cool in a light blue polo and navy-blue pleated trousers. I set my handbag on the table and took a seat next to him.

"So, Madis…." He winked, "What brings you calling on a devilishly handsome man like myself?"

"I've been talking to a friend of yours, Clara Bixby."

"Clara," he said. A smile broke out on his face. "I haven't heard her name in a long time. How do you know her?"

"We swim laps at the same pool. She told me about Gimpy's and how you, Sunny, and she were thick as thieves."

"Sure were," he said. "Those were the days." He closed the book on his lap and set it on the table.

"I have a confession," I said. He looked at me questioningly. "I've become a bit infatuated with Sunny Nigh. I'd love for you to tell me about her."

"It's hard for me to talk about Sunny. There was a time when I thought—" he raised his hand and waved it back and forth. "Doesn't matter what I thought."

"She meant a lot to you, didn't she?" I asked gently.

"She used to be my best friend. I hear you're helping with the retrospective."

"You know about it?"

"Sure," he said. "Her kids asked for my help. Acted like they were doing me a favor, but I told them what I thought about it."

"Does it bother you that Sunny's life will be on display?"

"Doubt I'll be around to care much. Besides, people won't get to know the real Sunny by looking at torn ticket stubs and old dresses."

"You knew the real Sunny."

"I thought I did, but you can't really know a person until you know yourself. I didn't know myself until I left Dallas. Saw the world. Lived my life. Got some perspective." Jack stopped talking and looked around the floor by his chair. He looked up and pointed over my shoulder. "Do me a favor? Hand me a bottle of water from that ice chest?"

"Sure." I stood and turned away from him for a moment, retrieved a cold bottle, and handed it to him. Condensation dripped onto the table and into my open handbag.

Jack took the bottle and nodded his thanks. He took a long drink and then asked, "Why so curious about those days? Shouldn't you be thinking about the future?"

I sat back down. "My business aesthetic comes from the past, but owning a business is all about the future. Projections, client appointments, new leads, and such. It's a delicate balance."

"Most people spend their lives looking backward. Trying to figure out what went wrong, or why things didn't go their way. When you live by improvisation, you learn to accept the unexpected. You can't change the past, but the future, that's where the true excitement is. Entire experiences yet to happen."

"Most people want a guarantee. Proof that they're on the right track."

"That's the problem," Jack said. "The world's obsession with tracks. Why go from point A to point B when you can meander around the middle? Maybe that's where life lies. Maybe that's where true happiness lies. The in-betweens. When you're not trying to get anywhere. Where you just are."

"You never found yourself chasing something you wanted so badly you felt you'd never catch?"

"Once. It darn near broke my heart."

# FIFTEEN

As much as I wanted to keep talking to Jack, I didn't want to pry open his old wounds. He was a delightful man with a trove of stories, but they all seemed tinged with a note of sadness. I didn't want to be a party to bringing him down.

I thanked Jack for his time and drove home. I pulled a set of Danish Modern two-tiered end tables out of storage. My Alfa Romeo was inconvenient when it came to furniture transportation, but the tables fit nicely. I drove to Mad for Mod. By the time I arrived, it was closing in on nine.

Business first. There was no reason in the world for my line of credit to be canceled, and as I faced down a one-month deadline on the biggest job on my calendar, the last thing I needed was to feel the pinch of a budget. The Ledbetters had given me a five-figure deposit to secure my schedule, but I used that money to pay back my quarterly installment on a business expansion loan. It seemed like a good idea at the time, but now, I was strapped.

I called Mitchell Moore. Mitchell owned Paintin' Place, a local paint shop where I frequently did business. Mitchell had become a friend, though the favor I needed today was business related.

"Hey, Madison. You wouldn't happen to need seven gallons of lilac paint, would you?"

"I don't think so. Why?"

"I used the wrong tint for a custom job and now I'm sitting on a rejected order."

"What's the finish?"

"Three satins, four gloss."

"Is that how the job came in?"

"No. After I got the tint right, I noticed I had the finish wrong. It's been that kind of day."

"I'll take it," I said, "but I need you to charge it to my line of credit."

In the past, I'd endorsed a line of paint at Mitchell's store. After a dry patch, interest in Mad for Mod came back tenfold and we'd expanded our partnership to include rag rugs and room dividers. Mitchell often paid me in paint supplies at his cost and counted the retail profits on our collab as store profits, which worked for both of us.

"How come?" he asked. "This was my mistake. I should give them to you."

"No," I said. "Ring them up now, please. I'll wait."

Mitchell placed our call on hold. When he returned, it was with the news I didn't want to hear. "There's something wrong with my credit machine," he said. "I tried your line of credit and three of the cards you have on file. Must be a hang-up with the banks. It's not a problem for me, so you can get them whenever you want. We'll work out payment later."

"Sure," I said.

Next, I called the number on the back of every credit card in my wallet. One by one, I was told some version of the same thing. My identity had been reported to the credit bureau as deceased and a credit alert had been placed on my profile. I would need to contact the credit bureaus and provide proof of identity before having my case reviewed and my credit reinstated.

All because of the error of a junior editor who was barely old enough to go to his prom. I was going to get Jimmy Nussbaum and the *Dallas Tribune!*

It was Sunday. Any bank business I wanted to conduct would have to wait until a business day. I cued up the Ledbetter file and typed up my notes from the morning: *Fallen tree. Need tree removal crew? Call local design school about work-credit program for interior rebuild.*

After recording the problem with the house, I made brief notations about the design element: *Refinish hardwood floors. Shampoo carpet. Check inventory for light fixtures, shelving units, sofa/loveseat/chairs/ottomans/coffee tables/end tables. Go through wallpaper stash.* I tapped the end of my pen on the paper and then added: *See how Linda feels about lilac.*

My next phone call was to Sue Niedermeier. "This is Madison."

"Hey," she said. Her voice sounded groggy and it occurred to me for the first time that even though I'd been up for four hours, I'd probably woken her. "Can you stop by my studio on Greenville? I'd like to talk to you about a few things I discovered at Sunny Nigh's house yesterday."

"Sure," she said. "I'll head there now."

Rocky settled in on his dog bed with a large stuffed carrot. I put on a pot of fresh coffee and vacuumed the carpet in the showroom, then unwrapped the protective plastic from the end tables, tagged them, and positioned them in the empty spot. I pushed a tropical-printed sofa into the space between the tables and moved a surfboard-shaped Danish modern coffee table to the front. I filled a glass bowl with colorful, individually wrapped hard candies, then removed the blue and pink ones from the bowl, leaving behind the shades that matched the green, yellow, and orange print on the fabric of the sofa.

Through the front windows, I saw a gray sedan pull up alongside the curb. It was Sue. Her hair was in a stubby ponytail, and the left side looked flatter than the right. She carried a coffee cup with her to the front door. She spotted me and waved, and I unlocked the door and let her in.

"Hi," I said. I pointed at her cup. "As soon as that's empty, I've got a fresh pot ready to give you a refill."

"It was a late night."

"Another homicide?"

"Saturday night karaoke. Ling wanted to close down the bar."

As long as I had a new seating arrangement in my showroom, it seemed convenient to use it. I led Sue to the sofa, and we sat side by side.

"What's happening with Renee?" I asked.

"She's still being held, but we don't have enough for a warrant. She's been completely cooperative. Every person we've spoken to says she and her brother were on good terms."

"Something happened yesterday," I said. "It might be nothing, but I thought I should tell you."

Sue nodded and gestured for me to talk while she drank her coffee.

"I went to Sunny Nigh's house at Renee's suggestion."

"How'd you get in?"

"Renee told me where Sunny kept the spare key." Sue shook her head at the laziness of that. "There appeared to have been a music recital in Sunny's living room not long ago. There was a microphone stand by the piano, and chairs were set up as if there were an audience."

"We know about that," Sue said. "Renee said there's a music coach in Lakewood who trained under Sunny in the eighties. She hosted the recital for her students. Sunny loaned out her house for the occasion."

"Is that relevant?"

"We still don't know if Punch Snyder's death had to do with his club or with Sunny. Renee fits the inheritance angle, but she claims she and Punch were working together on a project to honor Sunny's legacy. When I asked if she knew anybody else who might benefit from Sunny's death, she told us about the recital."

"Sunny was ninety-five years old. She wasn't murdered. Why are you investigating her death and not Punch's?"

Sue shook her head. "Right now we're operating under the assumption that the two events are connected. Her death can be explained through natural causes, but Punch's death on the heels of it doesn't feel random."

"What about the *Dallas Tribune?*" I asked. "The mistake with the obituary started there. Punch was pretty angry when we went there, and Renee said he threatened legal action against them."

"You think a small town newspaper with a staff of five ganged up on Punch Snyder at his jazz club?" She sounded skeptical.

"I thought it might be another avenue for you to check."

Sue shrugged. "It's something. There's not enough evidence to sell it to the judge. Considering Ms. Nigh's estate was split between Ms. Snyder and her brother, the inheritance angle is thin at best. The DA doesn't think we can get a conviction with what we have so we're still digging."

I wasn't used to getting information when it came to open cases. Tex was notoriously tightlipped about these matters, but Sue seemed willing to talk.

"You said there's a music coach in Lakewood who trained under Sunny? Is she still active on the local jazz scene?"

"She was seventeen when she trained with Ms. Nigh. Her parents moved her out to California to try to break into the movies, but aside from a few bit parts playing the singer in the background, she never made it big. She moved back to Dallas, got married, and started teaching privately. Why the interest in the recital?"

"One of Sunny's albums was on display by the bookcases. I noticed it when I first went in. It struck me as odd that she'd display her album at a recital in her house, almost as if she were asserting her celebrity lest someone forget it. After I checked it out, I spent several hours in the attic going through the memorabilia Renee told me about, and when I went back down, the album was gone."

Sue's eyes narrowed. "Gone?"

"Gone."

"You're sure?"

I nodded. "The record jacket was on a stand when I went into the attic. When I came down, it was missing."

"Did you notice anything else?"

"No. The house was completely still. I even called out, which was probably not very bright, but it was broad daylight, and I wanted to give the intruder the benefit of the doubt."

Sue took another drag on her coffee cup. The grogginess I'd noticed when she arrived appeared to be clearing with either the caffeine or the information.

"Did you lock the door behind you when you entered?"

"I closed it. I assumed it would lock behind me. I didn't take the time to throw a deadbolt once I was inside, no. Why?"

"If it was locked, then your visitor had a key. If you didn't lock it, someone could have come in behind you. Ling and I will check it out."

"I left in a hurry. The spare key from the rock outside is probably still sitting on the dining room table."

"I'll call the music teacher. If she doesn't have a key, her husband might."

"Why is that?"

"He's a realtor. Kip Bledsoe. His wife, Natasha, was the music teacher who hosted the recital."

## SIXTEEN

At the mention of Kip Bledsoe's name, I sat a little straighter. "I know Kip," I said. "He sold my client a house with a tree inside."

"Is that a new trend in decorating? I don't keep up with these things."

"It's not what the client had in mind," I said.

Sue finished her first coffee. She stood and wiggled her cup. I led her to my office, where I refilled her cup with fresh, steaming coffee from my electric coffee pot. It was a vintage West Bend Scandia 5923 percolator from the sixties, white with an abstracted blue floral design on the side. I probably drank twice as much coffee than I should simply because I loved interacting with it.

"Kip's wife is the music teacher who held a recital in Sunny Nigh's living room?"

"Yes. Does that mean something to you?"

"I'm not sure." It felt like too much of a coincidence, and Tex had taught me a long time ago that coincidences were rarely what they seemed. But if it weren't a coincidence, I didn't yet know what it was or how it related to me, Sunny, or Punch Snyder's death.

"Do you think I could come with you when you go to Sunny's house? I'd love to put that key back outside so I can keep going through the files in the attic."

"Madison, if the person who followed you into the house has something to do with the murder, then you going back would put you at risk. I can't have that. Until we know more, I don't want you going back to that house."

"But Renee thinks something in the attic might exonerate her from suspicion."

"Or Renee is the killer, and she made up an excuse to get you there. Did you consider that?"

I did not.

"Tell you what. If I can get Captain Allen on board, I'll have the files from the attic brought to the station. We'll get a team of unis to go over them there. It might be a dead end, but I'd rather flip those rocks and look under them than leave them unturned."

After Sue left Mad for Mod, I sat at my desk and checked my messages and email. That kept me distracted for about twenty minutes. I cleared my inbox and then opened a search window and looked up Natasha Bledsoe.

I recognized the woman on the screen. Natasha Bledsoe, realtor Kip's wife, had been in the car the day he met up with me and the Ledbetters to turn over the keys. Her hair was the same honey shade that Sunny had in her casket. Her brows were dark and arched, and her lips were a deep cherry red. Her online image was both airbrushed and retouched, a promotional picture intended to solicit bookings. Other pictures showed her performing in snug satin dresses and long gloves but it wasn't her attire that caught my attention. It was the uncanny similarities between her stage presence and the image I'd seen of Sunny Nigh on the album cover displayed in her living room. Natasha Bledsoe didn't seem to have studied *under* Sunny, she seemed to have studied Sunny herself. I wondered how much of this was for the sake of performance and how much was appropriation.

There was one way to find out.

At the bottom of the Bio page on Natasha's website was a phone number for bookings. The contact listed was Goldy Michener.

I called the number, expecting an answering machine, and was surprised when a female voice answered. "Dallas Jazz Studios, Goldy speaking."

"Goldy, you're just the person I hoped to reach," I said. "I didn't expect someone to be there on a Sunday. I'm coordinating a wedding vow renewal ceremony for a client, and I wanted to inquire about Natasha Bledsoe's rates and availability."

"I'm sorry," Goldy said. "Natasha's completely booked for the next six months."

It wasn't like me to name-drop to get results, but in this case, I had no other recourse. "The clients are Linda and Larry Ledbetter," I said as if the woman on the other end of the phone hadn't said a word. "They're sparing no expense on the event, and there will be extensive media coverage."

"When's the ceremony?"

"The beginning of next month." As soon as I said it, I heard how implausible it sounded that I might have waited this long to book the entertainment. I considered hanging up before she asked my name and I lost all credibility. I quickly added, "The

Ledbetters are huge fans of Addison Nigh. As morbid as it might sound, it was the news of Ms. Nigh's death that brought Natasha to their attention."

"Is that so," Goldy said idly. I heard something in the background, the clicking of a keyboard, maybe, and then she spoke again. "Natasha's schedule is clear for the first week in November. We'll require a ten-thousand-dollar deposit and the balance of her booking fee at the event."

"How much would that be?"

"Another fifteen."

I silently balked at the figure—twenty-five thousand dollars for what amounted to a vocal impersonator? —but agreed to the figure aloud. "The Ledbetters will be pleased. I'll have payment coordinated and add Ms. Bledsoe's name to the press release."

I hung up and immediately called Linda Ledbetter. "It's Madison," I said when she answered. "Quick question. How do you feel about having a vocalist at the ceremony?"

"We were planning on a band, something to get people dancing."

"After you left the property, I did a complete walkthrough. I can get the tree removed and the interior walls rebuilt, but that's going to eat up a sizable portion of our time. If we move the vow renewal ceremony to the backyard, it could be fun to convert the inside into an entertainment space. I was thinking of a jazz club. We could book a quartet and a vocalist performing standards."

"Is it right for the era? Jazz sounds like the twenties, not the fifties."

"Doris Day's musical career was at its peak in the mid-fifties. Same with Ella Fitzgerald and Addison Nigh."

"It *does* sound fun," she said.

While she was warm to the idea, I pressed her. "I have a line on a vocalist who trained under Addison Nigh who is available for your date. We'd be lucky to book her."

"We should grab her while we can. I bet her calendar's going to fill quickly now that Addison died."

It was a point I hadn't even considered, but Linda was right. Natasha Bledsoe was in the perfect position to benefit financially from Sunny Nigh's death. But what did that have to do with Punch?

Aside from the request that I pay Natasha's deposit out of my advance, the call went exactly as I'd hoped. I hung up, toggled to Natasha's website, and clicked around until I found an address. A phone call would have done, but now that I had an excuse to show up in person, I wanted to use it.

———

The Dallas Jazz recording studio was about four miles south of Mad for Mod in a part of town called Deep Ellum. The district had once been synonymous with live music. Somewhere in the nineties, the bars and music venues closed and chains of restaurants moved in. These days it was a family-friendly entertainment spot. It wasn't far from the pajama factory I'd inherited, so while I didn't spend a ton of time here anymore, I knew the area well.

I parked in the lot and led Rocky to the small house-turned-recording studio. Other properties along the street also shared commercial and residential designations: hair salons, tax preparation, pet grooming, and party planning. There were two cars in the lot. One of them was the red Lexus Kip drove to the Ledbetter property; the other was unfamiliar.

Rocky and I entered the building. My first impression was disorganization. Tables and chairs were stacked with paperwork; folders and files and promotional posters were strewn about. To the left of me was a check-in desk. I approached the sliding glass window and peeked through, but there was no one there.

"Can I help you?" asked a female voice from somewhere behind me. I turned around and faced a sixty-something woman with big golden blond hair, shiny gold button earrings, and gold-trimmed eyeglasses attached to a gold metal chain. The rest of her outfit was black.

"Are you Goldy?" I asked. The woman nodded. "I called earlier about booking Natasha for the Ledbetter event. I came by with the deposit." I gestured toward my handbag.

"We aren't usually open on Sundays."

"I was in the neighborhood and took a chance."

"Come to the window." Goldy stepped through a door and then met me on the other side of the glass partition. Rocky sat by my feet, the picture of a well-behaved dog. Goldy flipped through a desk calendar until she reached November, and then tapped a long, gold fingernail on the end of the month. "What day did you say this would be?"

"Saturday."

She grabbed a pen and wrote "Ledbetter." I pulled out my checkbook and wrote the deposit, then handed the check to her.

"Mad for Mod. Aren't you that decorator whose name got mixed up in the obituaries?"

Yes! Finally, someone who read the correction printed in the *Tribune*. "Mistakes happen, I've been told."

"That was a shame," she said.

I mistakenly assumed she meant the inconvenience caused

to me, and I said as much. "It's been a difficult couple of days, but I think the worst of it is behind me."

"I'm not talking about you," she said. "I'm talking about Addison Nigh. Every last drop of publicity her estate should have gotten when she died went to you."

# SEVENTEEN

"I don't think the estate is worried about publicity," I said.

"They should be," Goldy said. "That back catalog is only going to be worth money to the inheritors if they maximize opportunities to get her name in the papers. *Her* name, not yours. That mistake happened twice, didn't it?"

"Yes, but I can assure you it's not having a positive impact on my business."

She waved the check. "With clients like the Ledbetters, your business isn't exactly hurting either."

Goldy opened her desk drawer. She pulled out a black vinyl money pouch. Underneath it was a gun. I recognized the model: a .22 caliber semi-automatic. It was the same type I'd used when Tex took me to a shooting range. I mentally cataloged the details to tell him later. It's amazing what knowledge I picked up after we started officially dating; I briefly wondered if he could identify Franciscan Starburst dinnerware with the same ease.

Goldy looked up and caught me staring in the drawer. I looked away and pretended to study the lesson schedules. She pushed the gun out of sight and shut the drawer. She put my check in the money pouch then reopened the drawer and set the pouch inside. When she closed the drawer again, she locked it and pocketed the key.

To maintain the perception that I'd seen nothing unusual, I studied the posters on the corkboard. The most prominent one was from Eight to the Bar, and until recently, Natasha Bledsoe had been the regular headlining act. Again, the coincidence of it felt too obvious, as if I'd been led here by someone who wanted me to see this.

"Is Natasha here?" I asked. "I saw her car in the lot."

"She's rehearsing in a sound booth," Goldy said.

I pointed to the poster. "Does she perform regularly around Dallas?"

Goldy came out of her office and stood next to me. "Natasha has a standing gig on Friday nights. Recently, she's been in demand with private bookings. I tried to renegotiate her commitment, but the venue wasn't as understanding as I'd hoped. For now, she's on hiatus except for private parties." She reached up and snatched the poster off the board.

Her tone troubled me. I'd left her a ten-thousand-dollar deposit to book Natasha for a four-hour event, and that wasn't even half of her total fee. There was no way Punch Snyder paid her five figures a week to have her headline Friday nights at his club. If she were under contract, then she'd be expected to fulfill her end of things regardless of her rise in demand or rates.

I did some quick mental calculations. If Natasha performed once a month at the twenty-five-thousand-dollar per gig rate, she'd be making three hundred grand in a year, and once a month felt like a conservative estimate. Was her arrangement with Eight to the Bar holding her back? Exactly how not understanding had Punch been? Enough so that Natasha—or

Goldy, her manager—would have taken things to a more final level to free the vocalist from her contractual obligations?

I left the recording studio with Rocky in tow. He strained his leash when we reached the car and raised his leg to pee on the rear right wheel of the red Lexus. I called Sue while he finished. "How closely have you looked at Natasha Bledsoe?"

"For the murder?" she asked. "Her name came up in connection to the bar, so I took a statement from her. It checked out. Why?"

"She was the bar's standing Friday night act until recently. Punch was murdered on Friday night. I spoke to Natasha's manager who seemed to believe there's a lot of publicity to come from Sunny Nigh's death. She said Natasha's currently in-demand, but her booking calendar was wide open."

"How do you know that?"

"I hired her for an upcoming event."

I was met with silence. When Sue spoke, her voice was laced with annoyance. "I didn't ask you to solve my case for me," she said. "I asked you to keep Captain Allen out of our investigation for a few days."

"The line between those two things tends to blur."

"Have you seen the captain today?"

"He went fishing with Lloyd."

"Lloyd was here half an hour ago. He brought us the autopsy findings."

I smelled something fishy, but it wasn't freshly caught fish. "So you're saying Lloyd didn't go with Tex to the coast?"

"I'm not saying anything except maybe I was wrong to ask for your help. I thought you'd come up with a project for the two of you, or maybe even get him out of town for a few days. I don't want to find out you're putting yourself in danger because of this case. Do you understand?"

"Yes," I said reluctantly.

"Good. And Madison?"

"What now?"

"Thanks for the lead."

I drove back to Mad for Mod. The past twenty-four hours had been spent focused on elements related to Punch Snyder's murder, but I had more pressing things on my hands. I couldn't straighten out my business woes with the bank until tomorrow, but today was a perfectly good day to tackle work.

The first thing I did was send an email to the dean of the local design school. Occasionally I was invited to guest lecture on the merits of mid-century design, which I hoped would bring me goodwill in terms of asking for help. I sketched out my dilemma and timetable and clicked Send.

Owning a business is often not as glamorous as people might think. Admin work, logging payments, buying ads, maintaining websites all added up to the foundation of my design firm. Effie's employment took a portion of the load off my shoulders, but her ideas had added in projects I'd never considered. She moved my inventory to an online database that could be accessed remotely (previously it had been in a series of journals I kept color-coded on a shelf behind my desk) and expanded our reach with social media accounts (that I protested but allowed her to set up and manage as long as they remained focused on business). She could have handled more, but I found the business details oddly satisfying. It reminded me that this wasn't simply a hobby with a storefront. It was my life.

While Rocky, now tired out from his big day gallivanting around Deep Ellum, slept in his dog bed, I recorded the outgoing deposit in the Ledbetter file, and then added a few notes about a makeshift stage or performance area. Two months ago, I'd driven by an old dance school that was being torn down. Not one to ignore free mid-century-era building materials when they're piled up by the side of the road, I pulled over and approached the foreman. He'd been planning to take the torn-out floor home to install in his house, but his wife was tired of having a house filled with spoils from demo jobs and insisted on new wall-to-wall carpeting instead. Since he and I were of like minds, he agreed to meet me when his crew's workday ended. I left and rented a truck and returned at five. The two of us filled the bed of the truck with beams of wood from the well-worn dance floor plus the shock-absorbing underfloor layers, which now waited patiently in the back half of my satellite office for me to repurpose them.

In addition to the stage floor, I'd need to take measurements and figure out an exact layout of everything I planned to install for the big day, but tree removal was going to be task number one. Until I tackled that, the Ledbetter job would be little more than notes in a file.

I checked my email. There was a response from the design school, but it wasn't what I'd hoped. The class's graded off-site project had been assigned to an Italian restaurant in the West End. If my tree could wait until next semester, the dean felt confident we could work something out.

Well, that was just great.

Normally, I excelled at problem-solving, but this was a different kind of challenge. Removing the roof and hauling the tree out the way from which it had come was the most expensive option available. The roof was new, and I didn't much like the idea of spending that much of my budget on something that shouldn't have needed attention.

Often, my brain worked best when I didn't try to solve the problem at hand, so instead of sitting at my desk, staring at photos of the downed tree, I sought out a more satisfying distraction. The front windows were due for a refresh.

We were three weeks out from Halloween, and I'd recently discovered a pack of never-opened Universal Monsters masks from an old Five and Dime in my inventory. The masks were garish neon shades, the kind with the band of elastic around the back. I went to the front window and started clearing the current staged furniture display from the space. Once it was empty, I cleaned the inside of the window and vacuumed up any errant dust, and then I filled the back of the window with plants and trees that had been sent with condolence cards.

As I worked, passersby stopped to watch. It was all part of my marketing concept, to allow people to see how I did what I did, to give them a window into my creative process—a literal window. Word of mouth was a powerful thing, as was the desire of people to take photos and post them on their social media accounts. I'd had a sign shop print my store's name and logo in lettering that I rubbed directly onto the glass, so any images used on social media would instantly be tagged. I may not celebrate the idea of scrolling endlessly through posts, but thanks to Effie, I could certainly reap the benefits.

I tossed the condolence cards on the chair with my phone and used end tables and stools to stagger the heights of greenery and create a makeshift forest. I brought floor lamps of varying heights into the window and attached the Halloween masks to the outside of the glass shades with self-adhesive dots from the craft store, then changed each of the bulbs to purplish black. I added spotlights from the hall closet, changing out the bulbs to orange and green and aiming them from the ground pointing up. The light cast eerie shadows over the masks and the trees. I threaded a set of heavy black velvet curtains onto a tension rod at the back of the window as the finishing touch, then went out front to the sidewalk to assess the tableau with the spectators. Satisfied, I went back inside and adjusted the folds on the curtain.

The bell above the back door rang. I peered toward a convex mirror I'd mounted in the hallway that reflected the back entrance and saw Tex. He knelt and set a wriggly Shih Chi dog onto the carpet. The dog, Wojo, was both son and friend of Rocky. Wojo ran toward the front of the studio, and I walked toward the back, and by the time Tex and I met in my office, the two dogs were happily yipping in the showroom. Tex sat down across from my desk and I perched on the edge of it.

"This is a surprise," I said. Not wanting to let on that I'd spoken to Sue, I followed with, "I thought you and Lloyd would be relaxing on your boat by now."

"Lloyd blew me off," he said. "Autopsy results came in on Punch Snyder. I was in the area, and I saw your car."

"My car's parked out back."

"I may have pulled into your parking lot while I was in the area." He grinned. "Did you miss me?"

"You have no idea."

Tex being on vacation meant he had time on his hands, more so now that his fishing trip had been canceled.

"I know you're on vacation, but do you have any interest in helping me with a work project?"

"You're finally going to take me up on my offer to catalog your stash of post-war pin-up girl art? I'm in."

"Not so fast, soldier. It's a little more, shall we say, physical than that."

"Now you're speaking my language."

I told him about the downed tree inside the Ledbetter house, which felt like longer ago than yesterday. "The realtor is Kip Bledsoe," I said, hoping to detect some reaction in Tex's expression. Unfortunately for me, he perfected his expressionless cop face long before we met. "He's owned the place for three years and refused to show the interior."

"Did the Ledbetters get a good price?"

"It would have been an excellent price if there weren't a tree inside. He priced the property based on the lot value."

"Nothing unethical about that."

"No, but I have one month to turn a twenty-seven-hundred square foot house into a 1955's time capsule, which I could easily have done if not for two things."

"The tree and what else?"

"My credit's been frozen because of the obituary."

Tex's playful expression changed. His jawline clenched, and his icy blue eyes turned cold.

"It seems some entrepreneurial bank employee notified the credit bureaus, and they froze my credit. I'll straighten it all out when I meet with them on Monday."

"I don't like it."

"I don't much like going to the bank either, but in this case, it's necessary."

"Not that. I don't like how this obituary is following you around."

"Consider the alternative," I said. "At least it wasn't true."

Judging from the look on Tex's face, he was actively holding back a response to thoughts of the obit. I had half a mind to ask him to run Jimmy Nussbaum for jaywalking, but this didn't feel like the time to feed the fire with gasoline.

It also didn't feel like the time to tell Tex about my conversation with Renee at the police station, my time in Sunny's attic, or my trip to Dallas Jazz to book Natasha Bledsoe for the Ledbetter case. Nothing I'd done had been outside of the realm of my normal daily routine, but I'd been instructed to lay off. Ling and Sue had asked me to keep Tex out of the way while they investigated other angles to this case, and on short notice, there was pretty much one diversion left.

"Follow me to the Ledbetter house. You're going to help me assess the damage done by the tree."

———

After briefly discussing the best way to get a tree out from inside a house (Chainsaw? Chipper? Tow rig? Jeep chain? Beavers?), we altered our plan slightly. Tex followed me to Thelma Johnson's house where we dropped off the dogs and his Jeep. I drove us to the vacant property and parked in the driveway, then pulled two sets of coveralls from the trunk. I handed one to Tex.

"You like to present yourself as a big, strong man. It's time to show me what you've got."

"After all this time, you're questioning my manhood? Geez, Night, you're cold."

"You know my needs, Captain. Let's see if you can fill them."

Our playful joking around kept me from seeing anything off about the property, but Tex put his arm out and blocked me from moving closer to the entrance. "Hold on."

"What?" I followed his gaze, and then I saw it.

Yesterday, the biggest problem I faced with the Ledbetter property was the presence of a downed tree inside. But whatever challenge that tree removal brought on, it was isolated from a new issue: the front door was wide open.

# EIGHTEEN

Tex handed me his coveralls and pulled his handgun out of his holster.

"Is that necessary?" I asked.

"I hope not." He crept toward the house. "Wait here."

It had taken me a few years to understand in cases like this, Tex wasn't ordering me around as much as conserving energy. I stood by the entrance while he entered and cleared each room. A few minutes later, he returned. "There doesn't seem to be any new damage," he said. "I'm guessing whoever broke in expected to find something more valuable than a tree."

I held up my index finger and called Kip Bledsoe's cell. Seconds later, he answered.

"Kip, this is Madison Night. I'm at the property you sold to the Ledbetters, and the front door was open. You didn't happen to come back here after you left yesterday, did you?"

"Is that an accusation?"

I glanced up at Tex and then turned away from him. "No, it's a question. You're the previous owner and the realtor on record, so you're twice as likely to know something about the door being unlocked than anybody else."

"Maybe your clients christened the place after you left. Did you ever think of that?"

I hadn't, and I was embarrassed to admit that scenario was more likely than any involving Kip. "Have you had any vandalism or break-ins while you owned the property?"

"No," he said. "Listen, Madison, your clients bought an ugly house in a desirable neighborhood. If anybody vandalized it, it's probably one of the neighbors who'd rather see it bulldozed to make way for something from this century."

"You know, Kip, you sold a million-dollar property. That's the kind of thing that might make some people happy."

He hung up on me.

"I don't get it. This house has been vacant for three years. Why break in now?"

Tex shrugged. "Who knows it was sold?"

"Aside from the seller and the buyers, anybody who read the press release the Ledbetters sent out. The idea of them buying a million-dollar property for their vow renewal ceremony is unique, and they used it to bring attention to their existing businesses."

"What happened to privacy? Marriage should be between two people."

"And it was. Linda and Larry eloped twenty-five years ago when they barely had two pennies to rub together. Now they're two of the most successful residents of Dallas, and they want to have some fun with their money. Is that so bad?"

"You're saying that because their fun brought you the biggest commission of your career."

"I won't deny that."

"Then explain this to me. Why involve the whole city? Don't people ever do anything for themselves anymore?"

"I assume that's a rhetorical question."

"It's not. You've never struck me as the type who wants to live for other people, so explain why this doesn't offend you. What makes them different?"

"There's something about the two of them. They're in sync. Us, we've both had our share of bad relationships. We've seen people murder in the name of love. The Ledbetters," I said, gesturing to the empty interior of the house as if it represented Linda and Larry's love for each other, "they met when they had nothing. And they stayed together and grew closer through their struggles and their successes. And now they want to throw a party and invite every person who had a hand in their lives turning out the way they did. It's refreshing to see two people who, after all this time, want to celebrate the fact that they found each other."

"We found each other too," Tex said.

Tex's statement took me by surprise. We were all wrong on paper, but something about us worked. There were times when I slept next to him, when I curled up against his warm body with his arm loosely holding me in place, that I felt at peace. I'd always thought a part of us functioning so well was the fact that we didn't talk about it.

"I—we—I—" I grappled for words. "I suppose we did," I said. "We never should have met, let alone started a romantic relationship."

Tex approached me slowly. "But we did."

"Yes, we did."

He brushed my hair out of my face. "Maybe we were as destined to meet as the Ledbetters."

My breath caught in my throat. "Maybe."

"I want to spend the rest of my life with you, Night. I want to protect you and keep you safe."

What started as a sweet sentiment turned into a cliché. I leaned back, not fully willing to destroy the moment, but not sure I was willing to go all-in on his prehistoric views on love either. "I want you in my life too, but you know you can't protect me or keep me safe."

"You know what I mean."

"I'm not sure I do."

"I'm a cop. Facing danger is what I do. When I saw that obituary—when I thought you were dead—"

"—you put your fist through a wall." I studied his face. "I saw the damage."

Tex's face colored and his body went rigid. We were too close for me not to notice. Tension coursed off him, but neither of us stepped apart.

"Don't you realize that's exactly how I feel every time you get wrapped up in a case?" I asked gently. "I know you're a cop, Tex. I know your job is likely what will kill you. Yet I don't ask you to quit. I don't tell you your hours are crazy or accuse you of being married to your job. I don't pretend you don't rush toward danger. I know you do."

Tex's pent-up tension exploded, and his arms dropped off me. "But you're a decorator," he said. "How many decorators die in the line of duty?"

I stepped away and held up my hands. "Don't force me to be something I'm not," I said. We stood face to face, the playfulness shattered like a mirror that's been hit by a meteor. I reached my hand up and touched his cheek. "Maybe this is what we are," I said to him. "Maybe this is enough."

Tex put his hand over mine. The warmth flooded from my palm to my heart to my toes, and I felt alive with nerve endings.

For the briefest moment, I thought that was it, that I'd diffused the situation and he'd agree and we'd enter the house and assess the damage done by the tree.

"Why can't you be like other women just this once?" he asked.

"I am what I am," I said.

We stared at each other while an early October breeze alerted the leaves around us that a storm was coming. I didn't know what to say or do so I said and did nothing. After a stretch of silence, Tex raised my hand to his lips and kissed it, and then stepped back, dropped it, and walked away. I watched him pull out his phone and call someone, and then he continued walking until he was out of my sight, past the house, and down the street. He never once looked back.

I never thought it would be me. I never thought I would be the one to run away from commitment when it came back into my life. Tex's whole history, his whole way of life before we got together, centered around cop bars and strip clubs and a revolving door to his bedroom. I'd accepted that. But here we were at a crossroads, and I was the one who put on the brakes. I loved Tex's company. He made me think. He challenged me. He brought things out in me that other people didn't even know were there. So what was the problem? Had I been that burned by my last real relationship—did I believe that anyone who said they wanted to spend their life with me was ultimately lying?

There wasn't much I could do about the tree now. I walked the perimeter of the house and then spent the next two hours carrying tree limbs out to the curb. It was physically draining work that kept me from thinking too much about how things had gone with Tex, about the role I played in the situation, and about how my closeted skeletons were rearing their ugly heads. When I couldn't bear to lift another armload of branches, I left.

When I got home, I was greeted by Rocky and Wojo. I let them both out in the backyard where they ran around while I sat on the porch swing and stared at the sky. The moon was in the waning gibbous state, three-quarters visible, one-quarter in shadows. It mirrored everything, what we can see and what we can't. What we take for granted and think will always be there, and what we don't even know is right in front of us. What gives us light, and what cloaks us in darkness.

That night, I fell asleep alone with the moon visible from my bedroom window. When I woke up, it was gone. I felt its absence more than I ever would have predicted.

## NINETEEN

Of the various pressing issues I woke to on Monday morning, one met me face to face. Wojo, Tex's dog. He pranced over the covers next to me. He was a little guy, half the size of Rocky thanks to the Chihuahua in his mix, but in some ways, he was twice as feisty. As used to having him around as I was, I couldn't keep him indefinitely, and it seemed immature to wait for Tex to make the first move.

After getting ready, I let the dogs out for a morning run and called Tex. It was quarter to eight.

"Hey," he answered. His voice was low and gravelly, as if "Hey" was the first word he'd uttered today.

"Hi," I replied. I let the moment breathe before speaking again. "Wojo's in the yard with Rocky. I can drop him off this morning if you want."

"Wojo," he said. After another beat of silence, he said, "Can you watch him until tonight? I've got a busy day booked."

Relief flooded over me. Maybe we just needed to talk, to clear the air. "I'll bring him to your place after I close the store. Six thirty or seven-ish."

"Sounds good."

The phone went silent again and I wasn't sure if he had more to say or if he was giving me a chance to talk. "I should go. I've got a busy day too."

"Okay. Thanks, Night."

I didn't have time to sit around thinking about our argument if I could even call it that. Was it technically an argument when the point of contention was what felt like a proposal? Wasn't that what Tex had implied? And if it was, had I turned him down?

I packed up the dogs and drove to the bank. Pete Cross, the small business loan officer who managed my account, was in his cubicle. I told a greeter I needed to speak to him, the message was relayed, and a few minutes later, we were face to face. He stared at me as if he'd seen a ghost.

"I'm not dead," I said. Blunt? Yes. Necessary? Definitely. "My obit was a mistake. The newspapers printed a retraction."

"I'm sorry. I didn't know. I had the bank send a ficus tree."

"And I thank you for that. It was a lovely gesture, and it's now in the windows of my studio, though why you would send a condolence tree to my place of business if you thought I was deceased is beyond me."

"That's the address that was listed in the paper."

Of course, it was.

"I won't take up too much of your time, but this whole thing has affected my business. My credit's been canceled, and—"

"Identity theft is running at an all-time high. People get names from the newspapers and try to establish credit. Sometimes we don't discover it until it's too late."

"What happens in those cases?"

"We write off the debt. It's almost impossible to catch these people. It's better to head them off before they can act."

"What does that mean for me?"

Pete wriggled his mouse and then tapped and clicked a series of times until he had my account on his screen. "I'm going to need to contact the main branch to have your account reinstated. It'll take me a few days."

"What about my line of credit? I'm working on a big job. You'll see I made a sizeable payment toward my loan last month, but the balance isn't due until November when the job is complete."

Pete clicked around the screen some more. "Oh."

"What?" I asked. Pete stared at me for an uncomfortable amount of time. *"What?"* I asked again.

"Wait here."

I sat as patiently as I could with two dogs winding their leashes around my ankles while Pete went to see the bank manager. If identity theft was as big a problem as Pete made it out to be, there should be some sort of assistance for the victims. I hated wasting time when I had other things to do, and that's what this felt like: a waste.

The longer I sat waiting, the more tasks I thought of for my day. I wanted to keep busy so I didn't think about Tex. I'd locked myself out of Sunny Nigh's property, which severed my access to the memorabilia in the attic. All around me I saw difficulties that stemmed from my inextricable involvement with Sunny Nigh including Punch Snyder's murder. The fallout from that obituary error felt like drops of rain on a windshield; they didn't touch me, but I couldn't see anything without looking through them first.

Pete came out of the back room with a stocky woman in a light blue suit and chunky beige shoes. He led her to where I sat.

"Madison, this is the branch manager." He looked at her questioningly.

"We have a problem," she said. "In cases like this, a family member contacts the credit bureaus to put a fraud alert on the deceased's name, which is sufficient to protect the estate."

"I don't want to be rude, but I don't have any family members. I don't know a single person who would have made that call."

"That's the problem. Your credit history was frozen, not canceled. Someone notified us that you were still alive, that there was a mix-up, and that they feared there would be identity theft."

"All of that is true."

"Right. The problem is the person who notified us was you."

# TWENTY

There it was again: the reminder that someone out there was claiming to be me.

"I think I'd remember if I froze my credit, don't you?"

The bank manager held up her hands. "That's just it. One of my new tellers took the message and thought he was going above and beyond by handling it on my day off. He didn't know the person calling wasn't you, and I didn't know that the person called. We've been short-staffed for months. It's not uncommon for my employees to try to handle work as it comes in. Everybody's doing more these days. That's the new workforce."

"Let me get this straight. Someone called in and identified themselves as me and then requested to freeze my credit?" Both Pete and the bank manager nodded. "To what end?" I asked. "Aside from massively inconveniencing me, how does someone benefit from a move like that?"

Pete and the branch manager exchanged glances, and then she looked at me. "We don't know."

I'd completely forgotten about Jimmy Nussbaum's claim when I went to the *Dallas Tribune* that someone said she was

Madison Night and said I was an imposter. It seemed like a joke at the time. Tex putting me in handcuffs and leading me out of the building. But that call had come from somewhere. Who? Who wanted to be me? I could tell them a thing or two about being Madison Night these days. Maybe it would change their mind!

"Obviously, I didn't initiate this," I said.

"Obviously," the bank manager said. "We'll get this all straightened out with a minimum of fuss. First, can you show me two forms of photo ID?"

———

It took me two hours at the bank, but the time was well spent. I left with access to my business funds and a green light on the Ledbetter job and I hadn't thought about Tex once. I'd been so dedicated to my loan repayment schedule that not only did the bank reinstate my balances, but they also increased my line of credit. After a year of rebuilding and expanding, it felt good to know my efforts were paying off.

With two dogs in tow, I drove to Mad for Mod. Effie took Mondays off, and while I didn't expect much foot traffic, I needed time to regroup. I set the furry fellows up with plush vegetables (Wojo went for the peas; the other vegetables were bigger than he was), returned a few phone calls and emails, and then got to work on the Ledbetter plans.

Converting a house into a party venue required a completely different concept than converting it into a living space, but I wanted it to feel natural. Bathrooms would be seen by everyone by the time the event was over. The kitchen had to function at a professional level since food would be prepared, baked, broiled, and served from there. Linda made it clear she wanted it to feel like a mid-century party, so I'd outfit the kitchen with vintage appliances to be used by the team of bakers she'd hired to turn out cupcakes, petit fours, and Jell-O molds.

I downloaded the photos I took of the interior of the house during my first walkthrough and then printed five of each so I could make notations directly onto the images. I liked to work by hand with markers and colored pencils first. It helped me get a feel for what could go where, and how to transform, renovate, or undo previous renovations with the most impact. Where earlier I'd felt blocked now the ideas flowed easily. I sketched in a spot for Natasha Bledsoe's jazz quartet and seating arrangements scattered around high boy tables from my inventory. Each table would be lit with taper candles to mimic the interior of a club. Slubby barkcloth floor-to-ceiling curtains covering the walls would soften the environment and make the outside feel like a whole different scene. It would require some time digging through my inventory, and some special cleaning attention to remove the mothball odor from the fabric, but I had two full closets of curtain panels and I didn't doubt I could find the right thing in there somewhere.

The downed tree had demolished the wall between the foyer, the kitchen, and the living room, and I was troubled by how the dark jazz corner clashed with my plans for the rest of the living space. Great rooms weren't common in mid-century ranches, and while I needed a stage for the quartet, I needed a solution. Removing the tree would take two things: time and manpower. Once the tree was gone, I'd know how badly the floor had been damaged and what else might be needed. But a full interior reconstruction probably wasn't in the cards, not with the ticking clock I now faced.

I flipped through my idea file, a folder with clippings from otherwise damaged magazines I acquired in batches, and found the solution. Of course! A temporary wall made from breeze blocks! I had mountains of them stacked out back, surely enough to create a partial divider between a fifties-era sitting room and a makeshift jazz club.

As was often the case, designing a room took my mind off other things. I stopped for a break twice, once to get a fresh glass of water, and once for bathroom breaks for me and the dogs. I'd been sitting for so long that it felt good to stretch my legs on a walk.

We went around the block. On our way back, a medium blue Lincoln Continental with a white roof and white wall tires rumbled toward us. The car, a boat by modern standards, glided past us and parked alongside the curb by Mad for Mod. I slowed my walk until I recognized Clara Bixby's pert cap of white hair. I called out to her, but she didn't seem to hear me until I was a few feet away.

"Madison! I came here to surprise you and you surprised me."

Clara was dressed in a red skirt suit with a red and white striped shirt underneath. Her belt had a gold closure that matched her round button earrings. She opened the back door of her car and pulled a large plastic bin toward her. As she stood by her car, she reminded me of a patriotic fashion ad from the mid-sixties.

"Let me help you," I said.

"Pish posh," she said. "I can pull a cart."

The plastic bin in question converted to a pull cart, and once Clara had it out of the car, she tipped it and moved to the curb. She followed me into Mad for Mod, where she went to the newly arranged sofa and end tables and parked the cart. I suggested she have a seat while I get us coffee, then went to the office and poured us two cups. When I returned, Clara was bent over an open photo album. Rocky and Wojo were a few feet away tugging on both ends of the peas in a pod.

I dropped two coasters on the surfboard-shaped table, set the coffee cups on top of them, and sat next to Clara. She took a sip of coffee and then returned the mug to the coaster.

"You were asking me about Sunny," she said. "I remember how you like going through scrapbooks. I've held onto these for decades, and I thought you'd like to have them."

"I'd love to look through them, but I wouldn't presume to keep them indefinitely."

She held up a hand in protest. "Madison, you don't have to mollycoddle me. When I die, these things will be tossed in a landfill. Those days were important to a small number of people, and every day that passes, fewer of us are here to remember them." She tapped the brittle pages of the scrapbook on the table. The photos were affixed to the pages with little white corners holding them in place. "Take a look. See if you recognize anyone."

As I flipped through the pages, I occasionally found a spot of glue where a photo had once been.

"Where were these taken?" I asked.

"Gimpy's Jazz. That was the place to be in the sixties." She leaned closer and pointed to a photo of a woman in a long white gown on stage. Behind her, a ten-piece orchestra sat, each musician behind a small white stand with the letter G painted on it in gold. The woman's eyes were closed, her hands were up, and her body language was impassioned. A white flower was pinned to the side of her hair. She was familiar in an abstract way. I'd learned enough from Clara this morning to assume why I recognized her.

"Is that Sunny?"

"Yes. Wasn't she gorgeous?"

"She was. Were you in the audience?"

"No, this was after I started working at the club." She flipped the page. A new series of photos showed a young woman in a short uniform and fishnet-covered legs for days next to the glamorous singer. Both women's smiles were genuine, and I could tell this wasn't a staged photo. They were friends.

"You both look happy."

Clara sat back and looked at me. "You recognized me?"

"I applied a few deductions."

"Always sleuthing, that's my girl." She pointed to the photo. "I don't think I was ever as happy as I was when I worked at Gimpy's. It felt so wild. So free. Nothing like the debutante atmosphere of Dallas—always the same four hundred. Jazz was hot."

I let Clara talk. This was one of my favorite pastimes: letting someone from a different generation share their stories. Listening to Clara was no different. I dressed in vintage and decorated in the style of the era, but she'd been there. An idea formed, and I jumped on it before thinking twice.

"How would you like to be a consultant on a job of mine?"

"What job?"

"I've been hired to decorate a vacant 1955 ranch house into an era-accurate location for a private wedding ceremony. I've decided to convert a portion of the interior to a jazz venue, and I booked a student of Sunny's to perform. If you could help me envision what that part might look like, you'd save me loads of research." Lest she thought I was placating her; I added a final plea. "Between your memories and the photos in these scrapbooks, I'm hopeful we can nail the atmosphere. Maybe even recreate Gimpy's itself."

Clara radiated joy. "I'd be honored," she said. She glanced over each shoulder as though she suspected an eavesdropper.

She leaned close and lowered her voice. "I may know of a secret that will make your work even more authentic."

"What?" I asked. I leaned in closer too, and our heads nearly touched. Clara seemed to have de-aged into a younger version of herself, someone up for an adventure.

"Back when Sunny and I worked at Gimpy's, we used to hide things under the floorboards of her dressing room. She called it our time capsule."

# TWENTY-ONE

"When did Gimpy's close?"

"Ages ago," she said. "We thought the club would be there forever, and we used to talk about returning as patrons and sneaking into the dressing rooms to find our hidden stash."

My heart sank. Dallas didn't place as high of a value on its history as some other cities, and I'd seen building after building get bulldozed to make way for something newer, bigger, and potentially more lucrative. I'd never heard of Gimpy's before today, and that told me it was another part of the city's forgotten history. Whatever treasures Sunny and Clara had buried had probably become part of a concrete slab foundation.

"I don't suppose you thought to retrieve your time capsule before the building turned over to its new owners?" I asked hopefully.

"We were a lot of things, but visionary was not one of them. The building is still standing, and if the new owners had no reason to pull up the floorboards, then there's a chance...." Her voice trailed off.

"Do you mean to tell me the building wasn't torn down?"

"It's changed hands a few times, but it's still standing on Abrams Road like it was back then."

My spine started tingling, and my enthusiasm rose to meet hers. "You don't mean Eight to the Bar, do you?"

"That's right. Have you been there?"

"A few times," I answered truthfully, though I left out the more gruesome details about those visits. "I may be able to get access during the day."

I excused myself and went to my office. I called the police station and asked for Ling. By the time the detective came on the call, I had a plausible excuse to finagle a visit to her crime scene.

"This is Madison," I said. "Have you released the crime scene?"

"This morning. Why?"

"I've been talking to a consultant about a decorating job. My source used to work at that club back before it belonged to Punch, and she said there's a hiding space under the floorboards. She claims she and Sunny used to hide things there, glasses from the bar, matchbooks, nothing that would matter to anyone but a couple of twenty-year-old girls who thought they were getting away with something. It's a long shot, I know, but I wondered if I could check it out."

"You'd need Renee's permission. The club now belongs to her."

"Are you still holding her?"

"No, she went home this morning."

"Then I'd say this falls under her request that I review what she and Punch accumulated for their jazz retrospective."

"I'd feel better if I were with you."

"Your call. I'm heading there now." I hung up the phone and

turned around. Clara had followed me into the hallway, openly listening in on my call. "The police will meet us there."

"You called the police?" she asked. "I hardly think hiding matchbooks in the floor was a crime."

On the drive to the club, I explained the situation to Clara: how Punch Snyder owned the club and how his sister had been held in connection to his murder. I told her I'd spoken to Renee and wasn't convinced of her guilt, but that the police lacked other suspects. I told her not to let on that she knew any of that, realizing too late that I closed on what should have been the opener.

"This is so exciting!" she said. She held Wojo on her lap while Rocky sat at her feet. She pantomimed zipping her lips. "Mum's the word."

Ling and Sue were both waiting in the parking lot of Eight to the Bar when Clara and I arrived. They seemed surprised to discover my consultant was a woman in her nineties. I made quick introductions and explained why we were here.

"Clara used to work here with Sunny," I said. "She's the one who told me about the floorboards."

We all looked at Clara as if expecting some remorse for her act of theft. "Are you going to toss me in the pokey?" she asked the cops.

Ling and Sue looked at each other and then back at Clara. "Is that a confession to criminal misconduct?" Ling asked.

"We were girls," she said dismissively. "Girls do silly things."

Clara led us inside. The brise soleil blocked natural sunlight from filling the interior, and it seemed later than it was. All four of us switched on the flashlights on our cell phones. Clara took a minute to look around the bar. I wanted to hear her talk about what was the same and what was different, but we were here for a reason and nostalgia wasn't it.

"Clara?" I nudged.

"Right. We're here on a police matter." She led us through the hallway to the first dressing room on the right marked "Band" and turned the knob.

"I thought you hid things in Sunny's dressing room?" I asked.

"Back in the day, this *was* Sunny's dressing room," Clara said.

She entered the room and the three of us followed. A beat-up sofa was pushed along the far wall and covered with an array of shirts, neckties, and suit jackets. An upright bass was propped along the wall, and a set of bongos sat in front of a barrel-shaped stool. A half-empty bottle of Jack Daniels rested on the vanity next to a stack of newspapers. The room had been appropriated by the band, but traces of feminine glamour peeked through in the gilt-edged mirror, fat pink tassels on faded pillows, and a poster of Sunny from her heyday that hung behind the door.

Clara tapped the toe of her shoe on the floor in a few spots, and then looked at me. "Here," she said.

I suppose when you're in your nineties, you don't need to be the one to drop down onto the floor on your hands and knees, so I didn't complain about her expectation that I'd do it for her. I lowered myself slowly, favoring my knee, and ran my fingers over the rough wooden boards until I found a knothole. I fed my fingers in and pulled the board up. The inside was packed with items loosely wrapped in pages of newsprint.

"It's still there!" Clara exclaimed.

"Out of the way, Madison," Sue instructed.

I scooted backward and gave the detective access to the loot. She and Ling each pulled on latex gloves. Sue dropped down to a squat and reached into the floor, then pulled out a bundle and unwrapped it. Inside was a stack of money.

"Why, that's cash!" Clara exclaimed. She looked at me with a shocked expression. Her Fire and Ice lips formed an O. She looked from me to the detectives. "Sunny and I never stole any money. You have to believe me."

Sue handed the cash to Ling and reached in for a second bundle. Renee said Punch suspected someone of stealing from the bar, and the bundles of cash seemed to support that theory. But as Ling held the bundle of money, it was the newsprint wrapped around it that bothered me more than the cash itself.

It was the page from the *Dallas Tribune* that featured my obituary. Whoever had hidden this cash had done so recently.

# TWENTY-TWO

I stood up and joined Clara a few feet away. We watched as the detectives continued to unearth bundles of cash from the hiding space, each of them wrapped in a page from a recent newspaper. After a while, Ling's hand produced a black shoe.

"Well, I never!" Clara exclaimed. "That must be Sunny's missing shoe," she said. She looked at me. "I remember Martin—he was Sunny's manager at the time—coming in here looking for it. We must have forgotten to close up the hole in the floor. That shoe's been stashed in there since the fifties." She peered down at the floor. "Anything else?"

Ling set the shoe aside and reached back in, this time pulling out a never-opened gross of matchbooks with the word "Gimpy's" embossed on the front in a gold, cursive font.

"That was us," Clara said breathlessly. She reached her hands out for the matchbooks and Ling shook her head.

"Fingerprints," Ling said.

Clara looked disappointed. "There should also be napkins, cocktail stirrers, and glasses."

Ling pulled out a few additional bundles of bar supplies and then reached in as far as she could. "If there's anything else down there, it's out of reach," Ling said. "Someone will need to tear up the floor, and we don't have the authority to do that." She looked directly at me. "You don't either."

"Can I talk to you?" I asked her.

Ling turned to Sue, "I'm going to take Madison out front." Sue nodded.

The sun nearly blinded me as we exited the club. I shielded my eyes. "Remember how Renee told you Punch asked her to meet at the jazz club? How he thought someone was stealing from him?"

"Yes," she said.

"Have you corroborated her story?"

"If we had a forensic accountant on the force to review the books, we might have found something by now. I gave the bank ledgers to a couple of unis to go through but they haven't found anything unusual. Why?"

"The money you found seems to back up her suspicions."

"It does point in that direction. Or maybe she's the one who hid the money in the floor. Maybe she made up the whole embezzling thing to throw us off. If she planned to kill Punch and we can prove she hid the money first, it shows premeditation."

"The first bundle of cash you removed from the floor was wrapped in my obituary," I said. "There's a stack of newspapers on the vanity too."

Ling went back inside and returned with one of the newspapers in question. She flattened the paper against her thigh and then scanned the page for details, the most important one staring back at her from a headline. She looked up, surprised. "This was last week."

"Right. The cash you found had to have been put in the floor after this newspaper came out. A few days later, Punch Snyder was murdered. That's should shorten your timeframe."

"Good catch, Madison."

"What does this do to Renee's alibi?"

"Hard to say. She had every reason to be at the club, so the presence of DNA evidence doesn't mean much. We don't know their history. They might have been fighting about the club ownership, profits, money, or the inheritance."

Up to this point, I followed along and agreed with Ling about everything. "I thought the estate was split evenly between them."

Ling glanced over her shoulder at the club. "Everything except for Sunny's musical catalog. She left that to Punch." She sighed. "Renee said it had something to with the club. She didn't seem bothered by it."

"Did you check that out to see if it fit?"

"It does. I talked to the executor of the estate this morning."

"Then it proves Renee's telling you the truth. If she had something to hide, wouldn't she lie?"

"That's the thing. Now that Punch is dead, his estate goes to Renee. After Sunny died, that musical catalog quadrupled in value. If Renee is found not guilty, she stands to inherit the whole lot of it."

———

I didn't envy Ling and Sue. Their job was to string together the clues in a murder investigation and get enough evidence for the district attorney to feel confident about a conviction. In this case, there was reasonable doubt everywhere I looked. I didn't like seeing them zero in on one suspect above all others, but I knew how it worked. And because I was tangentially involved, I felt somehow responsible for the outcome.

After talking with Ling, I returned to the bar interior to find Clara. She and Sue were perched on stools, and Clara had been given a pair of latex gloves too. She seemed perfectly at home. It was as if she'd taken a trip down memory lane by coming into the bar, and despite the various updates to the décor over the years since she worked here, she was in her element.

"You won't believe it, Madison," Clara said. "Not only were the matchbooks still there but so was our secret bottle of gin."

"You hid your gin in the floor?"

"The wall." She picked up a dust-covered bottle that now showed fresh smudges from the gloves. "I used to sneak back to Sunny's dressing room for a nip while she was on stage." Her expression turned sad. "I sure do miss those days."

The bundle of matchbooks sat on the bar. "What's to become of those?" I asked Sue.

"The gin and the matchbooks were coated in dust. Nobody's touched them for decades. You can take them. We'll question Renee about the money and see if she knows anything about it."

"What about the other things under the floor?"

"The cash keeps the bar front and center of our investigation. If the public hears there was money buried under the floorboards, this place will become a sideshow attraction. I'm going to suppress that information for now. If that changes, I'll let you know."

I drove Clara back to Mad for Mod. It was after four. She left me with the package of vintage matchbooks to use on the Ledbetter job, and she left.

I went inside. Between Clara's photo albums and the trip to Eight to the Bar, I had more than enough inspiration for a makeshift jazz club inside the Ledbetter house, but instead of the job, my mind had something new to chew on. Namely, the money in the floor at Eight to the Bar.

Punch had asked me to meet him at his club to discuss a possible renovation, but the way he'd asked, pausing before he finished each sentence, had bothered me all along. Initially, I felt like he wanted to talk to me about something else, but he hadn't. I'd gone to the bar yes, partially because of the possibility of a job, but also because I sensed he wanted to talk about something else. But what if he hadn't been alone? What if the killer had been there with him at the time of the phone call? Was that phone call his Hail Mary, his last-ditch attempt to get someone to show up and save his life?

And like Ling said, this new finding neither proved nor disproved Renee's guilt. She was the one who confirmed the embezzlement. She could have put the money there to point the police in a different direction from her.

There was a third possibility. Punch could have been involved in something illegal. He could have wanted me there as a bargaining chip or an alibi. He could have been the one to take the money there, to hide it in the floor, to claim he was being robbed. If he wanted to make his story believable, he'd need a witness. I might have been the perfect one.

There was one thing I did when I needed to take a mental vacation from my life. I turned to Doris Day. I avoided the cheerier options for *Love Me or Leave Me,* the biopic she costarred in with James Cagney. It wasn't a happy story, but it felt timely. Plus, I was hoping to get some ideas.

My company's press release said I studied Doris Day movies to refine my eye for mid-century modern design, and for that reason, I tended to bypass period pieces. But Doris Day's performance as Ruth Etting in *Love Me or Leave Me* was undeniable. Much of the actress's legacy went back to her romcoms with Rock Hudson and James Garner, and I'd watched those movies so many times they were committed to memory. But knowing what I did about the unhappy part of the actress's life, I couldn't help but recognize the raw honesty in this performance. Had she used her relationship with her manager and husband at the time, who embezzled millions from her while they were married, to tap into the emotional core of the character she played? Interestingly enough, this was one of the few movies she made during their marriage that he hadn't produced.

The movie, with its jazz theme, gave me a few ideas for the Ledbetter job but provided little entertainment. When the movie ended, I switched off the screen and packed up for the day.

It was obvious my identity theft was tangled up in Tex's homicide. There was no point denying it. There was also no point pretending we weren't going to work together on this. Maybe the first few times something like this happened I showed up uninvited to the party, but like everything else, we were beyond that.

The problem with collaborating this time was we hadn't cleared the air from our argument, and I didn't know where we stood. I was due to drop Wojo off at Tex's house soon, and it made more sense to be adults and discuss the case than it did to allow our argument to balloon.

I said goodbye to Rocky and carried Wojo to my car. I cracked the back windows for Wojo and the front one for me. The air was neither hot nor cold, but it felt good against my face. It was a short drive, and it took longer for me to find a nearby parking space than it had to cover the distance there.

While I stood on his stoop, I braced myself for whatever

possible response I'd get when he opened the door. I debated whether I should ring the bell or go in when the door opened from the inside, and I found myself face to face with former police officer, security company owner, and all-around boss babe, Donna Nast.

# TWENTY-THREE

Donna Nast, known as Nasty in certain circles, had left the police force to start her privately-owned security agency. She was a successful businesswoman with a baby fathered by one of Dallas's wealthiest residents, yet she rejected his offers of money and marriage and held onto her independence. For probably the first time, it occurred to me that Nasty and I might have more in common than I ever considered.

"He's not here," Nasty said before I could ask. She stepped back from the door. "Come on in."

"I didn't know you were still his person to call in case of emergency," I said.

"You're the one calling it an emergency. Not me."

I followed Nasty up the stairs. Tex lived in a three-floor condominium with a rooftop deck. He was the last person to buy into the development and secured the place for a ten thousand dollar down payment. Everything about it was pure Tex: the black leather sofa, the big screen TV, the Bang & Olufsen home audio system with surround sound, and the Shi Chi puppy that tore the place apart when Tex wasn't there.

Nasty's baby, Huxley, was eighteen months old. He was on the living room floor with a shiny red toy Mustang in his hand. He drove the car across the carpet and made *vroom vroom* noises. Wojo approached him and Huxley forgot all about the car. He pulled himself up using the edge of the sofa, then stumbled after Wojo, reaching forward to try to pet the small dog. Along with the now-abandoned Mustang were a sketchpad and an assortment of crayons.

"Huxley, leave the dog alone," Nasty said.

"Dog—dog—dog," Huxley said. He pointed at Wojo, who ran in circles around Huxley's legs. Huxley turned around in a circle to try to keep his eyes on Wojo and then fell down. Wojo seemed to prefer seated-Huxley to chasing-Huxley. He went straight up to the toddler, put his paws on Huxley's chest and licked his cheek. Huxley squealed his delight. Nasty took all of this in stride.

The kitchen smelled like marinara. A tall silver pot sat simmering on a burner. Nasty went to the stove and stirred the contents, and the aromatic flavors boosted exponentially.

Nasty and I hadn't started as friends, but little by little, she gained my undeniable respect. She lived her life on her terms and was like Teflon when it came to what people said about her. Our conversations inevitably left me seeing whatever was on my mind in a different light, and tonight I was due for a shot of new perspective.

"Why didn't you marry Gerry Rose?" I asked Nasty directly.

She tapped the spoon on the side of the pot and set it on a spoon rest. "Hi, Madison. What's up with you?"

"You once acknowledged that we don't do the whole 'hi, how are you' routine." She tipped her head to the side as if agreeing with my point. "I know Gerry asked you to marry him. I know Huxley is his baby. That marriage would have given you and

Huxley financial freedom for five lifetimes over. Why did you turn him down?"

"I like my freedom. Just because I wanted to have a baby doesn't mean I wanted anything more than that."

"Then why Gerry? If you wanted to have a baby and nothing more, you could have gone to a sperm bank. You could have had a one-night stand. You could have approached any number of men in Dallas who I'm sure would have said yes." I stopped talking when I remembered Nasty and Tex had cohabitated briefly and he may have made that list.

Nasty rolled her eyes. "Please, Madison. The entire world doesn't want Captain Tex Allen. He's all yours."

"Then why are you here? Why did he call you to meet me here instead of being here himself?"

She set the ladle down. "You want to know why he called me? Because I'm on the payroll. My company runs security surveillance on a lot of businesses and private residences around town, and he's one of them."

"You're here… because… he pays you," I said.

"We had a relationship that didn't work, but we worked together before that. We've both moved on personally, but we both benefit from each other's professions. There was no reason to throw that away. The money keeps it less complicated."

"Then my question stands. You understand the importance of separating your personal life from your professional life, but Gerry Rose has nothing to do with your professional life. If it was all about having a baby and not anything more, then why Gerry?"

In the background, Huxley resumed his *vroom, vroom* noises.

Nasty picked up a leaf of basil from the countertop and rolled it up, then released it and smoothed it out with her fingers. I didn't need to prompt her to talk. I could tell she was thinking about the question, about the answer, and about whether she wanted to make either one public. She tipped her head to the side and pulled her long copper-streaked hair over one shoulder and then glanced up at me.

"How many people know what they want?" she asked.

"I don't know."

"Take a moment and think about it," she said. "You work with clients. How many times do people hire you and then expect you to tell them what they want?"

There was no point dilly-dallying with my answer. It wouldn't change. "It happens more often than not," I admitted.

Nasty started to chiffonade the basil leaf with a pair of kitchen shears. "I knew I wanted a baby. A lot of other things were vague. Gerry and I stayed up one night talking, and I realized he was one of the few men I've met in my life who had the same clarity toward getting what he wanted that I did. But here's the catch to all that: if I married him, if I took his money, if I became Mrs. Gerry Rose, anything I wanted would have gone away. I would have had to stop thinking about it. Big Bro Security? Freelancing on the side? Poof. I might not have known what I wanted beyond the next two years, but I knew I didn't want that."

"And Gerry understood?"

"How could he not? After twenty-four hours together, he claimed we were cut from the same cloth."

She took a pinch of basil and added it to her sauce and then swept the remnants of the leaf off the counter into the garbage disposal, turned on the water, and let it run down the drain. When she finished, she glanced back up at me. "You and Tex are like that," she said. "I thought you already knew that. Did he propose or something?"

"When that obituary came out, it's like for the first time it occurred to him that I might die. He's been weird ever since. I don't know how to get him—us—back to where we were. He's afraid I'm going to die, and he thinks he can protect me by keeping me at home while he goes out and slays dragons. I told him we're *all* going to die someday, and now I feel like I pushed away the one person I want in my life."

If Nasty were judging me, she wouldn't be the first.

I knew people criticized my choice of independence. Most people didn't understand what it felt like to be alone at an early age. To lose your family. To rebuild your life with just yourself. Most people didn't know what it felt like to trust that someone else would be there for your future and then feel the rug pulled out from under your feet.

It's one of the reasons Doris Day was such a huge influence in my life. We shared a birthday, and I'd watched one of her movies on that day every year. But when I lost my parents in my twenties, that ritual stayed. And I discovered there was so much more to the actress than the perky roles she played. I found out she knew tragedy too.

I long ago learned there was one person I could count on and that was me, and that made it difficult to let other people in. It was like I unwittingly played a giant game of hard-to-get, sometimes being surprised at how effectively it worked.

Back when I first moved here from Pennsylvania, I felt like a fish out of water. A woman who dresses in vintage—not high-priced and well-maintained designer vintage but the polyester double knit that filled a lot of closets in the sixties—and models her world after Doris Day, that's not the sort of woman who has a built-in social circle in a cliquey town like Dallas. I carved out a niche for myself and my business and lived a small life amongst other mid-mod enthusiasts. My handyman at the time was part of that life, professionally at first, but in time I gave in to the notion that I didn't want to be alone anymore, and we started to date.

To the rest of the world, we were perfect for each other. But to us, we were worlds apart. In time, I gave in to the notion that I'd rather be alone than settle. But Tex...Tex was infuriating, charming, exciting, loving. Tex was different.

Nasty stirred the sauce and then set the spoon on the counter. "I'll tell you what I like to think I'll tell my son someday: clean up your own side of the street. Nothing matters other than what you want. I don't say that to be cold or calculating like people think, but the more *solid* I am in life, the more *helpful* I am in life. If my days are steeped in obligation, then how am I ever supposed to know if I did what I wanted? But if I spend my life doing what I want, then I'm fully committed to everything I do. Most people don't get that."

Nasty needed to author a book of wisdom drops. The woman never ceased to amaze. Hearing her explain why she was the way she was was more of a revelation than if she explained how she functioned all day in four-inch heels.

"Do you think you'll ever get married?" I asked.

"If I want to get married, I'll get married. If I don't, I won't. That's it. That's all there is. This moment. Now. Whatever makes you happy."

"It seems too easy to view life like that."

"Life doesn't have to be a struggle, Madison. The sooner you understand that the sooner you'll start enjoying everything that comes your way."

Not for the first time, Nasty gave me something to think about. The conversation fell to silence as she removed a pot of pasta from the stove and drained it into a colander. Not seeing any dishes, I went to a cabinet, pulled out two pasta bowls, and set them on the table with forks and spoons. Nasty added a third bowl to a small highchair set up a few feet away from us and then strapped Huxley in. While she knotted on a bib, I poured us each a glass of wine from a bottle I'd left in Tex's fridge. I sat opposite Nasty while Huxley grabbed a handful of spaghetti and hurled it onto the floor.

"Huxley, no," Nasty said.

Huxley looked at her with wide brown eyes. Nasty spun her fork in her spaghetti and ate it. Huxley tried to mimic her with his green plastic spork, though at eighteen months, he didn't quite understand the concept of twirling spaghetti. A few noodles caught in the fat tines of his spork by accident and ended up in his mouth.

Amazing.

"Do you want to talk about Tex?" Nasty asked.

"What did he tell you?"

"Not much. He asked me to meet you here when you brought over Wojo. He said he had to see Lloyd about autopsy results." She swirled another forkful of spaghetti and held it while it cooled. "I didn't buy that for a second, but I figured whatever trouble was in paradise, it was his fault, not yours." She raised her fork to me as if toasting me. "Imagine my surprise."

I didn't realize how hungry I was, and at the moment, a simple spaghetti with a simple marinara was exactly what I wanted. Nasty and I ate in silence while Wojo romped around in the living room.

"So what's next for you?" I asked when I was done. "Do you know?"

"I thought I might go back to dating a cop." She glanced up at me and smiled. "Just kidding."

I finished first and took charge of cleaning up. Nasty had no compunctions about joining me and relaxed with her wine while Huxley pushed the toy Mustang around the living room floor. I transferred the remaining sauce to a Tupperware and cleared the dishes. After I finished, I thanked her for both dinner and her advice.

"It's not advice, Madison. I don't tell people what to do. I told you once that Tex has demons. Seems like you do too. This time don't throw yourself into work to avoid the problem. And don't place the blame on anybody but yourself. Find the root of your problem like you do with your business. Solve that and everything else will fall away."

## TWENTY-FOUR

The next morning, after another sleepless night, I showered and dressed in a powder blue pantsuit. I pinned a yellow and white metal cluster of daisies to my lapel and went next door to check my schedule from the satellite office. Effie had added an appointment with the Ledbetters at their new property. I had two hours before I was due to meet them, so I culled through the various notations and ideas scattered around my desk and organized them into a proper presentation. It felt good to focus on something I knew.

About two years ago, I'd come across a vintage Bassett bedroom suite in Italian Golden Bisque, an exotic mid-century description for a near-white shade. There was a bed frame with over-the-bed cabinets, a dresser, nightstands, and a mirror. I could picture them against the pink carpeting in the room, and with cheerful pink, yellow, and white floral curtains, it would have a feminine charm. With a little effort, I could match the paint technique on a pair of bookcases, which would be perfect for displaying a collection of reproduction Barbie dolls from the era. Those came from a toy store that had sustained massive water damage; a fire in the shop next door tripped the sprinklers and the inventory got waterlogged. Barbies are far less valuable in damaged boxes, so I got the whole lot for pennies on the dollar, and aside from the calluses I sustained while removing the dolls from the packaging (those people at Mattel take doll security seriously), the process of unpacking them took me back to my childhood.

For the other room, I planned to use the suite of Broyhill Brasilia that I'd recently stripped of paint. The newly exposed rich maple wood would contrast nicely with a Wedgwood-blue rag rug from my latest collaboration of home décor items for Paintin' Place, and the largest rug of the assortment would neatly fit with about eight inches to spare on each side. Occasionally I came across bins of Hot Wheels, which I never knew what to do with, but today I pictured an entire wall of them. I measured the wall twice and then sat back and ran some calculations. It would take over a hundred individually mounted shadow box frames, but if I backed each frame with shades of blue, the wall would serve as an accent, an art piece, and a slice of Americana. I'd rummage through the toy bins at the very back of my warehouse and find any additional car-themed objects to use on the nightstands or dresser. I made a note to check my curtains for something in the blue family, but nothing floral. A nice geometric would do the trick.

Satisfied with my concepts, I zipped my portfolio and drove to the property. I parked alongside the Ledbetters' SUV. I found Linda inside the house staring out the sliding doors at the pool.

"Hi, Linda," I called out. "You're early." I looked around for her husband. "Where's Larry?"

"He's not coming," she said.

"Okay, I didn't have time to copy my sketches, but I can go to the print shop after we're done and send a copy to your office if you'd like."

"That's not necessary," she said.

There was something off about Linda's attitude. Until today, every time I'd interacted with her, she'd been effusive. I'd marveled at how well she and her husband fit together, at how they proved a couple could both work and play together and thrive in both cases. But today, Linda was missing her spark. I hoped my designs would perk her up.

"Let's come to the kitchen," I said. I unzipped my portfolio and pulled out a sheaf of drawings and inspiration boards. I laid them next to each other so she could see the scope of the project and get a sense of how seamless the design would be.

When I finished unpacking my displays, I stepped back to make room for her. She glanced at the drawings and nodded her head. "They look nice," she said. "I'm sure whatever you have planned will be fine." A fat tear spilled out of her eye and ran down her cheek.

"Linda? What's wrong?"

She swiped at her face. "I'm sorry, Madison. It's not you." She waved toward the sketches. "And it's not your designs. It's Larry." She turned her head away from me so I couldn't see her face.

"Did something happen to him?" I asked. "Is he okay?"

"He changed his mind. He doesn't want the house and he doesn't want the ceremony. I'm not even sure he still wants to be married," she said. She reached into her massive tote bag and pulled out a full-sized box of tissues. She plunked the box onto the counter and pulled out two, then blew her nose. "I'm not usually so emotional. You'll have to forgive me."

I stood next to her, shocked. I didn't know what to say.

Linda Ledbetter was half of the most successful hotel management company in Dallas, and she didn't reach that position by playing a hysterical female. Even now, while faced with what most women would consider a crisis, she limited herself to one tear, one blow of her nose, and that was it. She even stepped forward and picked up a sketch, considering it as if she hadn't said a word.

I took the sketch from her hand and set it on the counter. "Linda?" I said. "Forget the sketches. Let's talk about this."

There weren't a lot of places to sit with the tree occupying the majority of the front living space, but women can be resourceful when necessary, so I led Linda to the bathroom with the Cinderella bathtub. We sat on the two sides that weren't wedged against the corner walls, with our feet resting in the empty basin. It surprised me to realize how few Cinderella tubs I'd come across in my decorating career.

"Larry and I made each other a promise when we got married. We wouldn't do things I wanted or he wanted. We'd do things we both wanted."

"That's a tall order. You're two different people."

She shrugged. "It's not that we expected to agree on everything. That's not plausible. But we wanted to look at life as a unit, not separately. We started out with nothing and if we hadn't both agreed to live that way while we were starting out, if we hadn't both fallen in love with an abandoned hotel that used to be a minimum-security prison, if we hadn't both believed that we could turn it into something the city needed, we wouldn't be here. Everything we are today was built on the fact that we looked at life the same way."

"Linda, spending time around you and Larry is inspiring. You two are the most perfect couple I've ever met."

"There is no such thing as a perfect couple. We work well together, and we're best friends, but maybe we don't know each other as well as we thought. Maybe we've been fooling ourselves."

"What did Larry do?" I asked.

Linda stretched her legs out and rested her heels on the bottom of the tub. She tipped the toes of her shoes apart so her feet were in a V, and then brought them back together. She did this three times while I waited for a response, and by the time she spoke, I'd convinced myself he cheated or threw out her childhood collection of Madame Alexander dolls or some other unforgiveable act.

"He asked me why I wanted this." She was silent for a moment, and then she made a sweeping gesture toward the property.

"'This?'"

She made a sweeping gesture toward the house. "This."

When Linda and Larry Ledbetter first approached me, I'd been bowled over by the scope of the job. My business had expanded to include commercial properties and apartment complexes, but the idea of being given carte blanche in a genuine 1955 ranch house that had been vacant for an undetermined amount of time was huge. Cool customer that I am, I tamped down my initial response and represented myself as the most capable person for the job.

I saved my happy dance until their SUV left my parking lot.

But I couldn't put my business needs above those of my client. Not when she was clearly in turmoil.

"What did you tell him?" I asked.

"I said I thought we both wanted it, and Larry said he went along with it to make me happy. That goes against the very foundation of our marriage." She shook her head. "It's like I'm married to a stranger."

I didn't see much point dragging out my meeting with Linda, so when she was ready to leave, I left too. If she and Larry called off their ceremony, then they'd probably call off my contract too. Sure, they'd paid a non-refundable deposit, but a portion of that had gone to Goldy for Natasha, and the rest had floated bills I'd paid along the way. With a job of this size, I'd cleared my schedule of other clients so I could proceed without interruption. After the wave of cancellations that came when clients thought I was dead, I had nothing on the horizon. I needed this job more than the Ledbetters needed me.

I'd welcomed the meeting with Linda Ledbetter to take my mind off the murder, but now, as I watched her drive away, I wanted something to take my mind off Linda.

Clara's scrapbook was in the back seat of my car. I pulled it to my lap and flipped through the pages of the scrapbook. About halfway, I came upon a photo that felt vaguely familiar. It had three women: Sunny flanked by Clara and another cigarette girl. I ran my fingertips over the photo and thought back to where I'd seen her before, and then it came back to me. The newspaper clipping that had been inside the record album displayed in Sunny's living room.

I flipped through the entirety of Clara's scrapbook once, and then twice, hoping maybe Clara had clipped out the same notice from the paper and preserved it, but I was out of luck. Aside from the photo of the three of them, there was no mention of the missing cigarette girl. I called Clara, hoping her memory might provide some missing detail.

"It's Madison," I said. After a brief exchange of greetings, I said, "Can you tell me anything else about the night Julie went missing?"

Clara accepted my curiosity about those days without question. "It was an odd night. Sunny got a last-minute gig in Houston, and her manager drove her there. Jack left that night too. I've always suspected Sunny told him she was running away with Martin, maybe she even told Jack her plans to marry him. It was a surprise to the rest of us, but if she were going to tell anyone, it would have been Jack. By the time Sunny and Martin came back, Jack was playing with a jazz combo in Paris."

"What happened when Sunny returned?"

"She was pregnant. After she had her baby, Martin started sending her out on the road more frequently. Mr. Gimpy auditioned for a new vocalist, but nobody could fill Sunny's shoes."

"What happened to Martin?"

"He died of a heart attack in his fifties."

"What about Jack? He came back eventually, didn't he?"

"About a year later. Jack and I tried to console each other in the wake of Sunny's marriage, but that kind of consolation wears thin. Jack quit the club circuit and made a living as a song plugger—playing in department stores and music shops to demonstrate the pianos and the sheet music."

I thanked Clara for the information and made plans to get coffee after lap swimming later in the week.

There was something about that night in question. Something that didn't jive. I wished I'd held onto that newspaper clipping that fell out of the missing record album the day I'd been at Sunny's house, but someone had beaten me to it.

I carried the scrapbook back inside the house. Particles of dust filled the air, mixing with allergens and making my eyes itchy and irritated. I opened my handbag and rooted around the bottom for a bottle of eye drops but discovered something else instead.

Under my wallet and spare tissues, sunglasses case, cosmetic bag, and plastic pouch of doggie treats was a key. And not just any key—the key to Sunny Nigh's house.

I'd thought I left it inside on Sunny's dining room table, but it appeared as though I'd had it all along.

# TWENTY-FIVE

I had no recollection of putting the key into my handbag. Had I done so unconsciously? It didn't seem likely, except the evidence indicated I had. I pulled the key out and held it as if the inanimate object's vibrations could help me remember something about my actions that day, but all I remembered was leaving in a hurry. I'd even told the detectives that I left the key behind.

I returned to my Alfa Romeo. On the way to Sunny's house, I drove through an In-N-Out Burger. It was a fifteen-minute drive. I could have saved myself both gas and time if I'd discovered the key before I left Thelma Johnson's house this morning, but I'd been preoccupied with the need to stay busy.

Discovering the key was fortuitous. I wasn't completely ignorant of the dangers involved in my return trip, though, so I called Sue and filled her in on my plans.

"Did you ever talk to Captain Allen about moving the files from Sunny's attic to the precinct?"

"There hasn't been time. Why?"

"I've had the key to Sunny's house all along," I said. "I

thought I left it on the dining room table, but I found it in the bottom of my handbag. I'm headed back there now."

"Is that wise?"

"It is if you meet me there."

"I'm a detective working this case. I can't go inside that house without a warrant or explicit permission from the owner." She paused for a moment and then added, "I'll send a patrol car to the neighborhood."

I arrived at Sunny's house a minute later. It took me a moment to unlock the door. The key fit into the lock, but it wouldn't turn without a fair bit of jiggling. I didn't remember having this much difficulty with it when I'd been here the last time. The tumblers eventually fell into place. The knob turned, and I pushed the door open and stepped inside.

I took my time getting to the attic. The living room appeared largely the same as it had when I was here before. The chairs for the recital were still set up facing the piano. The empty display stand sat next to the empty turntable. If I hadn't seen the album cover with my own eyes, I wouldn't have noticed its absence.

After a brief walkthrough, I pulled on my cotton gloves and climbed back up into the attic. This was the real reason I was here both officially and personally: access to the collection of jazz memorabilia that Renee and Punch had amassed. The boxes were as I'd left them. I opened two trunks and found stage costumes, long silk dresses, beaded gowns, and matching headpieces. It was a costume historian's dream, but it wasn't mine. I closed the trunks carefully.

The next box I opened was filled with archived concert posters announcing Sunny and the Syncopated Six's performances. Someone, Renee or Punch, likely, but maybe Sunny herself, had organized the posters chronologically. The posters were each in parchment paper sleeves to protect them from dust, humidity, and finger oils, and the contents were divided by year.

I closed that box and pulled out a photo album similar to the one Clara had loaned me. It must have been a current style at the time, and Clara had said how close the two of them had been. I opened the front cover and saw the same photo of the two of them smiling at the camera, Sunny in her gown and Clara in her cigarette girl costume of short dress, fishnets, and black Mary Jane heels. They had that conspiratorial look on their faces, two friends who believed their friendship could withstand anything the world tossed their way.

I flipped through the rest of the pages. Inside were photos similar to the ones Clara kept, documenting what Gimpy's jazz club looked like in the mid-century. These pictures were filled with inspiration for the Ledbetter job, and I could tell from the atmosphere depicted that the club really swung. There were pictures of Clara and Sunny, of Sunny and Jack, and one of Sunny with her band. Someone had conveniently written details of the photos on the back of each one, making identification easy. What struck me was there were no pictures of Sunny with Martin Snyder, her manager, yet she'd gone on to marry him.

The scrapbook ended in May of 1955. I couldn't ignore the significance of that date; it lined up with the newspaper clipping that fell out of the now-missing album jacket. Yet if I'd never seen that newspaper clipping, I wouldn't even know about the missing cigarette girl who'd disappeared from the club that night.

I was lost in the momentum of history and nostalgia. This happened when I buried myself in other people's stories. I could almost hear the music, almost feel the rhythms, almost smell the booze and the sweat from drinking and dancing.

Even though I was fully immersed in the past as inspiration for a job, I couldn't shake the notion that something in this attic meant more than the rest of it.

I set my sketchpad down and went to the banker's box that held the concert posters, then nimbly flipped through them until I reached the one for Sunny's gig in Houston. I opened the parchment paper envelope and slid the poster out, gingerly holding it in my gloved hand. The poster was an uncomplicated design in black and white and featured a pencil sketch rendering of Sunny's face along with her name: ADDISON NIGH, ONE NIGHT ONLY, IN-PERSON! The date, ticket prices, and organizers of the event were listed along the top and bottom of the poster. A dotted line ran down the left side of the poster and bent around the bottom left corner into an arrow, reminiscent of Googie design, which pointed to details about ticket sales. Otherwise, it was clean and modern and could have been used as a template for a promotion today.

I gently eased it back into the parchment paper sleeve. It caught on something inside the envelope. I set the poster on top of the box and peered inside the sleeve. A slip of paper was at the bottom. Finger oils were the devil when it came to preserving documents, and even though I wore the white gloves, I didn't want to potentially leave dust behind, so I opened the envelope wide and tipped it, letting the stuck piece of paper fall out. It was a voided check.

The check was made out to Martin Snyder. The memo field indicated the payment was for Sunny's May 26 performance at the Astrodome. The check had been made out on the same day. None of that was suspect.

What was suspect was the notation scribbled across the front of the check. *Void: cancellation of concert due to no show of performer.*

Huh. The night Sunny was unexpectedly booked in a last-minute gig in Houston, she hadn't appeared to perform.

I took a picture of the check and the poster, then returned them to the archives in the same condition I'd found them. The spell of nostalgia had been broken. On the bright side, everything I found pointed to a crime in the fifties, not the one that had taken place at Eight to the Bar last week, which meant I'd successfully avoided the open Punch Snyder murder investigation—or so I convinced myself.

I descended the attic stairs and folded them back up, then scanned the interior of Sunny's house for anything I might have missed. That's when I saw the key on the dining room table, exactly where I thought I'd left it the first time.

# TWENTY-SIX

I reached into my pocket and closed my fist around the key I'd found in my handbag. If the one on the table was the one from the rock out front, then where had the one I'd used today come from?

"Hello?" I called out, much like I had the first time I'd been here. And much like that first time, I received no response.

I left the house and locked the door behind me. A red Lexus had parked me in. I hadn't expected company, least of all Natasha Bledsoe. What was she doing at Sunny's house?

The vocalist looked far less glamorous than her headshots, but still, I recognized her. Her honey-blond hair was pulled back, and her face was flushed. Natasha didn't have the benefit of already having researched me as I had her, and she seemed at a loss by my presence. Several different emotions, from surprise to anger to confusion back to surprise showed on her face. Natasha may have a beautiful singing voice, but I doubted she'd ever have a career in acting.

"Natasha," I said coolly. I descended the stairs, thankful for the rubber treads of my sneakers against the smooth wooden incline that led from the back door down to the driveway. "I'm Madison Night. It's nice to meet you face to face."

"Do I know you?"

"I'm a decorator. I'm working on the million-dollar property your husband recently sold. I spoke to Goldy about booking you for an event."

All but one of the emotions that played with Natasha's features dropped away, leaving confusion. Her mouth pulled into a small O. Her forehead didn't move other than a small twitch by her eyebrows—I suspected Botox, and for the briefest moment wondered how that might affect the two Sues' job. It's probably difficult to get a read on a suspect when their features are frozen due to injectables.

"Goldy doesn't handle my schedule anymore."

"She may have been filling in for whoever does."

"You're not listening," she said. "I fired Goldy two weeks ago."

Of all the things Natasha could have said, that was the least expected, and my expression turn into a mirror of hers. My voice trailed off as I remembered that trip, the black vinyl money pouch in the drawer with the gun. Goldy had been the only one there. I thought about the deposit I wrote out, the ten thousand dollars, paid to Dallas Jazz. Was it possible that Goldy had me write her a five-figure deposit that went no further than the lining of her own pockets?

"There must be some mistake," I said.

"Stay out of this, Madison. It doesn't concern you." Natasha turned on her heel and strode to her car. Seconds later, she drove away. I was not far behind her.

My mind spun with questions. Why was Natasha at Sunny's house? Why didn't she know about the Ledbetter job? Who had put the extra key into my handbag? And what had Goldy done with my money?

In every direction I turned, I found complications. Doors shut in my face. Even the Ledbetter commission, a job that was made for me, was at a standstill.

I was doing what I always did, the very thing Nasty had cautioned me against. I was keeping myself busy by throwing myself into work and staying distracted by talking to all of the people who had nothing to do with my world, but I couldn't stop myself. One of these issues affected me more adversely than the others, and I couldn't sit by and do nothing.

I drove to Dallas Jazz. By the time I parked in the lot, I was convinced this was more about me than the murder. Natasha claimed to have fired Goldy as her manager, but I was unclear on whether Goldy had other clients or whether Dallas Jazz was her business. Either way, I braced myself for an altercation.

Since my first visit to the recording studio, someone had tried to organize the place. The stacks of sheet music that had been piled around were all gone, leaving behind clean tabletop surfaces and plenty of accessible seating. The posters that had been tacked to the cork board outside of Goldy's office had been swapped out with ones for future bookings. There was a space where the Eight to the Bar poster advertising Natasha's appearance had been.

"Hello?" I called out. The doors had been open, but the studio was empty.

I approached the glass window and peered behind it. The desk and the file cabinets had been tidied up much like the rest of the office, almost as if a cleaning crew had been brought in to tackle the place. The wastepaper bin behind the desk was full.

A cleaning crew would have emptied the bin.

I leaned back from the window and called out again. "Hello?"

It appeared as if I were alone.

I checked over each shoulder, convinced someone was going to appear from a sound booth or bathroom and discover my presence at any moment. Swiftly, I turned the knob and entered the front office. I tipped the wastepaper bin onto the desk and sorted through the trash. I wasn't looking for anything specific, but I was too far down the rabbit hole to consider the futility of my actions.

Three-quarters of the way down the bin, I found my check. It had been endorsed by Goldy. She'd ticked the box that said, "mobile deposit." I opened my bank account and sure enough, the money had been drafted out.

I set the check aside and pulled out a bent poster for a gig last month. It was the one that advertised Natasha's performance at Eight to the Bar. I cringed as I shifted dirty tissues out of the way and pulled up a square torn from the daily calendar that sat on the desk next to the phone. Something had been written on it and crossed out. I held the paper up to the light to try to read past the ink, but no luck.

The calendar was open to tomorrow's date. A cup filled with pencils and pens sat not far away. I pulled out a pencil and lightly shaded the fresh calendar page to reveal an impression. It was a phone number.

I pulled out my cell and typed in the number, then held the phone to my ear while it went unanswered. After four rings, a voice came on. "You've reached Punch Snyder. Leave me a message after the beep."

I heard the beep as the phone fell from my hands.

A million questions sprouted in my consciousness like a time-lapse video of a garden. Goldy had called Punch? How did they know each other? When did this call take place? Was this about Eight to the Bar? Or Natasha? Or something else?

I had a bad feeling, the kind that radiates deep within my chest and moves outward, making my arms heavy and my legs wooden. I put my hand on the upper right drawer and slowly opened it. The last time I'd been here, the drawer had contained a black vinyl money pouch and a .22 caliber pistol. Today, the drawer was empty.

A new rhythm permeated my brain: Goldy was missing. Goldy had a gun. Goldy had ten thousand dollars and a head start. Goldy knew Punch. Goldy knew Eight to the Bar.

Goldy. Goldy. Goldy. Goldy. Goldy.

I picked my phone up and hovered my thumb over Tex's name. We still hadn't cleared the air, and my being here felt like a middle finger to his request that I not take unnecessary risks. I pulled up my call logs and hit Sue's number instead.

"Niedermeier," Sue answered.

I turned my back on the front window and identified myself. "I'm at Dallas Jazz, and I found something that might give you a new lead on the Punch Snyder case."

"I'm listening," she said.

"Have you come across the name Goldy Michener?"

"Natasha Bledsoe's manager, right? She came up in a routine background check of Punch Snyder. Why?"

"I paid her a ten-thousand-dollar deposit to book Natasha for an event in November, but I found out today that Natasha fired Goldy two weeks ago."

"That sounds like a separate crime. If you want Goldy investigated for fraud, you'll need to call the FBI and open a case with them."

"Goldy called Punch the night he was murdered," I said quickly. "I found his phone number in the trash written on a page from her desk calendar. It's the date of his murder."

As I told Sue what I found, I wandered away from the desk.

Despite the front door being unlocked, the empty environment had lulled me into a false sense of confidence that I wasn't going to be discovered. I rounded the table that sat behind the desks and everything I thought about my personal safety went out the window.

Goldy Michener was lying dead on the floor.

## TWENTY-SEVEN

"I'm wrong," I said. "Goldy didn't leave town."

"Hold up, Madison. Give me time to check this out."

"She's here," I said, "and she's not going anywhere."

Being on the phone with the police at the moment of discovering a body had its benefits. Sue gave me instructions: don't leave the premises, and don't touch anything (else).

First on the scene were the same officers who arrived at Eight to the Bar. I directed them to where Goldy's body lay and then waited in my car. Sue and Ling arrived next, and then Lloyd. It was like showing up at a play for an encore.

Sue joined me by my car. "I need a formal statement," she said. She held her phone out. "What's your connection to Dallas Jazz?" she asked.

"I'm working on the vow renewal event for Linda and Larry Ledbetter."

"The hotel couple?"

"Yes. They bought an old ranch house and want it retrofitted to 1955 designs. I suggested hiring Natasha Bledsoe, and when they agreed, I came here to put down a deposit."

"Why Ms. Bledsoe?"

"She studied under Sunny. With all of the recent press, hiring Natasha felt timely."

Sue narrowed her eyes. "What brought you here today?"

I sighed. There was no avoiding this part. "I was at Sunny Nigh's house earlier today, and I ran into Natasha. She said she fired Goldy two weeks ago. If that's true, then I'm out ten thousand dollars. I wanted to confront her about it, and I thought that meeting would be more effective in person."

Sue scanned my powder blue pantsuit. "So this was a business call."

"Something like that."

"Did she cash your check?"

"It's in the trash. There's a notation on the back that says, 'for deposit only.'"

"Then your money is probably sitting in her bank account. I'm sorry, Madison, but that's not a police matter."

"But anything related to Goldy and Punch is, right? The first time I was here, Goldy had a .22 caliber gun in her desk drawer. I saw it when I dropped off Natasha's deposit, but it's gone."

"The gun is at the station. You told me about Ms. Michener on Sunday." She ran the back of her forearm across her forehead. "Look, there might be a connection between Ms. Michener and Mr. Snyder's murders, but this doesn't appear to be a self-inflicted wound, so I'm going to say the killer is still out there."

"What's the connection between them? Why would she call him the night he died?"

"Maybe they had a personal relationship."

I stared out at the parking lot. The last time I'd been here, two cars had been in the lot. Goldy's and a red Lexus. At the time, Goldy had said Natasha was in a sound booth, but that didn't fit with Natasha having fired Goldy.

"What about Natasha? She worked at the club and Goldy was her manager. There might be something there."

"We collected a statement from her in our initial round of investigating and ruled her out. She and Punch seemed to have little interaction. She told me her manager landed her the gig at his club, but she'd been dialing back on her booking schedule and had asked Punch to find a new act to take her place."

"Did she say why?"

Sue shrugged. "Age? Married life? Tired of being hit on by saxophone players? Maybe all of the above. She teaches voice lessons locally. That's not something an up-and-coming talent adds to her resume. Seems to me Natasha Bledsoe wanted out of the limelight."

"What about Kip Bledsoe? Natasha's husband?"

"What about him?" Sue asked.

"Did you question him?"

"Aside from his relationship with Natasha he has nothing to do with our investigation."

"Does he have an alibi?"

Sue appeared to be losing patience with me. "He was at a real estate convention." She paused. "You can't accuse innocent people because you don't like the direction the evidence points."

I knew Sue was right, but something didn't fit. I couldn't help thinking there was something else at play here, something that had nothing to do with Eight to the Bar or Sunny Nigh's estate. That somebody was adept at lying and was on the verge of getting away with it.

It was a long, lonely night. I drove home and changed into a bathing suit, then went out to my new inground pool for a late-night dip. I kept the water at eighty degrees, and after my temperature adjusted, I floated on my back and started to itemize everything on my plate.

No. For once in my life, I would not throw myself into a project as a distraction from my problems. I wouldn't practice avoidance. I would ask myself the tough question: Why was I so afraid of intimacy?

I closed my eyes. I put my arms out on either side, and the water supported my body. Like always, Nasty had a point. If I didn't face my demons, my life would stay in park while everything, everybody I cared about, moved forward.

The night was quiet. Crickets chirped and somewhere in the distance a cat howled. Water sloshed into my ears, dulling the sounds. The sky was a thick navy blue with a sprinkling of white dots scattered about. Unexpected beats. Some bright, some barely there. A pattern that seemed abstract but formed an array of stars that were millions of years old. Like jazz. Like life.

And as I lay there, buoyed by the water, I knew I wanted to talk to Tex. I wanted to tell him about finding the money in the floor of Eight to the Bar, about the timeliness of the newsprint that wrapped it. I wanted to tell him about my trip to Sunny's house and my meeting with Natasha Bledsoe. I wanted to tell him how someone had tried to hijack my bank account. I wanted to tell him about the Ledbetters, how they weren't as perfect as they seemed.

But I didn't want to just tell him the bad stuff. I wanted to tell him about the bathroom with the Mamie pink tiles and the Cinderella bathtub and the black shag carpet. I wanted to let him know the bank upped my line of credit. I didn't want to just share the bad stuff; I wanted to tell him my good news as well.

I got out of the pool and dried off quickly, then scampered to the house. It was nine thirty. There were three missed calls from him on my phone. I hit Redial before stopping to think about what I would say, but it wasn't Tex who answered his phone. It was Sue.

"Madison," she said. "Where are you?"

"I'm at home. Why do you have Tex's phone? Can I talk to him?"

"I'm sorry, Madison. You can't. I'm at Baylor Hospital. Captain Allen's been shot."

<h1 style="text-align:center">TWENTY-EIGHT</h1>

Half an hour later, I found Ling and Sue in the hospital waiting room. They both wore the same clothes they'd worn at Dallas Jazz. Sue held a cup of coffee. She saw me first and called me over.

"What happened?" I asked.

"We don't have details. A call came in while we wrapped up at Dallas Jazz. Armed robbery in progress at a business downtown. Right after the call came in, Captain radioed that he was in the area and he'd check it out."

"You didn't say you spoke to him when we were at the recording studio."

"We heard you two were on the outs," Sue said. "It seemed better to steer clear of the subject."

———

I spent the night in the waiting room dressed in a white vintage terrycloth pool coverup over my now-dry bathing suit—no, I hadn't taken time to shower off the chlorine and change into something more suitable. As the hours ticked by, the seats vacated, leaving me with the detectives. We took turns nodding off, waiting for an update or the word that we could see him, whichever came first. We didn't get either until the following morning.

I wasn't prepared to see Tex lying in a hospital bed. His eyes were closed, and an IV ran into the back of his hand. I glanced at the screen monitoring his vitals—blood pressure, oxygen, pulse—all seemed normal.

"Are you his wife?" an intern asked.

"Partner," I said.

"I thought he was the captain."

"Life partner."

She nodded as if she understood. In a flash, I saw how overcomplicated I'd made my relationship with Tex in my mind and how easily those two words defined it.

"What happened?" I asked.

"He took a bullet in the shoulder. The bullet grazed his subclavian artery, which feeds the main artery of the arm as well as the large nerve bundle that controls arm function."

"Will he recover?"

"He'll need physical therapy and time. He was conscious when he came in, but we put him under to operate. About half the victims of gunshot wounds to this area of the body need follow-up surgery, but he might fall into the lucky half."

I had a tough time justifying "lucky" with "he got shot" but in terms of hospital-speak, the intern seemed to think Tex was in a good place. There were questions, lots of questions, populating my mind, but before I addressed any of them, I reached my hand down and curled my fingers around Tex's hand. His skin was warm and rough.

Tex opened his eyes. "Hey, Night," he said. His voice was

raspy and low, a combination of whisper and hush. I picked up a plastic cup of water and held it out to him. He released my hand and took the cup, sipped from it, set it back down, and curled his fingers around mine again. "What brings you here?"

"I was in the neighborhood," I said. "and if you think this somehow makes your point about the fragility of life and how it can change in a moment, it doesn't. The newspaper only *said* I was dead. You getting shot was unnecessary."

He smiled and closed his eyes. He rolled his head away from me and coughed, and the pain he felt was immediately evident on his face. His hand gripped mine tighter. "Now you know how it feels."

While the intern recorded Tex's vital signs on a computer, I pulled up a chair and settled in. It wasn't that I had hours to spare; I didn't. But for right now, everything else fell away. This was where I wanted to be.

The last thing the intern did before leaving was adjust the bed so Tex was sitting up. After she left, I asked the obvious question.

"What happened?"

"I finished eating at Terry Black's Barbecue when a call came in about a robbery in progress. I was already in the area, so I checked it out."

"You're on vacation."

"Cops don't take vacations."

*Neither do decorators,* I wanted to say, but this didn't seem the time.

"The intern said you were lucky. The shooter used a low caliber gun, though I would argue that any caliber gun is still a gun."

Tex glanced at the door. "Are Tsu and Niedermeier still here?"

"They were when I got here."

"Tell them to come in."

I went out front and found the detectives in the waiting area. A TV was mounted in the corner of the room, and Tex's picture was on the screen. "Earlier today, a police captain was critically wounded after responding to a call about a robbery in progress. Captain Thomas Allen was taken to Baylor Hospital where he is being treated for gunshot wounds. At this time, his condition is unknown."

"He's awake," I told them. "He wants to talk to you." I stared at the TV and then turned back to them. "Have there been any updates?"

Ling shook her head. "No." They exchanged a glance. "If he's awake, maybe he can tell us something."

Ling pointed to the TV. "The news kept things vague at our request. If someone saw what happened, they might come forward. Nobody has to know he's going to pull through."

Having a front-row seat to a police investigation had taught me a thing or two about how to lure criminals out of hiding. People liked to believe the system was at war with itself: reporters versus police versus legal counsel versus district attorneys. But the system was designed to catch the bad guys while protecting the good ones, and it wasn't uncommon for the supposedly warring factions to come together to mete out justice.

Tex had been a part of the community justice system his whole adult life. He worked his way up through the police academy, first as a uniformed officer, eventually getting promoted to detective, lieutenant, and now captain. He changed the face of the force by recruiting new talent and made what was once a boy's club atmosphere more reflective of the

Lakewood community. It was nice to see the community had his back.

I followed Ling and Sue back to Tex's room. He looked at the three of us. "Night, I need to talk to the detectives about what happened. It will compromise our investigation if you're a part of that conversation."

"Of course," I said. "I'll wait in the lobby."

"Hold up," he said. He looked at Ling and Sue, and then back at me. "Call Nasty. Ask her if she'll hold on to Wojo for a few more days. She'll be our best source of non-police intel. Tell her what happened and tell her to keep it quiet. She has resources. She might hear something we won't."

"Done."

Something was bugging me, one small detail from Tex's account of what had happened that didn't ring true, but I felt guilty even believing for a moment that he was lying to me.

I had the same feeling of déjà vu that I'd had outside Tex's townhouse the night Nasty had been waiting for me. The sense that my problems had started with the obituary of Sunny, that my stolen identity was tangled up in Tex's homicide. Only this time I saw it differently. Tex was on vacation, so it never should have been his homicide. The case belonged to Ling and Sue.

But Tex didn't sit idly by while his detectives investigated a case whether he was on vacation or not. It was what his team both loved and hated about him. He didn't stop being a detective when he got this promotion, which challenged them to bring their A-game to every case.

Tex claimed he took the robbery-in-progress call because he was already in the area. He said he was eating barbecue when the call came in—more accurately, he was finishing his meal. I remembered how the scent of the barbecue smoke had gotten into my dress the day he and I ate there recently. Whatever he was wearing would have been soiled from the gunshot and the odors, and I doubted he'd want to put those clothes back on when he was discharged.

I stopped by the nurses' station. "Hi," I said to the head nurse. "I'm here for Captain Allen. Can you tell me what happened to his personal belongings when he came in? His clothes and wallet and whatnot?"

"In gunshot cases, we put everything in a plastic bag and secure it. The police may need to examine it for evidence."

"Evidence of what?"

"DNA, gunshot residue, whatever they can find."

"Did they smell?"

She looked at me as if the question were somehow offensive. "Fabric picks up odors. Food smells, cigarette smoke, perfumes. Did his clothes carry any odors that might indicate where he'd been?"

"I didn't notice anything, but working here, your sense of smell tends to deaden."

"Can I—could I see him again?"

"Sure," she said. "He's due for another round of painkillers in about twenty minutes, and they'll probably knock him out."

I didn't think Tex and his detectives would much like me coming back into his room after they'd asked me to leave, but I didn't need a lot of time to check what I already suspected. As I entered the room, the three of them looked up at me.

"I'm sorry to interrupt," I said. I looked back and forth at Ling and Sue. "Can I have one more moment with your captain? There's something I need to say and I'd like some privacy to say it."

They nodded and then left us alone. I went back to Tex's bedside and took his hand again. I stared down at him, into his face, lined from stress and sun and a life lived on the edge. I squeezed his hand and bent down to kiss his forehead.

"Don't go soft on me now, Night," he said.

"You know me better than that, Captain." I touched his lips and then pulled my hand away. "Besides, I'm not the one who lied."

"Come again?"

"You lied. About being at Terry Black's Barbecue. You smell like strawberry Jell-O, not brisket. Now, do you want to tell me what you were doing in the area when you caught that bullet in your shoulder?"

# TWENTY-NINE

If there were one good thing about Tex being in a hospital bed, it was that there wasn't any place he could go to get away from me now. I could tell from the look on his face that I was right. I could also tell he hadn't even considered that a detail that small would give him away.

"You said you had finished eating barbecue. We both stripped in the living room and showered after we ate there. There's no way you wouldn't still smell like it, and don't tell me they gave you a sponge bath, because I already talked to the nurse. They cleaned your wound so they could operate. You're otherwise as dirty as you were when you came in, and yes, that works as a double entendre."

He grinned. "In another life, you were probably one heck of a policewoman." He reached his hand up and rubbed his eyes, and then blinked a few times. "I was going to eat barbecue after I went to the *Dallas Tribune*."

"The *Tribune*? Why did you go there?"

Tex shook his head. "After the murder, I requisitioned Punch Snyder's cell phone records. They came in earlier today. He made several calls to the *Tribune* before Addison Nigh's memorial. Before the paper printed your obituary."

"Before?" I asked.

"Yes."

"That doesn't make sense."

"That's what I thought. I went down there to check it out in person."

"Is that when…" I glanced at Tex's shoulder.

"The robbery call came in before I got to the paper." Tex reached behind his head and adjusted his pillow. "I did find out one interesting thing, though. The *Dallas Tribune* let their liability insurance lapse two months ago. If Punch went through with a lawsuit, it likely would have put them out of business."

"But again, Punch wouldn't have threatened the paper with a lawsuit before the obituary ran. Maybe he called them about the jazz retrospective. Renee said they circulated a press release."

"When did you talk to Renee?" His clear blue eyes held nothing more than curiosity.

I held Tex's hand and looked at the door. "Maybe I should ask Ling and Sue back in here for this. It's their investigation."

"Talk to me, Night."

I couldn't fault Tex for lying to me if I withheld information of my own, so I pulled up a chair and filled in the gaps of my recent days. "Punch and Renee were working on a retrospective of Sunny's life. The memorabilia is in Sunny's attic, and Renee asked me to look through it. I may not have been the only person interested in accessing the material." I cut a glance toward Tex. He raised his eyebrows. "It seems while I was there, someone entered the house."

"How do you figure?"

"There was an album on display when I arrived that was gone when it was time for me to leave."

"Could it have blown over?"

"Maybe if Puff the Magic Dragon made a surprise visit, but otherwise, no. The windows were sealed and the air in the house was still."

"Why'd you notice the album?"

"It was one of Sunny's. It seemed unusual that she'd put one of her albums on display, almost like she didn't want people to forget her. The record was on the turntable and the jacket was on display, but when I came back down, both were gone."

"Someone took both," Tex said. "That makes it seem as if the album had some value. Did this person know you were there?"

"I was in the attic, but the pulldown stairs were extended and my car was parked outside. If they know my car, they could easily deduce it was me. I had permission from the next-of-kin. I do this sort of thing all the time. There was no reason to hide."

"Was anything else missing?"

I shrugged. "Other than the record album, I wouldn't know. I'd never been there before."

"Is that it?"

"No, that's not it. Remember I told you Kip Bledsoe sold the Ledbetters their wedding vow house?"

"Yes."

"His wife, Natasha, is one of the preeminent jazz vocalists in Dallas. I booked her to perform at the Ledbetter ceremony."

"Why does that sound suspicious?"

"Natasha studied under Sunny Nigh."

"Night—"

I held up my hand. "There's nothing curious about that. We were lucky to get her."

Despite the drugs in his system, Tex's BS meter appeared to be functioning. "I'm surprised her calendar was open."

"She was the regular performer at Eight to the Bar until she quit. She fired her booking manager, who failed to indicate that fact when I booked Natasha for the Ledbetter event and now I'm out half of her fee."

"How much are we talking?"

"Ten thousand dollars."

Tex whistled.

"I know. And you might already know this last part, but Natasha's booking manager's body was found at Dallas Jazz earlier tonight. In the interest of full disclosure, I'm the one who found it."

"I suppose you had a good reason for going to Dallas Jazz?"

"I had ten thousand good reasons."

Tex and I had been down this road more than once. In the beginning, his response was the expected warning to steer clear of his investigation, but then I'd been right about something he'd failed to see because his perspective was clouded. He'd shown interest in understanding what it was I saw how and how I'd managed to see it when he didn't, and we'd eventually reached a place where he was willing to listen to a unique perspective if it helped him or his team solve a case.

It wasn't until this very moment that I realized how far Tex had evolved from the man he'd been when we first met, and if he'd changed, then I probably had too. We were different people now, different every single day, than the person we were the day before. External factors forced us to adapt if we wanted to survive, not just physically but emotionally, too. Where I'd once had walls so impenetrable only the love of my puppy could get through, I now had friends, colleagues, employees, and, yes, a relationship. How had I not seen it? It was as if *I* were the time capsule—pretending I was the same person because I maintained the same style, even though I'd undergone structural improvements.

"Night, can you get the two Sues to come in here?"

I nodded. I left his room and found Ling and Sue in the waiting room. Ling was watching the local news on the corner TV monitor, and Sue stood by the vending machines with a scowl on her face. She had her phone up to her ear and didn't look happy. A family of four sat in a row of chairs under the windows. The mother read a paperback while the remaining three played with their cell phones.

I headed to Sue. She held up a finger and said into her phone, "I expect this matter to be resolved by the end of the day." She hung up.

"What's wrong now?" I asked.

"The vending machine ate my money." She punched the display above the coin dispenser and a hollow *thunk* resounded. "Are you heading out?"

"Not yet. Captain Allen would like to talk to us together."

"Okay." She turned away and then kicked the machine with the sole of her boot. Several coins dropped into the change dispenser and her eyes lit up. She pulled the coins out and stared at them. "Great. Now I have to call them back and cancel my complaint." Ling joined us while Sue pocketed the change, and then we went back to see Tex.

By the time a nurse came in to give Tex his pain medicine, Ling and Sue were caught up with everything I'd told Tex: the connection between Natasha Bledsoe and Sunny Nigh, the financial benefit Natasha had in Sunny's death, and the missing gun from her now-deceased manager's drawer. Whatever the two Sues thought of Tex letting me in on the details of their investigation, they kept to themselves.

The three of us clustered out of the way in a corner of the room while the nurse practitioner administered Tex's medication. When he finished, he approached us. "If you have anything else to discuss, you better do it soon. He's probably going to nod off in about," he checked his watch, "ten minutes."

Ling nodded. We moved back to Tex's bedside, with me in the lead. "Don't be stubborn," I said. "Let the staff take care of you."

He nodded. His eyelids looked heavy, and I could already tell he was feeling the numbing effects of the drugs.

"Thanks, Night." He squeezed my hand and then I went to the door. "Hold up," he called out. I stopped and turned back around. "You need to be careful out there. Call Nasty and have her security company keep an eye on Mad for Mod, your house, and the Ledbetter property."

"But—" I started to protest, and then, realizing it was the smart thing to do, agreed. "Okay. Do you need me to watch Wojo?"

"Wojo's with Nasty. See if she'll keep him a few more days."

"Anything else?"

"Yeah. You need to call in a chip."

"From whom?"

"From Jimmy Nussbaum at the *Dallas Tribune*. He needs to write a new obituary."

No matter how much Tex had evolved over the past four days, there was no way he was suggesting the newspaper report me as dead again, which left one other possibility.

"I don't like where this is headed," I said.

"It's the fastest way to flush out the shooter." Tex held my stare. I could already tell he'd worked the idea over in his mind enough times that he was convinced. "He needs to report that I'm dead."

"What good will that do?" I asked.

"You saw the news out there, Madison," Ling said. "If the person who shot Captain Allen thinks they killed a cop—"

Sue interjected, "—a *captain*," she added.

Ling nodded and pointed to Sue. "What she said. If somebody thinks they shot a police captain, they're going to either panic or brag. We might draw out a witness or a confession."

I didn't like it, and I said as much. "You've spent years working toward stronger community relations. Won't this undo all of that when the truth comes out?"

"Shooting a cop carries a heavy burden," Ling said. "If we don't respond with urgency, it'll send the wrong message. I don't like this us versus them tactic any more than you do, but it's the most effective strategy.

Ling and Tex were on the same side of the scenario, but Sue had been quiet through most of it. I nodded my head and then asked Sue to talk to me out front. I turned back when I reached the door, and my eyes connected with Tex's. I turned back toward the door and left.

I led Sue to a quiet corner of the waiting room. "You don't like this plan," I said.

"Ling and Captain Allen are right. It's the most effective way to force the shooter to either come forward or hide. If this was an accident, the shooter will come forward. If word on the street reveals someone bragging, we'll be looking at a whole different angle."

"Do you think this is related to Punch Snyder's murder?" I asked. "Where are you on that?"

"If it's connected, we'll find out soon enough. We released Renee on Monday. There wasn't enough evidence to get a warrant, and now this will take top priority. I'm not going to let that case go cold, but for now, Ling and I will have to juggle. It won't be the first time."

I left the hospital. It wasn't like Tex to ask me for favors related to his cases, but Jimmy Nussbaum owed me. Plus, it was a great big distraction that, if played correctly, would give the police the time they needed to catch whoever did this.

Now that the immediate concern about Tex was in the past, I had time on my side. It was shortly after noon. I went home to shower and change out of my bathing suit and into a red shirtwaist dress and white Keds. I clipped on Rocky's red leash and we left. On the way, I called Nasty.

"I need to hire you. Your security company, Big Bro. I need security at my studio, Thelma Johnson's house, and the Ledbetter property."

"This wouldn't be you freaking out because Tex got shot, would it?"

"It was his suggestion. The LPD is investigating the murder of the man who inherited Sunny Nigh's estate. Thanks to the obituary mix-up, I'm tangentially related to the whole thing. It might be nothing other than coincidence, but with his detectives now juggling the case and a shooting, he thought it would be wise."

"I'll have a team set up remote cameras at all three locations right away. Anything else?"

There was no sense having Nasty keep up security surveillance on Tex's townhouse if he wanted people to believe he was dead. "Tell your team not to monitor his place for now."

"Don't be naive, Madison. Tex is a cop. This shooting could have nothing to do with you and everything to do with him."

"Trust me. And if you hear any rumors about Tex, call me before you do anything."

"What are you up to?"

There was no point telling her the plan if I couldn't put the plan into action. "You're using your resources, and I'm using mine."

I hung up and went into the *Tribune*.

The room was empty. Brown cardboard boxes were stacked by the file cabinet, and Jimmy Nussbaum sat at the back of the room feeding paperwork into a shredder. I approached him. He recognized me when I got close, and his face went white.

"Can't you people leave me alone?" he said. "I already told the cop everything I know."

I pulled out my driver's license and held it out. "I'm Madison Night. The real Madison Night. I'm not an impersonator, and I'm not dead." When he didn't take my license, I set it on his desk and pushed it toward him. "Look at it."

He did. And then he looked up at me, back at the license, and up at me. When he seemed convinced, I took it from him and put it back into my wallet.

"I need a favor that only you can grant, and you're going to grant it because my life has been miserable since you printed my obituary."

"I don't have a lot to say about what we print," Jimmy said. "Especially after I screwed up your obituary."

A middle-aged man in a Hawaiian shirt came out from the back. "What's going on here?" he asked. "Who are you?"

"I'm Madison Night."

"She is," Jimmy said. "I checked this time."

"Ms. Night, I'm sorry about what happened." He glanced at Jimmy. "I can't fire him. He's my sister's kid. I told her I'd get him some experience for his transcripts."

"I already told you I don't need it," Jimmy protested.

The editor ignored him. "We printed a retraction and a new obituary, and Jimmy called every local paper and asked them to print corrections too. We're on our last legs here. You can move forward with the lawsuit if you want, but we're closing our doors at the end of the week, so you won't win anything. I don't know what else we can do."

"Now that you mention it, can we talk in your office?"

It was a point in Tex's favor that I had experience being recently deceased. After convincing the small newspaper to print a fake notice of Tex's death and having them sign a confidentiality agreement that I made up on the fly, I left.

I drove home to check on Rocky and make a list. For this story to be believable, I'd have to go through certain motions: notify the bank. File a fraud alert on Tex's credit. Send flowers to the precinct. Notify Tex's sister to not answer her phone for at least a week.

Tex's idea, though possibly well-intentioned in terms of drawing out a shooter, had put me in a corner. If I interacted with people I knew, they'd expect me to respond accordingly to the news. And if I told anyone the truth, his plan could backfire.

The easiest way for me to sell the story was to withdraw. So, I did. I left a message on the Mad for Mod answering machine for Effie that I was going to work from the satellite office and I'd come in later to collect the Ledbetter file.

I understood why Tex punched a hole in the wall of his office. The ripple effect of my death having been reported, and the night spent believing it to be true. Even after he learned the truth the following morning, he'd been surrounded by the constant reminder that it could have been true every time a fresh order of flowers arrived.

This must have been what Tex felt. And I was finally starting to understand why he reacted the way he had.

THIRTY-ONE

The *Dallas Tribune* obituary was printed the next morning: *Local Police Captain Dies from Complications from Shooting.*

Jimmy emailed me the obit before it ran so I knew what details would be contained. It wasn't a love letter to Tex, but it had the necessary facts: local boy turned cop, a lifetime of service to the Lakewood PD, a steady career climb to captain. Career highlights included capturing the Pillow Stalker, exposing a counterfeiting ring, and solving a string of abductions and murders. I'd been involved in all three cases, and therein lay the thin connection to me in the whole darn thing. I'd even asked them to keep his sister out of it, though this whole scenario warranted an explanation via phone call. I hoped Ling and Sue could flush out the shooter with this cockamamie plan quickly.

I dressed in a green polyester knit pantsuit. The pants had an elastic waist and the tunic top had a small stain on the hem. I had piles of clothes with irreversible stains and kept them in a cardboard bin for use while painting, stripping wood, or hanging wallpaper. Polyester is remarkably resilient, and you can't ruin an already ruined garment. It's like double jeopardy.

I ate a bowl of Special K, kissed Rocky goodbye, and then left. The Ledbetter house had stood vacant for three years while on the market, and I doubted anyone who'd heard about Tex would come looking for me there, which made the silver Saab and cargo van in the driveway all the more curious. The Saab belonged to Nasty, and the cargo van, a nondescript white number with tinted windows in the front and no windows in the back had surveillance written all over it. That or something more nefarious, which I pushed out of my mind.

I approached the house. Nasty stood with a squad of young men waiting by the front door. "Madison," she said. She said something to the men and then joined me halfway. "I saw the news."

I ushered her out of earshot of her team. "He's not dead," I said in a hushed voice. "He was shot in the shoulder. It was a .22 caliber bullet and for some reason, the police say that was a good thing."

"Smaller bullet means less internal damage. How is he?"

"Groggy when they give him drugs but otherwise alert. Angry that he's confined to a hospital bed."

"Whose idea was it to leak that he died?"

"His."

"Figures. I'll keep my ear to the street. Who's running point?"

"Ling Tsu."

Nasty nodded. "She and Sue are good detectives. If Tex isn't careful, I might recruit them out from under him."

"You wouldn't dare."

"I'll give him time to recover before I give them my pitch."

Behind her, a member of her team propped a ladder against the house and climbed up. Two men stood by the bottom staring into a screen. A few seconds later, one of the men on the ground gave the man on the roof a thumbs up.

"What is all this?" I asked.

"Security detail. Provided by the Lakewood Police Department. If I were you, I'd use them to deal with that tree while they're here."

"They work for you?"

"Yes, and for now, they work for you."

"Why?"

"That's your question?"

"No," I said. I looked past her at the group of men. They were young and fit, two of the most important qualifications for what I needed to accomplish here. "How long do I have them?"

"How long do you plan to work?"

"When I get going on a project, I keep odd hours."

"Then you'll have them round the clock. I installed closed-circuit cameras to monitor the entrance. If someone tries anything, we'll see them. I'll send a fleet of food trucks this way around lunch. And before you think you owe me one, remember: this is business." She stuck her index finger in the air and made a circle. "This whole set-up is going to give me a down payment on a vacation house in Miami."

Nasty introduced me to her team of security bros and stayed while I unlocked the front door and showed them the tree. It seemed far less overwhelming in relation to the rest of my problems. There was nothing I could do while they worked, so I left while a team of twenty-somethings came up with their own plan that involved a lot of noise.

I drove the short distance to Thelma Johnson's house. I was surprised to discover a white van with the Paintin' Place logo on the side parked alongside the hedges out front.

I parked behind the van while Mitchell Moore got out.

Today the paint store owner wore a black T-shirt and black Dickies. Traces of dirt, dust, and paint showed on his garments, making the color a poor choice. His dirty blond hair had grown long and hung in a ponytail halfway down his back.

"Did I know you were coming here?" I asked.

Mitchell straightened. He put his arms around me and hugged me. It took a moment to remember that, to the rest of the world, Tex had died. That's the thing about fake deaths— they're easy to forget. When he released me, I tried my best to look sad. Tex's plan had effectively added a time delay to everything I tried to accomplish, and at this rate, I was never going to get anything done.

Was that the real reason he'd done it?

I pushed that suspicious thought aside. Rumor has it when you find yourself in a relationship, you're supposed to trust your partner.

"Madison, I'm sorry for your loss. I know you and the cop were close."

"Thank you. I know this may sound cold, but I'm throwing myself into work to keep my mind off what happened, and I'd rather not talk about him."

Mitchell nodded. "That's how I dealt when my dad died. I arranged to teach a month of DIY classes at Paintin' Place. Passed by in a blur. I still don't remember painting the exterior of my shop green." He glanced down at my green polyester pantsuit. "Your cop would probably appreciate knowing you were getting on with your life."

Yes. Yes! I'd finally landed on a plausible explanation for my lack of remorse.

"Thank you for understanding."

"Sure," he said. "We all grieve in our own ways, right? Maybe I can help with yours." He turned toward his van and opened the doors in the back. Inside sat several gallons of paint, rollers, drop clothes, and brushes. "I threw in the drop clothes for free and charged the rest to your line of credit."

"The sale wasn't declined?"

"Nope, went through like lightning. Probably a system malfunction. I rebooted this morning."

As I stood by the van assessing the painting supplies, it struck me that everybody might grieve in their own way, but no one was grieving the death of Punch. I'd spoken to a handful of people who knew him, people I viewed as suspect, but wouldn't visible grief be one of the easiest ways to look innocent? Even Renee hadn't shed real tears. No one had. I'd been met with anger, ambivalence, and annoyance, but not sadness.

Was it possible that Punch Snyder made more enemies than I originally thought?

"Mitchell, I stopped home to check on Rocky, but I'm on my way to a client's house. There's a team of men working at the property where I'm going to use this paint. Would it be possible for you to deliver it there?"

"Sure," he said. "I didn't know you had a plan for it. I thought you'd put it in storage."

I gave him the address for the Ledbetter property along with information about Nasty's security bros. Mitchell was sixty-five going on twenty-five. He'd probably fit right in with them.

Mitchell's unexpected visit left me with two overriding concerns: one, I needed to find out if anybody was mourning Punch's death, and two, if I wanted to downplay suspicion, I needed to appear at least slightly upset about Tex.

I went inside to change into something a little less perky. I selected black and white checked trousers, a sleeveless white shirt, and a black cardigan. It was the sort of vintage outfit that could have been purchased today. I pinned a black and white enamel daisy to the band of a black bowler hat and pulled it on over my ashy blond hair. Between the daisy pin on my head and the Keds on my feet, I looked enough like me to move on with my day.

I found myself wondering about the link between Punch and Goldy. Were their deaths connected? It seemed unlikely that they weren't. That put the focus on Natasha or her husband, Kip. What about Tex? Was his shooting truly accidental, or had someone been gunning for him too? I had a new plan forming in the back of my brain, and it required me to speak to Natasha alone. I wanted—no, needed—to convince her to perform at the Ledbetter ceremony. It wasn't an excuse to get closer to her, it was part of my job.

Plus, I knew she knew Punch, and I knew she knew Goldy. I wanted to talk to her about them. I wanted to see her emotions play out on her face.

There was one big problem: Kip. Sue may have ruled him out as a suspect, but I couldn't. Conventions were nebulous in terms of an alibi; once you're registered, you can come and go as you please. With hundreds of attendees, it would be difficult to determine Kip's exact location for the three days of the weekend, and aside from the panel he spoke on, he might as well have attended by proxy.

And then, it hit me. Kip was at the Ledbetter property on Saturday morning to hand off the keys. I knew, because I'd been there too.

He lied about being at a convention, and I wanted to know why.

# THIRTY-TWO

I couldn't show up at Natasha and Kip's house if I believed one of them was capable of murder. I couldn't take that risk. I also couldn't ask anybody I knew to lure him away with the false promise of a house showing for the same reasons. That left me with precious few options. Turns out Tex and I called the same person in the event of an emergency: Nasty.

"I need another favor," I said.

"What?" Nasty asked.

"I need to talk to Natasha Bledsoe about a booking, but I don't want her husband to be there. He might be dangerous."

"He's a realtor."

"That doesn't mean he's not capable of murder," I said. Nasty's side of the conversation went silent. "Or some other act of violence like shooting a cop."

"I signed several real estate agencies up as clients for Big Bro Security. Kip's is among them. If you need me to get him out of the house while you talk to his wife, I can see him about business."

This time I was quiet. "You still there, Madison?" Nasty asked.

"I didn't expect you to agree so fast. Do you believe Kip Bledsoe could be behind this?"

"I think based on the rising crime rate, I can get Kip to sign on for a more expensive security package. Give me half an hour. I'll text you when the coast is clear."

What I used to dislike about Nasty was what I'd come to respect the most: she looked out for herself. Always. She was the center of her universe, and that made her choices easy.

I let Rocky out. He ran back and forth a few times and then pooped in the corner of the garden. The last of the tomatoes were a sad crop, rotting on the vine. Some critters had come upon them, nibbling at what had fallen, helping the fallen fruit along in the decomposition process. Maybe next year I'd put some effort into my garden, encourage the vegetables to grow and can them in the basement. Maybe not.

Nasty's text came through while Rocky sniffed a row of crabgrass. *Bledsoe meeting me at Big Bro in 10 min. Wife at home.* A second text came through, this one a map pin to an address in West Highland Park.

I set Rocky up in the Glenn Den with a plush rocket and left. It was a short, three-mile drive from Thelma Johnson's house to the Bledsoe residence. Highland Park was one of the wealthier parts of Dallas, and despite my trepidation, I was curious to see how Kip and Natasha lived. Kip had been sitting on a million-dollar property for years, so they couldn't be hurting for money.

I parked along the front property line. The house was a ranch, cream-colored brick exterior with chocolate brown trim. The lawn was neatly maintained, like every other lawn in Dallas, brighter green than seemed natural, squared-off hedges that implied regular maintenance, and dots of red flowers blooming in the beds by the entrance and on either side of the sidewalk. I approached the front door and rang the bell, unsure what sort of reception I'd get when Natasha opened the door.

"Madison," she said. She seemed surprised, but not angry, by my presence. "What are you doing here?"

You could catch more flies with honey than vinegar, so I channeled Doris Day. "Hi, Natasha. I wondered if we could talk. I really would like to discuss a possible job with you."

"Come in," she said. She stepped backward and held the door open for me.

It's impossible for me not to profile people based on their living spaces. A painting, sofa, floor lamp, or wallpaper choice can speak volumes about a person: how they live their life, what they prioritize as valuable, and who makes the decisions for the household among them. The Bledsoe house may have been bought and paid for by Kip and his real estate connections, but the person who lived here was Natasha.

The living room was similar to Sunny's: large black piano, microphone stand, floor-to-ceiling bookcases filled with record albums and sheet music. A large, abstract painting filled the wall, though the longer I stared at it the more I could make out a jazz quartet and a vocalist, rendered in thick paint smears on the canvas. The colors, bold red, cool blue, and fiery orange, together with the subject, radiated energy. Below the painting was a blue sofa. A pile of sheets was folded on the end on top of a bed pillow. The bedding took up no more than a square foot of space in the room but told me more than I'd bet Natasha wanted me to know.

I looked away from the evidence that someone had likely slept on the sofa and not in their bed and followed Natasha to the kitchen. She pulled two clear mugs out of a cabinet and handed me one, then poured herself a mug of tea from a pot on the stove.

"Would you like tea? I can make coffee if you prefer."

"Tea is fine," I said.

She reached across the table and filled my mug, and then carried over a tray with honey, sugar, milk, and mint. I added a dollop of milk to mine while she doctored her own. We were spending time on an unimportant ritual, but this visit wasn't meant to be a bonding exercise.

"Natasha, I booked you—or thought I booked you—for an event in early November. My clients are Linda and Larry Ledbetter. They bought a property on Northwest Highway from your husband. They hired me to convert it to a 1955 experience where they're going to renew their wedding vows and throw a party. I pitched them the idea of having you sing, and Linda loved it."

"Why me?" she asked.

"I learned that you studied under Addison Nigh," I said. "It would be fitting to have a vocalist who captured her essence."

"I'm sorry about earlier today," Natasha said. Her face grew red and her lips pressed together. She fought back tears, and the whites of her eyes got bloodshot in the process. She was holding something back.

"I know it's none of my business, but I couldn't help noticing the sheets on the sofa. Are you and Kip having problems?" I asked. Natasha nodded. "What have you been fighting about?"

"What every couple fights about: money. Kip invested in properties all over Dallas, lots he expected to explode in terms of value. Thanks to me, he has to sell off some of his real estate holdings prematurely."

"Was the property on Northwest Highway one of those?"

She nodded. "As the rest of the neighborhood flipped, he

expected the property values to rise. He was in no rush to sell that one in particular because of the tree damage. Every year that passed, the lot became more valuable because other developers invested in the neighborhood."

Now I understood Kip's hostility when the Ledbetters bought the house. He never expected a pair of impulsive, wealthy residents to come along, especially ones who wanted a 1955 ranch and didn't care that they couldn't conduct a walk-through. The highway-facing property would have been a ripe target for a business, or even to raze and pave as a parking lot for something nearby. Kip had been sitting on that property for three years. With the recent ups and downs in the market, he probably about broke even.

"Your fight with Kip—that's why you've been spending time at Sunny's house, isn't it?"

She nodded. "Kip kept a key to the house your clients bought. He was sleeping there, but after the sale went through, he came back here. I had to get away."

So Kip had lied about being back in the house. I wondered what else he lied about?

"Did Kip know Goldy?" I asked suddenly.

"Of course," she said. "He's the one who got me to sign with her. Sometimes I thought the two of them were more invested in my career than I was."

"Were you at Dallas Jazz on Sunday?"

"No," she said. "I already told you, I cut ties with Goldy, and we didn't end on good terms. I don't care if I never see her again." Natasha added a spoonful of honey to her tea and watched it dissolve.

"Back to Sunny's house. You were there when I was in the attic, weren't you?"

"Yes," she admitted. "I didn't know where else to go, and I

had a spare key from the recital, so I let myself in. I forgot to take my amplifier with me when the recital ended."

"Surely you have more than one amplifier," I said.

Natasha turned her head away from me and bit her lower lip. Tears spilled out of her eyes and slid down her cheeks and she didn't bother brushing them away.

"I faked my performance at the recital. My computer was hidden in my amp. I've been diagnosed with polyps on my vocal cords. That's a death sentence for a vocalist like me."

## THIRTY-THREE

Watching Natasha acknowledge that it was a medical condition, not a cover-up, which kept her from accepting the Ledbetter job was like watching a pressure release valve in action. She pulled several tissues out of a box that sat on the edge of the table and dabbed at her eyes and nose. The rising color on her face dissipated, leaving behind little more than a girlish flush. The tears that had been streaming despite her attempt to control them subsided too. Her breath was still ragged, but she was getting it under control.

"How long have you known?" I asked.

"I was diagnosed earlier this year. I told Goldy I wanted to scale back my performances, but she kept booking me. I lied and said I was going out of town with Kip when he went to his real estate convention, but Kip and I had a huge fight the night before he left. He's been sleeping on the sofa ever since he got back."

"Wasn't it risky to sing at the recital?"

"Addison asked me to close with her signature song. She was my mentor. I couldn't turn her down, not after all she'd done for me. But my throat—my voice—couldn't handle it, so I used an isotrack from an earlier performance."

"What's that?"

"An isolated vocal track. In the recording studio, each track to a song is recorded as a separate file. The vocals, the piano, the bass, and the drums. Anything else, too, if we layer it in. That way the song can be remixed in multiple ways. My vocals can be layered on top of a different arrangement if we want to release the song a second time, maybe with a Latin flavor or soft and slow as a ballad."

"You had your prerecorded vocals play and you lip-synched at the recital?"

"Yes." She looked embarrassed. "I downloaded the vocal performance to my laptop and hid the laptop inside the back of my amp. I ran the microphone through the amp, so nobody would notice."

"How did you sync it with the piano player? Was he in on it?"

"Are you familiar with the song?"

I shook my head.

"It starts with the vocals. The piano comes in on the fourth beat. I chose that song for a reason. Once the recording started, the piano follows my cues until the end of the piece."

"So you came into Sunny's house to get your amplifier and any evidence of the isotrack," I said. "Was there an album on the turntable?"

"Yes," she said. She seemed surprised by the question. "I played it the night before and forgot to put it away. I like things to be neat, so I put it back on the shelf before I left. Why?"

It was my turn to be surprised. "Could you find it again?"

"Of course," she said matter-of-factly. "The albums are organized alphabetically. It's the only blue album that starts with an 'F.'"

I'd made so much of the album that had gone missing from the display, yet I'd never even noticed the presence or absence of an amplifier not three feet away. So much for my powers of observation.

"Did you know I was in the attic while you were there?"

Her face colored again. "I recognized your car from the day you went to the Ledbetter property. I didn't see you when I went in, and the pull-down stairs were down, so I thought I could be in and out without you knowing I was there."

"Does anybody else know about the isotrack?"

"No."

"Not even Kip?"

"No. The only people who knew about my condition were Goldy and Punch."

"Punch Snyder knew?"

Her face colored. "I used to sing at Eight to the Bar, but I had to quit. After how things ended with Goldy, I didn't feel good about having her notify Punch. That's why Kip and I fought. I told him about the polyp diagnosis and how I backed out of all of my commitments, and when he heard I sang for free at a neighborhood recital, he hit the roof."

"Why didn't you explain it to him? Surely he would have understood. He's your husband."

"He wouldn't listen. He accused me of faking my condition. He stormed out of here and said he had to do damage control. He couldn't handle the idea that the venue manager might leak the word of my diagnosis. He couldn't accept that I'd never sing again."

"Natasha, this is your health. You can't perform a full set backed by a live quartet with prerecorded vocals no matter how much Kip wants you to. Even I know that."

She pulled two fresh tissues out of the box and blew her nose. She balled the tissues up, let them go, and took another.

"What do you think Kip meant by 'damage control?'"

"I don't know."

Love could blind people, and whether Natasha wanted to admit it or not, she was still in love with her husband. I wanted to shake her, to tell her to snap out of it and start making her own decisions instead of letting a manager or a husband make them for her, but I didn't know anything about Natasha Bledsoe's life other than what I gleaned from recent observations.

The thing was, Natasha's attitude, her willingness to say and do what her manager and her husband arranged, felt familiar. I already knew these kinds of things happened to women in the thirties, forties, and fifties. Doris Day thought her first salary was twenty-five dollars per gig, but after the fact she learned it was double that but the venue manager had kept half for himself. Her third husband embezzled millions from her, a fact she didn't learn until after he died an untimely death.

My mind was buzzing with new information, and I had to talk to Ling, Sue, or, preferably, Tex. It had been hours since we last spoke. I wanted to bypass the chain of command and go directly to him, to share with him what I'd learned and learn from him what he'd figured out while lying in a hospital bed. *If* he were lying in a hospital bed.

Which, now that I thought about it, I knew he wouldn't do. Tex wasn't the kind of guy to sit on the sidelines, even if he was supposed to be dead.

I finished my tea and thanked Natasha for confiding in me. She appeared to be in shock. I stood and gathered my handbag, and she followed me to the front door. When we reached it, I turned back around.

"Natasha, when's the last time you spoke with Kip?" I asked gently.

"Saturday," she said.

"I thought Kip had an out-of-town work commitment."

"He checked in from home but didn't go until the last day. We had a huge fight that night and we haven't spoken since."

THIRTY-FOUR

I couldn't get into my car fast enough. Kip went to see Punch the night Punch was murdered. He didn't attend the convention until the final day. He checked in remotely, giving him an alibi. I had to get this information to the police.

Punch Snyder's murder was one thing, and the police were focused on that. I may or may not have had a ticking clock on the Ledbetter job, depending on the rift between Linda and Larry, and a possible lingering case of identity fraud. I'd already suspected that there was a connection between my problems and Tex's case, and my conversation with Natasha reinforced that suspicion.

I drove to the police station. It was shortly after noon, and with any luck, Ling and Sue would still be at the hospital. The rest of the department knew the truth about the shooting so I didn't have to keep up the pretext of Tex's death around them. I entered the precinct and approached Imogene. Her eyes were rimmed with red as if she'd been crying intermittently.

"Madison," she said. "You don't look upset."

I lowered my voice. "You know he isn't dead, right?"

"I know. I'm the face of the department, though, so I have to look upset to anybody who walks in." She opened her drawer and pulled out a jar of menthol. She dabbed it under each eye and instantly tears poured out. "I read a blog. This is how they get actors to fake-cry in Hollywood." She held the jar toward me. "Want some?"

"No, thank you." I glanced around the empty police station. "Where is everybody? There are always officers here."

"Everybody's out on patrol. Killing a cop is a big thing, and there has to be a massive police presence on the streets."

"Is there any word on the shooting?"

"No, not yet. It's starting to look like it's not gang related." She sounded disappointed.

"They'll catch the person who did this. They always do."

"No, Madison, they don't. In fiction, you're expected to wrap up all the loose ends and make sure the bad guys get caught, but that's not how it works in real life. I try to tell the editors that, but they don't want to listen. Everybody expects justice to be served by the last page."

"Did something happen that I don't know about?"

She picked up a sheet of pink paper and handed it to me. It was a rejection letter. I scanned the contents and handed the letter back. "At least they addressed you by name," I said. "That's something, right?"

"That's why I printed it on pink paper." She opened a file that was otherwise filled with yellow pages. "The yellow ones are form letters addressed to 'Dear Author.'"

Imogene was preoccupied with her latest rejection letter, which I took to be a good sign. There were far more pressing issues afoot. This told me the crisis with Tex had passed.

While I stood at Imogene's desk, the front door to the precinct opened. I turned around to see which of the officers had returned and found myself face to face with a construction worker. He wore a neon yellow vest with reflective tape over a long-sleeved black T-shirt, beat-up jeans, and lace-up Timberland boots. I didn't know any construction workers personally, but this one was more than familiar: under the hard hat, the glasses, the mustache, sideburns, and reflective-taped regulation wear, it was Tex.

When he saw me, he froze. My breath caught in my throat. The door closed behind him, and he stepped forward to avoid being hit.

"Hi, Bob," Imogene said. She turned to me. "Madison, this, uh, is Bob. He works on the construction crew by the side of the building. He sometimes comes in on his break."

"Hello, Bob," I said coolly.

Bob looked from my face to my black bowler hat with daisy pin and back to my face. I could tell he wanted to comment. Of all the kooky items in my wardrobe, he had the most to say about the hats.

Imogene spoke up. "Madison, I should probably talk to Bob, you know, because he doesn't have a lot of time before he's due back at the job site."

"Of course," I said. "I'll wait here until you finish." I smiled at both of them and then pretended to study the wall of notices behind me. Notices for babysitters wanted and yard equipment for sale were tacked on a board alongside posters for the tipline and a schedule of performances for an all-cop outlaw country band called Frank Cannonball Run.

Imogene came over to me. "I didn't want to say anything, but I'd like to talk to Bob alone if you catch my drift."

"Well," I said. I looked at the construction worker. "Bob is probably a stand-up guy, but considering he looks like he stepped off the set of an adult film, I think I should stick around and make sure you're safe."

Bob spoke. "My office. Now." Imogene started toward him. "Not you. Her."

Imogene looked at me. "It's okay, Imogene. I have a can of pepper spray in my handbag and I'm not afraid to use it."

I followed Tex to his office. He opened the door and the overpowering sickly-sweet scent of flowers assaulted us. He pulled the door shut and stormed halfway back to Imogene's desk. "Get those flowers out of my office," he commanded.

"Where do you want me to put them?"

"I don't care. Make them go away. Crack a window while you're at it." He turned back and grabbed my hand, then pulled me to the same interrogation room where I'd talked to Renee. It felt like a year ago, not merely days, when the detectives had her here for questioning and she told me about the jazz retrospective, Punch's suspicion of embezzlement, and his pending lawsuit against the *Dallas Tribune*. So much had happened since then that I very nearly forgot about all of the other leads Ling and Sue had to chase down in addition to a possibly unrelated cop shooting.

Tex reached up and disconnected the camera mounted in the corner of the room and then pulled off his sunglasses and hard hat. He set both on the worn wooden table and then put his hands on either side of my face and kissed me.

When we pulled apart, I looked directly into his eyes. "You didn't have an ulterior motive for disconnecting the security camera, did you? That interrogation table isn't my idea of a romantic setting."

His eyes twinkled. "I'm still recovering from getting shot, but in my mind, this whole scene played out a little longer."

"Nice to see some things don't change."

He eyed me up and down. "Ditto." He scratched his mustache, and then peeled it off and set it on the table with the glasses and hard hat.

"Where'd you get the costume?"

"Borrowed it from Jumbos. They keep props on hand for Ladies Night. I asked for the cowboy but the girls said it was too close to the real thing."

"Comedians *and* dancers. I had no idea the ladies of Jumbos were multitalented." Tex grinned. "I didn't mean it like *that,*" I said.

Long before Tex and I met, he, along with the rest of the police force, frequented Jumbos Strip Club in the off hours. It was one of those pieces of information that formed my initial opinion of him. Since then, I'd gotten to know the owner, a former dancer herself, and discovered Jumbos was a business like any other business in the Lakewood area. I'd also learned she was a friend of Tex, of the police force, and I considered myself lucky that she'd become a friend to me too.

"I hate to tell you, but Porno Bob is close to the real thing too. If you want to go undercover, you should dress like a businessman. Shirt, tie, suit, the works."

"I tried it. Looked like the cover of a Billionaire Romance for women over fifty."

"I see your opinion of yourself hasn't been affected by the shooting."

"I got propositioned in the parking lot outside of Jumbos. They wanted to know if I was available for private parties. I went back inside and changed into this."

We spent a few more minutes on Tex's injury with a small

lecture from me for him to take it easy. I fully expected him to tune me out, so I switched gears into more—maybe "different" is a better word—pressing matters.

"Imogene said you haven't heard anything about the shooter."

"Nothing. I thought for sure someone would take credit. If this were cop related, there would be something by now. Problem is I put myself in a corner. I've got to stay under the radar and let the two Sues close this case before I can have the paper print a correction."

"Have they uncovered any new information?"

"Nothing you haven't heard yourself."

"I may have uncovered something when I spoke to Natasha Bledsoe earlier today," I said.

"Let's have it."

I told Tex what Natasha had confided in me. "She has polyps. Her singing career is all but over. She's afraid to let it become known publicly. She's the one who came into Sunny's house the day I was in the attic. She used a prerecorded track of vocals for her performance at the recital at Sunny's house and came back to get her amplifier and the laptop with her isotrack."

"Isolated vocal track?"

"How did you know that?"

"I guessed."

"You guessed correctly." I paused for a moment. "She was also responsible for the missing album."

"Why'd she take it?"

"She didn't. She said she likes things to be neat, so she put it away. It's the simplest answer and it never occurred to me."

"Don't beat yourself up, Night. That one might have gotten past me too."

"I did find out that Kip and Natasha fought. He wanted her

to keep singing at Eight to the Bar, but she'd already told Punch about her diagnosis. Kip stormed out of the house and said something about damage control. He didn't want anybody to know she couldn't sing."

"Ling said Kip Bledsoe was at a real estate convention in Austin on the night of the murder."

"Ling confirmed he was registered for the convention, but Natasha said he checked in from home. He was here on Saturday—that's the same Saturday he turned the keys over to the Ledbetters. Natasha said she and Kip had a huge fight that night and he went to the convention for the third day."

"That was the day of his panel."

"He could have been here to kill Punch. He could have killed Punch Friday night, turned over the keys to the Ledbetters on Saturday, fought with Natasha on Saturday night, and been back at the convention for Sunday."

"What's his motive?"

"Money." I told Tex about Kip's plan to invest in properties around Dallas and wait for them to become so desirable to developers that he doubled his investments, how this left him strapped, and how angry he'd been when Natasha gave up her career.

"I don't like it. If Kip talked Punch into giving his wife her gig back, then it seems Kip and Punch didn't have a problem."

"Or maybe that meeting didn't go as well as planned," I said.

"This all seems conveniently incriminating coming from the angry wife," Tex said. "Could be she made it all up to cover her own tracks."

"Don't you want to check it out all the same?"

"I'll check out both of them. If he has a motive, then she does too."

"What's hers?"

"Maybe she wanted out of the marriage. Getting the husband convicted of murder is convenient grounds for divorce."

## THIRTY-FIVE

I hadn't wanted to consider that angle, but it stared me in the face just the same. "I imagine if Kip were convicted of murder and Natasha filed for divorce, she might be entitled to *more* than half of his assets."

"A good lawyer could probably make that argument."

"According to Natasha, Kip was in debt due to his real estate investments. His whole business plan was to buy properties and sit on them until some developer with deep pockets came along. That's why he's been so annoyed at the Ledbetter transaction. He wanted to sell it for ten times what they paid. That was going to be his lottery ticket."

Tex's forehead creased. "I thought they paid the asking price of a million dollars."

"They did, and they didn't blink at his terms of purchasing the property without an inspection or an interior walk-through. At the time, I thought he was the luckiest property owner in the state. There's a tree inside the house, for God's sake. I couldn't fathom why he wasn't happy."

"That's the kind of price tag that dissuades ninety-nine

percent of buyers, and the terms probably knock out most of the remaining one percent. Did anybody pull up the assessment?"

"I don't think so. Why?"

Tex pulled out his phone and made a call. "I need you to check the assessed property value for—hold on." He pulled the phone away from his ear. "What's the address?" I told him and he repeated it into the phone. "I'll hold." A few seconds later, he said, "That's all? What?"

He hung up and pocketed his phone. "That house your clients bought? Guess what the assessed value was."

I shrugged. "The listing said it was priced for the value of the lot. The house was never considered to be part of the sale."

Tex's eyes narrowed. He pulled his phone back out and made another call. "When did the designation on the property change?" He paused. "Thanks." He hung up again.

By now, I was on the edge of my seat. "What?" I asked. "Don't leave me hanging."

"Kip Bledsoe paid about a million dollars for that property."

"Three years ago?"

"A couple of other lots in the area sold for close to two. In both cases, the lots were valued at a couple hundred thousand dollars and the owners hit paydirt when the planning commission decided to add a new exit to the highway. Seems Bledsoe gambled that the same thing would happen to his property."

"It does butt up against Northwest Highway," I said. "Which makes it possibly worth something for the planning commission but not particularly desirable as a residential property."

"Right. His gamble didn't pay off and every year that went by he needed a bigger payoff to earn back his investment in mortgage payments and taxes alone."

"None of this has anything to do with Punch Snyder," I said. "It doesn't cast Kip in the best light, and it would explain a conflict between him and the Ledbetters. It explains why he and Natasha were estranged and why she was hiding out at Sunny Nigh's house, and it could even extend to the rift between Natasha and Goldy. If any one of them were the victim here, this would feel like a lead, but what does any of it have to do with Punch?"

Tex scratched his fake sideburn. "I don't know."

After discussing details that may or may not have related to the case, I asked, "I suppose your construction disguise means the hospital freed up your bed."

"I can't lie around in a hospital. You know that."

"Right. But you can't be seen going into and out of your house, or visiting me, or crashing on a sofa at Jumbos." I paused for emphasis. "Where are you staying?"

"Can't say."

"You don't know?"

"I have a place where nobody'll think to look. It's best if you don't know where it is."

"Sure, I understand."

Tex picked up his mustache and pressed it back into place. He turned to me and I adjusted it so it was less crooked. I handed him the mirrored aviators and he checked his reflection in the lens. Satisfied with his Village Person appearance, he turned around and led us out of the interrogation room. After a few steps, he stopped in his tracks and I bumped into his back.

"What's wrong?" I peered over his shoulder and saw what had given him pause.

Imogene was in the process of relocating the flowers from

Tex's office like he'd asked—into the empty lock-up cell. All around the perimeter of the otherwise dismal cage sat baskets, vases, trees, and in one case, a wreath of roses with a ribbon that said RIP. If ever there were a time to be arrested by the local police, it was now.

Tex stared at the display. His mouth opened as if he were about to say something, but then he closed it and shook his head. He turned his back on the cage and walked to the exit. Right before he left, he turned back around. "Be careful out there, Night."

"You too, Bob." I gave him a bittersweet smile, and he left.

I gave Tex a five-minute lead and then left the police station. Imogene's decision to move the flowers to lockup had simply given the pungent odor space to balloon. Now the Lakewood Police Department smelled like the perfume counter at Macy's.

The sun was bright, casting the neighboring streets in an idyllic glow that made us think nothing bad could happen. It was the great lie we all wanted to believe: bad things only happen in the dark. But it was so not true that it made me question other universal beliefs like karma. Sometimes what came around didn't go around; sometimes the bad guys got away.

Imogene's rejection letter had rubbed off on me.

The air was warm but tinged with a cool note. I buttoned my cardigan and got into my car. There weren't many places I could go where I wouldn't get approached with condolences about Tex, including my showroom. Effie was of the generation who got the majority of her news from social media, and I couldn't predict if Tex's death had made her algorithm. I called the studio phone instead of her cell. Donut phones are remarkably effective when you prefer to avoid caller ID.

"Mad for Mod," she answered.

"Effie, it's Madison. I'm not coming into the studio today."

"Sure, Boss. Anything I need to know?"

It seemed she hadn't heard. I relaxed. Just knowing I didn't have to keep up the pretext for the thirty seconds or so that this conversation would last was a relief. I hesitated. Effie's breezy tone was welcome, but when she heard the news, which was bound to happen thanks to her connection to me, she might question my lack of sadness. "Yes. You're going to hear some news about Captain Allen. Don't—" I was in a corner. There was nothing I could say that wouldn't jeopardize Tex's plan, but there also was no way I could effectively run my business without letting Effie know the truth. I started again. "Captain Allen is—"

"I know, Boss. He's dead wink wink."

"He's—what?"

"He came here dressed like Bob the Builder. He told me who he was and threatened to bury me in parking tickets if I let it get out that he was alive."

"Did he say what he wanted?"

"Yeah, he said you needed the Ledbetter file."

"I have the Ledbetter file."

"I know. I told him that."

"Effie, did you question why Captain Allen was dressed like a cartoon contractor?"

"It's almost Halloween," she said. She sneezed. "I figured he was in costume."

"Then why did you say he was dead wink wink?"

"Because I know about the fake obituary. Hold on," she said. The phone went silent and I heard what sounded like a foghorn. She returned to the phone. "I know about the shooting. Jimmy told me when he stopped by. Don't worry, I can keep my mouth shut." She sneezed again.

I was shocked. Tex's whole plan hinged on the public at large believing he hadn't survived the shooting. If Jimmy were out there telling people the obituary wasn't real, it would undermine everything.

"Why did Jimmy come to Mad for Mod?" I asked, fighting to keep my voice steady.

"He dropped off your file," she said. "It's a bunch of stuff the paper compiled for the obituaries. You want me to toss it?"

"No, hold onto it. I'd like to take a look."

"Whatever you say, Boss." She sneezed again.

"Effie, are you sick? Do you need to go home?"

"No, I'll survive. I'm on my second dose of Claritin and it's barely making a difference. You think this place was full of flowers before? You should see it now."

I couldn't in good faith threaten to dock Effie's pay if she let word get out, so I let Tex's threat about the parking tickets stand. I told her I'd be there shortly and we hung up. A few minutes later, I was parked out back.

Effie hadn't been kidding. Along the exterior wall of the building, young trees in modest glazed ceramic pots sat in two neat rows. More than half of them were tied with black ribbons. I went in through the back and my eyes instantly started to itch. A narrow walkway remained between an aisle of flowering plants. I heard a sneeze and stepped over a basket of stargazer lilies and joined Effie in my office.

"Hey Boss," she said. She pulled a tissue from a box directly in front of her and blew her nose. "If you had any doubts about whether people know about your relationship with Captain Allen, consider them crushed."

"Right." I pulled the card off a small basket of white daisies. They were my favorite flower, the most Doris Day bloom in the botany world, and they seemed an unusual choice for a condolence gift. I slid the card out of the envelope and read:

*Sorry for your loss. We're here for you.* It was signed Hudson and Jules James.

Hudson had been my handyman when I moved to Dallas, and then he'd been more than that. He and Tex had a confusing history built from the kind of mistrust that comes from the detective/wrong suspect paradigm. I'd recently met his fiancé in a completely unrelated set of circumstances, and while we'd never be friends, I couldn't find fault with her. The card told me everything I needed to know: Hudson and Jules were now married, there were no hard feelings, and they'd heard the news about Tex. I held onto the card, feeling for the briefest moment a memory of the days when Hudson, Tex, and my lives were tangled in a way that felt like it would go on forever.

"Anybody good?" Effie asked.

"Just an old friend." I slid the card back into the envelope and nestled the envelope back amongst the flowers. It was official; I needed to find a new handyman.

There would be no business happening at Mad for Mod, not while the showroom was in an allergy-inducing state. I flipped the Open sign to Closed and spent the next hour side by side with Effie moving flowers to the parking lot.

When we finished, I told Effie to take the rest of the day off with pay. I went back inside and called Larry Ledbetter. My enthusiasm for their job had waned, not because of the concept, but because I found myself designing a house my clients might not want. Mid-century modern design provides a certain note of whimsy, but whimsy can be like whipped cream. It makes already good things better, but it has little lasting value on its own.

"Larry, this is Madison. Would it be possible for us to schedule a meeting?"

"Sure," he said. "Give me a second to pull Linda's schedule."

"No," I said. "I met with Linda earlier in the week. I'd like to talk to you."

"What did she say?" Larry asked.

"I'd rather talk about this face to face."

Larry, to my delight, was willing to come to me. Their office wasn't far, and he entered through the back door about ten minutes later. I locked the door behind him, and he followed me to the Mondrian seating area.

"She told you about what I said, didn't she?" Larry asked.

"She said you asked her why she wanted the house."

Larry fiddled with his wedding ring. "Did she tell you about our promise?"

"She said you both agreed you wouldn't do her things and you things, but you'd always operate as a unit."

"That's right. When you're eighteen and broke, it sounds romantic. Always having someone agree with you. Never having to fight for what you want. After twenty-five years of marriage, do you know what I want?"

I didn't want to risk guessing incorrectly, so I simply shook my head.

"I want to surprise my wife." He looked up from his ring to my face. "Is that so wrong? I want to make a grand romantic gesture and see pure delight on her face. We haven't made a move in twenty-five years without talking about it first. I want to mark the occasion by doing something spontaneous without asking her, something that's going to blow her away."

"That's it? That's why you asked her why she wanted the house?"

This time Larry nodded.

I leaned forward. "Larry, your wife thinks she pressured you into something you didn't want to do. She's questioning the foundation of your marriage because she thinks you didn't want to buy a mid-century ranch house to mark your anniversary."

"Well," he said. He tipped his head from side to side. "She's not entirely wrong about that."

"You spent a million dollars for a property you don't want?"

"The house is fine. It's better than fine. But I would have been happier with a mid-century split level."

"Well," I said, trying to hide my relief. "There's always next year."

I sent Larry home with an arrangement of blue delphiniums (after removing the Sympathy ribbon) from the local contractor who'd installed my pool and then returned to my desk. It was then I saw the file from the *Dallas Tribune* on my desk.

On the outside, Jimmy had written: *~~Madison Night~~ ~~dancer~~ ~~decorator~~ pain in my butt.* The paper may have finally printed the correct obituary for Sunny, but there was no mistaking that the notes written the folder pertained to me.

I opened the folder and flipped through notations and quotes about my life and Sunny's life. There were a few black and white pictures of Sunny from her performing days along with a sealed white envelope marked Confidential. I turned it over in my hands, volleying arguments for and against opening it. Jimmy hadn't proven himself to be the most detail-oriented employee I'd met, so before I did anything, I called the paper. After I got Jimmy on the phone, I explained the situation.

"This is Madison Night," I said. "I'm the one who's still alive."

"I printed the cop's obituary like you told me," Jimmy said. "I swear."

"That's not why I'm calling. You dropped a folder of notes off at my studio. There's a sealed envelope marked confidential inside. Was that meant for someone else?"

"No, that's for you. It's from the guy you came here with last week. The one who said he was going to sue us."

"Punch Snyder?"

"Yeah, that's him. He gave it to me before I screwed up his mom's obit."

"Before?" I asked. "Are you sure about that?"

"Sure. Before the error, he was a lot nicer."

"Did Punch come into the *Dallas Tribune* a lot?"

"Yes," he said. "He dropped off a press release about a jazz retrospective, and he used to give us notices about his club. I haven't seen him for about a week. Maybe his lawyers told him to stop talking to us."

"Jimmy, do you still work on the obituaries?"

"Heck, no. My uncle doesn't trust me with anything other than shredding."

I thanked Jimmy and hung up, then used a vintage letter opener to slice through the flap of the envelope. I pulled out a letter addressed to Jack Folly.

It was a love letter. An apology letter. And a letter that contained a secret.

It was a letter from Sunny Nigh to Jack Folly that explained the choices she'd made seventy years ago.

It also said Jack was Punch's father.

## THIRTY-SEVEN

I pulled Jack's calling card out of my handbag. I needed to talk to him, and I had the perfect excuse.

On the back were the details regarding Sunny's public memorial. What had he told me? The mix-up with the obituaries had created a problem in scheduling the memorial service, so they kept the one I'd been at for family. A public memorial for Sunny's fans was scheduled for next week. But it *was* next week. Maybe I couldn't make a show of giving away the flowers that had been sent to Mad for Mod, but I had an idea of where they would be appreciated.

"Jack, this is Madis," I said, using his nickname for me.

"You can't stop thinking about me, can you, pretty lady?"

"You're a difficult man to forget." I scanned the mass of floral arrangements in my parking lot. "You mentioned the public service for Sunny was this week. I'd like to donate some flowers to the memorial."

"The service is on Saturday, but the Church of St. Monica's has been accepting donations all week."

"Great. I'll have them sent tomorrow." I set Jack's card on my desk, and then, rather spontaneously, asked, "You wouldn't happen to be available for dinner tonight, would you?"

"I'm in my nineties. I ate my dinner at three thirty." He paused. "But if you're free, I'd love some company. I'll even change out of my pajamas."

Jack Folly only half kept up his promise and wore a gray silk dressing gown over matching pajamas and cordovan leather slippers. A pitcher of limeade sat on the table next to him with two empty tumblers and a bottle of tonic water. By the time I joined Jack, the tumblers were full. I carried Clara's photo album with me and set it on his table.

"Mocktails," he grumbled. "Lime and tonic. My doctors say I can't have the hard stuff, but I can't say it would matter much either way." He held out a tumbler. I took it and we clinked glasses. I took a sip and was surprised to discover how good it was. As I was about to take a second sip, he cautioned me. "Better slow down there." He winked. "You have to help me keep up the illusion that these are real. Otherwise, I might be tempted to go against the doctor's orders."

"Sure," I said, winking back. "I'll pace myself."

"What's the haps, Madis?"

"'The haps?'" I couldn't help chuckling. "Is that jazz lingo?"

"Nah, it's new. I'm testing it out."

"It suits you," I said. I finished my mocktail and Jack offered me a refill. "No thank you, I have to drive."

While we sat together, a woman in a white chef's shirt carried a tray of cheese, crackers, and fruit outside and set them on the table. Jack thanked her. "Figured you were hungry if you invited me to dinner," he said. "That's my caretaker. She probably couldn't beat Bobby Flay, but she makes a mean cheese board. Help yourself."

"Thank you," I said. I sandwiched a square of cheese and a ring of pepperoni onto a cracker and popped it into my mouth, then followed it up with a grape. Before I reached for more, I pushed Clara's photo album toward Jack.

"Is that Sunny's?" he asked.

"No, it belongs to Clara. I'm creating a fake jazz club inside a house for a decorating job, and she loaned me that to get ideas."

My motivation for meeting with Jack was purely selfish. I needed a place to go where nobody would ask me about Tex, and Jack fit that bill. But as I sat across from him, watching his hand shake as he turned the pages of the photo album, I felt guilty. I wasn't mourning but Jack was, and the photo album in front of him brought his old feelings to the surface.

I set my glass down on the table. "Jack, what do you remember about the night of May 26, 1955?"

Jack's hand stopped shaking. His glass was raised to his mouth, but he didn't take a sip. He lowered the glass and held it in his lap. "What makes you think something happened that night?"

"I found a newspaper clipping inside a record jacket at Sunny's house. It was from that date, and it was about a missing cigarette girl named Julie May. Since then, I've learned she worked at Gimpy's with Sunny and Clara, or she did until the night she disappeared." I studied his face. "I think some other things may have happened that night too."

Jack took a drink of his mocktail. The ice clinked in the glass. He lowered the glass and held it while he stared out over his vast front yard. I could tell he had something to say, but I had a strong feeling that whatever it was, he hadn't spoken about that night for a long time.

"I went to Sunny's dressing room between sets. I wanted to surprise her with a weekend getaway. I knocked, but nobody answered. I was about to leave when I heard a sound. I went in and found Julie on the floor. Someone had tried to choke her."

"Was she alone?"

"I thought so but I was wrong. The room was dark. I went in to help her and someone shot me." He tapped his thigh. "Bullet's still in there. Been using a cane ever since."

I imagined the setting that Jack described. "You should have gone to the hospital immediately, but you tried to save Julie's life instead."

He remembered the details with remarkable clarity. "That's how Sunny found me. She saw the blood, and she saw Julie, and she thought the worst. I knew how it looked, but I couldn't leave Julie there. She had nobody. The jazz life tends to attract free spirits and adventure seekers, but I couldn't leave her lying on the floor of a dressing room while I chased after the woman of my dreams."

"What happened when you talked to Sunny?" I asked, though I probably knew more about what happened next than Jack did.

"I don't know. That night was the last time we spoke. She left town for a gig in Houston. Martin knew how it looked and he said he'd fix things for me. He sent me to a doctor to get stitched up and then arranged for me to join a combo playing in Europe while the scene calmed down here."

"When did you return from Europe?" I asked.

"About a year later. Everything was different. Sunny and Martin were married. She had a recording contract and a baby boy."

"What happened to Julie?"

"I don't know. When Martin said he'd take care of things, I thought he'd take care of her too." Jack stared at the contents of his mocktail. "I don't like to dwell on the past, but it has a way of creeping into my nightmares. I don't know what happened, but lately, I've started to believe Martin wasn't the hero of the evening."

I'd come to believe the same thing.

# THIRTY-EIGHT

"Martin told Sunny he'd take care of things and he did—for himself," I said. "He didn't take care of Julie in the way you thought. He murdered her. He sent Sunny to Houston and you to Europe, not to protect either of you but to drive a wedge between you. Sunny was in shock too. She didn't know how to process what she saw when she walked into her dressing room and saw you holding Julie, but she knew in her heart you weren't to blame. She didn't love Martin. She married him to protect you, and she stayed with him because she was afraid of what he'd do to you if she left." I didn't add the final piece of that thought, that when Martin had died, Sunny had been too embarrassed over her choices to admit to the truth. If she had, she could have saved them both years of loneliness and heartbreak.

"How do you know all this?"

I reached into my handbag and pulled out the letter. "From this letter. I believe it was intended for you."

I handed the envelope to Jack. He slid it out of the envelope and scanned the words.

"Punch was my son," Jack said. "I've always wondered, but I never let myself believe it." Jack looked up. "Who gave you this?"

"The *Dallas Tribune*," I said. "Punch wanted them to print it. He must have found it. I think he wanted the truth to come out. I think that's why he sought out a relationship with you, not because you were one of the last musicians left from Sunny's club days, but because you were his father."

Jack held the letter up. "Is this why someone killed him?"

"I don't know."

The early evening air swept over us. Overhead, a cloud cover hid the moon and stars. I felt insignificant in a way I hadn't since the obituary ran in the papers.

"I should be going," I said. "Thank you for the drinks."

"Thank you for the company," Jack said. "Take care of yourself, Ms. Madison Night. Life is shorter than you think."

———

I left Jack's house and drove aimlessly for about twenty minutes, my mind wandering this way and that. I couldn't stop thinking about Larry and Linda Ledbetter, two peas in a pod who almost ruined everything by thinking they weren't allowed to disagree. Kip and Natasha Bledsoe, who barely occupied the same living quarters. And Jack and Sunny, two like souls who'd spent most of their lives apart because they'd let pride come between them. I also couldn't stop thinking about what Jack had said about true happiness lying between the ups and downs, when we're not trying to get anywhere. What he called the in-betweens.

I viewed my romantic past as touch points: relationships and break-ups but I never stopped to focus on the times when I wasn't moving toward or away from anything. And like Jack said, that's when I'd been the happiest. Maybe that's what I'd been trying to say to Tex. Maybe where we were was an in-between, but in a life filled with chaos and drama, the in-between felt like an oasis. Beginnings assumed endings, but maybe getting to this part should be the goal. The amorphous, never-ending, always expanding space between constantly moving bases.

My involvement in these people's lives had come by accident. A fluke that inserted my history into another person's narrative. But that fluke had led me down a path of love, loss, and secrets. I found myself chasing answers to the crime that had happened seventy years ago, not the one that happened last week. Of the two crimes, it was the one that included roads not traveled. It was the one that reminded me the most of myself.

While driving without direction, my phone rang. It was Renee. "Hi," I said. "I was going to call you tomorrow."

"Did you find anything in my mother's attic?" she asked. "I was there earlier today, and the key was missing from the rock out front. That was you, right? Thank you for not disrupting things too much. Did you find anything that might lead back to Punch's death?"

Her words came out in a rush, like machine-gun fire. I'd been so preoccupied with Tex and the shooter, with the tree in the Ledbetter property, with what I'd learned about Sunny and Jack, that I'd forgotten all about how what this past week had been like for Renee.

"I'm sorry," I said. "I haven't finished going through the files."

"Do you think you could come to Eight to the Bar? A local realtor approached me about listing the club for sale."

"Kip Bledsoe?"

"Yes. Why?"

I felt that familiar tingly sensation when something feels

significant. "I'm not sure. He seems to be popping up a lot lately."

"I know it's a good offer, but I can't make any decisions about that until I go through Punch's things, and I'm a little overwhelmed."

I didn't like the idea that Kip was sniffing around the jazz club, but I didn't want to alarm Renee. "I'm in the area," I said. "I can be there in ten minutes."

"Thank you, Madison."

After reading the letter Sunny wrote to Jack, I felt I knew Sunny, Martin, and Jack. The person I didn't know was the cigarette girl, Julie May. She was not only the victim of a murder, but she was a victim of time: the time that had passed while her life was slowly forgotten. A portion of that time had ticked past at Gimpy's. I didn't know anything about those days, but one other person did: Clara.

I called her. After identifying myself, I got down to it. "Remember how you said you and Sunny hid things in the floor of Gimpy's?"

"Sure," she said. "Why?"

"Did anybody else know you did that?"

"I'm sure the other band members knew. Martin caught me the day he was trying to find Sunny's shoe—you remember, the one we found the other day? And Jack, of course. There might be other things down there. Why?"

"Just curious," I said. It was exactly the information I needed to hear. "Thanks, Clara. I'm at Eight to the Bar now. If I find anything, you'll be the first to know."

It was a little after eight when I pulled into the parking lot behind the possibly closed-forever jazz club. Renee's car was in the lot. I left one space between us and went in through the back door.

When Renee saw me, relief showed on her face. A newspaper was open in front of her. The bar was covered in glassware, some wrapped, some not. She systematically pulled a fresh sheet of newsprint, set a glass onto it by the corner, and then rolled the glass up in the paper and slotted it into an empty cardboard box partitioned to hold a dozen bottles of wine.

"Thank you for coming," she said. "I've been keeping busy, but I honestly don't remember what I've done from one moment to the next. Yesterday when I went home for the night, I found a carton of sheet music in the living room. They were marked up with the International Phonetic Alphabet, so they probably belonged to my mother at one point, but I have no recollection of finding them. I'm running on autopilot."

"I felt the same way when my parents died," I said. "I don't know how I made it through that year. I do believe our brains have a fail-safe mechanism to buffer us from our emotions while we do what needs to be done."

"How old were you?"

"In my twenties. It was unexpected."

"Like Punch," Renee said.

I didn't want to tell her no, it was nothing like Punch; my family died in a car crash and Punch was murdered. Loss was loss and grief was grief, and by not dealing with my emotions, I'd made poor personal choices that ultimately led to my move to Texas and my need for a fresh start.

There was a time I resented the hand I'd been dealt. When I wondered why me? When it felt like forces conspired to keep me isolated and alone. Now, I saw it completely differently. Every single moment added up and brought me to where I was today.

"It gets better," I said. Renee looked at me questioningly and

I continued. "I know you don't want to hear that now. I know your grief is the one thing that keeps you connected to your brother and you're afraid if you let it go you'll forget him. You won't. I promise you that."

By all accounts, Renee should have been upset. Her words indicated a measure of sadness that I wanted to believe, but I'd yet to see her shed a tear.

"I'm numb," she said. She held a shot glass in either hand and dangled her arms by her sides. "I want to feel something, but I don't. I can't sleep. I can't eat. I can't cry. I've tried. I keep waiting for the emotions to hit me."

"They'll come when you're ready to feel them. Don't try to rush things. Healing takes time."

Renee nodded, but I couldn't tell if she'd even heard me. She set the shot glasses on the countertop, pulled a fresh sheet of newspaper off the pile, and wrapped the glasses together. Any thoughts of small talk led back to Punch, to Sunny, to the exhibit, or the bar, or any number of things that were part and parcel of the unsolved murder and Renee's future, and I didn't want to push her into talking about things she wasn't ready to face. The bar fell silent save for the sounds of glasses clinking and newspaper crinkling until the newspaper was used up. We were only halfway through packing up the barware.

"I'll be right back," I said. I headed into the hallway to the dressing room where Clara and I had found the money in the floor.

"Where are you going?"

"There's a stack of newspapers in the band's dressing room." I put my hand on the knob and turned it.

"Don't go in there!" Renee cried out.

But it was too late. Inside the dressing room, the floorboards were pulled up, exposing embossed napkins, bundles of matches, cocktail stirrers, and a case of booze.

The hole in the floor also revealed a skeleton that had been there for a very long time.

# THIRTY-NINE

———

"I told you not to come in here," Renee said. Her face tightened into a mask, rigid and angry. Her hands, previously busy with the business of wrapping glassware in pages of newsprint, now held a gun pointed at me.

I couldn't believe how wrong I'd been about her. From the beginning, I thought she was an innocent woman railroaded into being the number one suspect. I'd pushed Ling and Sue to investigate Goldy, Natasha, Kip, and the *Dallas Tribune*. All because Renee gave me access to files I never would have otherwise seen.

"That's Julie May," I said. "How long have you known her remains were here?"

My brain scrambled to find connecting thoughts, discarding unrelated ones that had preoccupied my mind for days. Renee—Renee? —Renee—Sunny—Punch.

The bar.

The exhibit.

The estate.

The murder. The *first* murder.

"You and Punch were working together on an exhibit that would have cemented your mother's legacy. You were close. What happened?"

"Punch found something in the archives. Information that implicated our father in a murder and made our mother out to be a weak woman who stood by and did nothing. It might have sold tickets, but it would have destroyed her legacy."

"But you and Punch didn't have the same father," I said.

"Where did you hear that?"

"In a letter your mother wrote to Jack Folly," I said. "The letter that confirmed your dad killed a cigarette girl in this club and then framed Jack for the crime. Punch found out, didn't he? He learned the truth after being lied to his whole life. He found out Jack was his real father, and his surrogate father was a murderer."

"He found something, but he wouldn't tell me what. He said he'd been in touch with a local newspaper about publishing an exposé about Addison Nigh's sordid past." She made finger quotes with her left hand around the last four words, keeping her right hand on the gun. "I tried to tell him that story would ruin her legacy. We had a chance to squash it. Destroy the evidence. Make it so it would never come out. But Punch didn't care. He said the story would put his club on the national stage."

Pieces of information dropped into place like a neat tile pattern on a renovated floor. Punch had been in touch with the *Dallas Tribune* before the mixed-up obituary. It hadn't added up when Tex first told me, but now I understood. Punch had contacted the paper about the murder of Julie May. That's why Jimmy had photos of Sunny, Clara, and Julie in a folder on his desk. Punch had a story about events at a jazz club in the fifties, and he planned to leverage it for publicity. That's why he was so upset about the obit mix-up—not because of an innocent mistake, but because his big publicity plan never got off the ground.

"You met Punch here the night after the memorial," I said. "You tried to convince him that the obituary mix-up was a good thing."

"He brought me here to show me what he found." She cut her eyes to the pulled-up floorboards. "He wanted to use it for publicity. We could have lived comfortably for the rest of our lives if we managed our mother's estate properly," she said. "We could have kept all this quiet. Punch's way would have taken a match to the house and burned it to the ground. But Punch didn't care. I had to stop him. Now I'm the one with the matches."

"You murdered your brother," I accused.

"I did, and I'd do it again. We should have been a team. But there was no changing his mind. Punch would have survived, but if he destroyed our mother's legacy, then I'd have nothing."

"And Goldy Michener? Why did you kill her?"

"She knew too much," she said. "Punch needed a partner, and when I refused to help him, he approached her. He told her everything. She asked me to meet her at Dallas Jazz, and when I got there, she said she knew everything. I couldn't take the chance of her turning me in."

"Why hide the money in the floor?" I asked.

"Diversion. I had to make it look like someone was embezzling from the club so Punch would turn on his staff. I never could have predicted you coming in with the cavalry." Her eyes glowed. "That's when I knew you were my golden ticket. You know, I really should send a thank you note to Jimmy Nussbaum."

"But why send me into your mother's house? Why ask me to go through the boxes in the attic?"

"Punch found something in the attic that tipped him off to the murder my father committed, and I had to know what it was so I could destroy it. Giving you access was a stroke of genius. You built your business on digging through other people's estates. No one questioned you being there. I had the benefit of knowing your life story from the obituary. I knew how to keep you spinning."

"But impersonator—that couldn't have been you."

"Of course, it could. I called the *Dallas Tribune* the night you went there with Punch. When the intern said you were there too, I told him *I* was Madison Night and *you* were a fraud."

"And the bank? How did you shut down my credit?"

"A simple phone call to the bank," she said. "Identity theft is their number one concern. Just the whiff of an accusation was enough for them to freeze your accounts."

"You killed your only remaining family," I said. "How could you do that?"

"My father died when I was five, and in my mother's eyes, I was always second best. Now I'm free. We're the same, Madison. Remember? We have nobody. You're just like me."

But we weren't. My emotional scars hadn't faded, they'd healed, and I emerged stronger than I ever might have been. I wasn't like Renee or Addison or anyone else.

As I scrambled to think of a way out of the club alive, I saw the reflection of headlights as a car pulled into the lot. The windows were thick with grime, and I wasn't close enough to see who had arrived. A few moments later, a cheerful female voice called out from the entrance to the club.

"Madison? I knew I'd find you here."

It was Clara Bixby. Curious nonagenarian that she was, her presence made me more nervous, not less. I didn't want to put her in harm's way, but if she came in far enough to see Renee holding me at gunpoint, I doubted Renee would let her turn around and leave.

So many things about this showdown didn't make sense. Where were Ling and Sue? Where was Tex? Why had we set up surveillance at my studio, Thelma Johnson's house, and my client's property, but not at the site of the murder?

Sounds carried to us from out front: the dull thud of glasses bumping up against each other. Something fizzy being uncapped. The *glug glug glug* of a beverage being poured. A clunk, and then the hallway was flooded in light. Renee kept her eyes on mine.

"Let me tell her to leave," I said. "She's an old lady. She doesn't deserve this. Let me send her on an errand so she's not here when you—" I gulped. "Please."

Renee waved the gun toward the door. "Five minutes," she said.

I moved toward the door. I was shaking, but this was no time to panic. I found Clara by the bar. Bottles of tonic water and gin sat next to a red leather ice bucket. Tongs sat on the bar top. Clara was a one-woman party.

"This isn't a good idea," I said. "It's late."

"Pish posh," she said. "It's seven thirty." She picked up one of the glasses and handed it to me. I took it but didn't drink. The last thing I needed was to compromise my judgment or reaction timing.

"I thought of something," Clara said. She went behind the bar. She tapped the toe of her shoe on the floor. "It sounds different over here," she said. "Listen." She tapped in a semicircle and then stomped her foot in one spot. "I don't think Sunny and I were the only ones to hide things under the floorboards." She demonstrated remarkable agility for her age by getting down on all fours, and before I could tell her no, she tried to pry the floorboard loose. "Help me, would you?"

I looked over my shoulder and then back at Clara. "Let's talk about this tomorrow. We don't have the right tools tonight." I glanced at the gin and tonic. "You didn't drive, did you?"

"Of course not," she said. "I always have a driver after five."

I packed up Clara's portable cocktail party and ushered her toward the door. She didn't seem bothered by my brush-off.

After Clara was out of harm's way, I went back to the dressing room. It felt like hours since I went out front to meet Clara, not the promised five minutes. Renee sat on the edge of the vanity. She pointed at the clock with her gun.

"Cutting it close, Madison. Tsk, tsk."

Out front, Clara's voice called out, "Madison? I'm back. Do you know how to use a crowbar?"

Renee turned toward the door. It was my only opportunity. I grabbed a stack of *Dallas Tribunes* and swung them against Renee's gun. The gun went off. The impact knocked me backward. I glanced off the arm of the sofa and fell to the floor. And while Renee scrambled to find the gun, Clara crept into the room and smashed her treasured bottle of gin over Renee's head. The newspapers that I'd used to defend my life were scattered across the floor. It was the edition with my obituary.

It was almost poetic.

———

The next day, a team of investigators came to Eight to the Bar. Two hours later, the remains of Julie May were on their way to a forensic examination. It wouldn't be official until Lloyd confirmed her identity through dental records, but there was one clue with her that told me everything I needed to know: remnants of her fishnet stockings loosely covering her bones.

Two murders solved for the price of one.

# FORTY

There were over four hundred attendees at Addison Nigh's public memorial. The Ledbetters, who'd spontaneously purchased a vintage Airstream camper and decided to renew their vows privately and then explore the country, had fallen in love with my design and greenlit it for Sunny's memorial service. They had a two-part plan for the property: add it to the Ledbetter Hotel portfolio and promote it as a novelty vacation rental when they returned.

As guests milled through the 1955 ranch, pausing by the fifties-inspired buffet on the dining room table or milling around Bixby's, my makeshift jazz club, the atmosphere was convivial.

There was a part of me in everything I designed. Sure, I listened to the clients' hopes and dreams. I walked their living spaces and asked to see items they cherished. Often it was a ten-dollar lamp from a yard sale or a treasured relic from a now-deceased family member. It wasn't just the item that gave me a window into their style, it was the joy they displayed when they showed their possessions to me. Society wants us to believe we need a never-ending stream of newer, bigger, and better to satisfy our cravings, but sometimes we need to get quiet and see that we already have the things we want.

My relationship with the bank worked in my favor. Once Natasha confirmed that she wouldn't be singing at the event, the money that had been deposited into Goldy's account was reversed and returned to me. I hadn't pressed Natasha to sing now that I knew about her vocal condition, but I'd asked her to coordinate the talent instead. The same talent that had performed at the recital at Sunny's house came here, this time dressed in vintage gowns from the trunks in Sunny's attic.

Jack Folly had warned me from the start: jazz wasn't for sissies.

Possibly the biggest surprise to come out of the last few days was the sneakiness of Jack. I'd spent a week suspecting all sorts of people of all sorts of things, but I never once realized that when I dropped by to visit with the elderly jazz man, he'd dropped a key to Sunny's house into my handbag. I'd never have a chance to know the real Addison Nigh, but thanks to Jack, I knew her better than most.

Tex had been hiding out on his boat while Ling and Sue caught up with the shooter, a petty criminal who'd been in and out of the system for years. Tex was still recovering from his gunshot wound and wore a sling. The injury crimped his style in more ways than one. He turned the keys to his boat over to Lloyd and his cousin and spent the week floating around my pool.

He found me sitting at the back of the jazz club while a young woman sang "Ten Cents a Dance." He pulled a dime out of his pocket and set it on the table in front of me. I followed him to the dance floor. He put his free arm around my waist, and I put mine around his shoulders.

"Penny for your thoughts?" Tex asked.

"Big spender," I said. We swayed to the music in silence. It felt good to be close to Tex again. "I've pushed you away," I said. "I've lost a lot of people. People I thought would be in my life forever."

"Do you miss them?"

"Some," I admitted. "But not all." A few bars of music filled the air. "I'd miss you."

He raised my chin with his hand. "Why so contemplative?"

"This case felt different than the others. Seventy years ago, a man got away with murder. He used Sunny to give him an alibi, and he extorted marriage from her in exchange for not framing the man she loved. Lives were ruined by one man's need for domination. Two people who were very much in love spent their lives apart because of it. If Martin Snyder hadn't murdered Julie May in 1955, a lot of lives might have turned out very differently."

"Maybe Sunny and Jack were never meant to be together. Maybe their mutual sacrifices allowed them each to show their love in a much bigger way than they might have otherwise."

I studied him. "That's either morbid or romantic. Is that how you see us?"

"You want to know how I see us?"

"Yes," I said. "Yes, I do."

"We're two people who cheated death this week and lived to tell about it. We've already defied the odds."

"What do you think that means?" I asked.

He leaned close and whispered in my ear. "It means we are what we are, Night, and I wouldn't change a thing."

Want more Madison?
Preorder Please Don't Push Up the Daisies, Madison Night
Mystery #11, coming June 2023!

# ACKNOWLEDGMENTS

Thank you for reading *Love Me or Grieve Me*! This book marks the ten-year anniversary of the publication of *Pillow Stalk*. That's when I first introduced Madison Night into the world. I'm delighted that you've continued to read about her decorating, personal evolution, and mystery solving in each case since. As always, a huge debt of gratitude goes out to Doris Day, the inspiration behind Madison Night and the series. Without your vast body of work, a life of ups and downs, a talent that knew no bounds, and a passion for friends, costars, and animals, I'd have nothing to inspire me. Wherever you are, I imagine you're lighting up a star.

Writing requires a healthy mix of feedback, support, and research. Thank you to Amy Ross Jolly, Madison's first reader. I love that you can see where I'm going and when I'm not quite there. Your gentle feedback manner is perfect!

Thank you to *Atomic Ranch* magazine and MakeItMidcentury.com for delivering the kind of hard-hitting journalism I love, and RoadsideArchitecture.com for your culled collection of mid-century modern churches. To the Dallas Observer for a piece on Soul City, the sixties club that changed Dallas music forever, RetroRenovation for a piece on Cinderella bathtubs, and various online maps for helping me keep track of every location in the book.

Thank you to members of the Weekly DiVa Club for joining

my orbit, especially everyone who volunteered to be a dead person. I love you all for hitting reply on an email with that subject line! Special thanks to Melissa Kay, Louise Pledge, and Tracy Hartman for the use of your names.

Thank you to the Polyester Posse for your ongoing support of Madison, with special shout-outs to Barb, Sandy, and Janet for your eagle eyes. As always, I love reading your reviews!

And lastly, thank you, dear reader, for selecting this book out of millions of choices. I appreciate you more than you could ever know.

Xo,

Diane

# ABOUT THE AUTHOR

National bestselling author Diane Vallere writes smart, funny, and fashionable character-based mysteries. After two decades working for a top luxury retailer, she traded fashion accessories for accessories to murder. A past president of Sisters in Crime, Diane started her own detective agency at age ten and has maintained a passion for shoes, clues, and clothes ever since. Find out more at https://dianevallere.com/

# ALSO BY

<u>Samantha Kidd Mysteries</u>

Designer Dirty Laundry

Buyer, Beware

The Brim Reaper

Some Like It Haute

Grand Theft Retro

Pearls Gone Wild

Cement Stilettos

Panty Raid

Union Jacked

Slay Ride

Tough Luxe

Fahrenheit 501

Stark Raving Mod

Gilt Trip

<u>Madison Night Mad for Mod Mysteries</u>

"Midnight Ice" (prequel novella)

Pillow Stalk

That Touch of Ink

With Vics You Get Eggroll

The Decorator Who Knew Too Much

The Pajama Frame

Lover Come Hack

Apprehend Me No Flowers

Teacher's Threat

The Kill of It All

Love Me or Grieve Me

Please Don't Push Up the Daisies

<u>Sylvia Stryker Outer Space Mysteries</u>

Fly Me To The Moon

I'm Your Venus

Saturn Night Fever

Spiders from Mars

<u>Material Witness Mysteries</u>

Suede to Rest

Crushed Velvet

Silk Stalkings

<u>Costume Shop Mystery Series</u>

A Disguise to Die For

Masking for Trouble

Dressed to Confess

www.ingramcontent.com/pod-product-compliance
Lightning Source LLC
Chambersburg PA
CBHW060918190726
48286CB00002B/554